Hardcover ISBN: 13- 9798475209486
Paperback ISBN: 13-9798475207987
Ebook ASIN: B08R3CNCC8

Edited by: Star River Author Services
Cover Art: Nola Marie
Photographs: Konradbak, Paulista, Thebault Trillet
Library of Congress Control Number:
Printed in the United States

Contents

Thank you to everyone who reads my books, messages me, or supports me in any way. Always remember, your scars don't define your present or determine your future. Under those scars is where your heart lies and what makes you all as beautiful as a shooting star in the rain.

Playlist

Under Your Scars – Godsmack
All Our Own – Radio Company
All Around Me – Flyleaf
I Want to Know What Love Is – Foreigner
Painkiller – Three Days Grace
Heaven (Little by Little) – Theory of a Deadman
Not Alone – Red
Stand By Me – Florence and the Machine
Ashes of Eden – Breaking Benjamin
Let Me – Zayn
It's Not Me, It's You – Skillet
Bitter Taste – Three Days Grace
You Can Still Be Free – Savage Garden
Can't Help Falling in Love – Ice Nine Kills
When they Call My Name – Black Veil Brides
Forget the Lies – Quietdrive
My Champion – Alter Bridge
Innocence – Nathan Wagner
Rise Above This – Seether
Best of You – Andy Grammar (with Elle King)
I Wanna Be There – Blessed Union of Souls
Best I Can – Art of Dying
Call On Me – Angel Falls
Hold Me Now – Red
As You Are – Daughtry
I Can't Breathe – Bea Miller
I'll Be – Edwin McCain

1

In My Arms – Plumb
Pieces – Red
Lovely – Lauren Babic, Seraphim
Yellow – Coldplay
Unlearn – Benny Blanco, Gracie Abrams
Start of Something Good – Daughtry
Rise – State of Mine
Let Me Love You – Ne-Yo
Reaching Out – Dillon Francis
Count on Me - Default

Prologue

Damn, I'm running late. I should have known better than to let Old Man Kramer into the shop five minutes before closing. Especially with Gramps and Jay already gone for the day. The old man is constantly bringing in his car with imagined problems. And it never fails that I spend half an hour convincing him that his car is fine.

I fly into my apartment, tossing the keys to my motorcycle on the counter as I race to my bathroom. Shoes and clothes get strewn behind me as I step into my shower, not even giving it a chance to heat.

Nerves hit about the time the spray of the shower warms. I want everything to work out, but if they don't, it can go epically bad. For a moment, I second guess myself. I am risking a lot.

Two years ago, I came home from UCLA after busting my ass to graduate a year early. I was ready to be back home with my family and friends.

I felt like I'd missed so much over the last three years. My best friend, Dane, found his two younger sisters. Ryder had his heart ripped out in a way I can't even imagine. Maddox discovered his friend in an alley and then in his bathroom with blood everywhere a year later.

I'd met Dane's sister, Tori, a few times on my trips home. She'd join us at Lucky's or at Maddox or Ryder's for a party. I'd never gotten the chance to meet his youngest sister, Cara.

When I did, I wasn't surprised that she and Tori looked so much alike. What I wasn't expecting was the visceral reaction I had to her. I'd never felt so much as a twinge for Tori.

But the minute I laid eyes on Cara, the world shifted.

And I was going to hell for it.

I couldn't think of more ways that it was wrong than the blatantly obvious one.

She was my best friend's *sixteen*-year-old sister.

Wrong. Wrong. Wrong.

But I couldn't take my eyes off her dark ones filled with so much life and brilliance they showed like black diamonds against her creamy skin and wheat blond hair. That pale blond hair, a few shades darker than Tori's platinum locks, hung down the middle

4

of her back. The way she tossed her head back when she laughed made my insides tighten.

Wrong! Wrong! WRONG!

For two years, I've choked down my need to have her. Pushed away the jealousy when Dane would complain about her boyfriends. Gritted my teeth against my envy at her ease with Ryder and Maddox. She saw me as nothing more than her brother's friend.

It has been eating me alive, and no matter how many other girls I dated or fucked, I still wanted her.

Tonight, with any luck, that all changes. I am going to Lucky's for her eighteenth birthday party. I am going to charm the fuck out of her. I will get her to agree to go out with me.

I hope.

And I hope I don't lose my best friend or any teeth.

I stare into the mirror, giving myself a pep talk. I feel stupid for being so nervous. I've never been nervous about a woman. Ever.

"I've got this," I tell my reflection as I rake my hands through my dark, unruly hair, attempting to tame the curls. I shrug on a blue t-shirt, dark jeans, and my boots, ready as I'll ever be.

I grab my keys and my bass, ready to leave when a tapping starts at my door just before I reach it. I open it to find blond hair and blue eyes I haven't seen in months staring back at me. "Peyton?"

"Hi Jake," she says softly without meeting my eyes. "We need to talk."

"I was actually just heading out," I tell her, confused why she's here or what we could possibly have to talk about.

5

"I'm pregnant, Jake," she spits out, but it doesn't clear things up for me. "It's yours, Jake," she continues when my brows furrow in confusion.

I feel all the blood rush from my face. My stomach drops, and my knees begin to shake. "*That* is not possible," I tell her more calmly than I feel. "We haven't been together in years."

"Nathan's party a couple of months ago," she says quietly but firmly. Like that is supposed to explain everything, but it doesn't.

I remember the party. I remember getting blackout drunk because the hangover was massive. I remember waking up on Nathan's sofa the next morning. I even remember seeing Peyton there. Half the place was packed with friends from high school celebrating Nathan coming home from the Marines.

But I do *not* remember fucking her.

"What are you trying to pull, Peyton?" I demand as anger takes hold of me.

Her eyes fill with tears. Peyton was always great at crying on command. "I'm not lying, Jake," she produces a black and white photograph.

I take it, looking at the obvious sonogram picture. It's proof of a baby somewhere. I shove the picture back at her. "This doesn't prove anything."

"Jake, I swear I'm telling the truth," she pleads. "I need you. We need you."

I scrub a hand down my face. Everything in me says she's lying.

But what if she's not? What if I don't remember because I was too drunk?

If she's not lying, that means I'm about to be a dad. That my responsibilities and priorities just changed.

My shoulders fall along with my head. I open the door wider and step back so she can come inside.

And that fast, my world changes, and my dreams turn to dust.

Cara

    I look through my list again, ensuring I have everything I'll need for the next several weeks. Electrical adapters, laptop, clothes, shoes, toiletries, and hair accessories are all there, but I feel like I am missing something. The threat of panic pushes its way up my throat as I try to figure out what it could possibly be.

    I hate those feelings of anxiety that creep up on me. They slither in like a serpent threatening to cut off my breathing and vision. It constricts and tightens around my throat until I'm clawing and gasping for air.

    I want to say I never struggled with this as a kid, but it's not true. I just hid it well. After my mom died, I struggled every day just to smile, but I did it. And I sought control because I couldn't control the cancer that took her from me. I couldn't manage how sick and frail she was or how much pain she was in.

When I moved in with Dane, he immediately got me into therapy. I was a very depressed thirteen-year-old girl, but I was also very traumatized and full of anxiety from watching the cancer suck the life from my mom. Watching her go from beautiful and vibrant to a shell of herself. A person I didn't recognize as my beautiful, loving mom at times because the cancer slowly changed her personality too. I realize now that it was not my mom. That it was the disease that infected her brain and changed her. But that little girl I once was, took a very long time to get there

Therapy helped me learn that my mom loved me. It helped me cope with that loss. And it helped me to focus on things I could control.

After Chicago, everything changed. I couldn't force a smile if I tried. I couldn't focus on things I could control because I felt like everything was out of control. I felt like I couldn't trust myself, my judgment. I just wanted to huddle in my bed and never come out.

Stop it! This isn't anything worth panicking over. If I forget something, I can just buy it later.

With my eyes closed, I inhale. I force my fingers to unclench as I exhale. On another inhale, I roll my head back and forth a couple of times, then open my eyes on my concluding exhale.

"Hey, brat, are you all right?" my brother asks from the doorway.

I turn to see him leaning his shoulder on the frame. His blond hair is a little longer now. On top, anyway. I don't think he'll ever let it get too long again after the mohawk the guys forced him to wear. His bright blue eyes are lined with worry, and I know that worry is for me.

I give him a reassuring smile, making sure it reaches my eyes because he will notice if it doesn't. "I'm fine. I just feel like I'm forgetting something."

"It's not too late to change your mind, Cara. You don't have to go."

This isn't the first time he's said that to me. He's given me whiplash lately. One minute, he seems thrilled that I am going on tour with his band, Sons of Sin. The next, it seems like he is trying to talk me out of it.

Cami, his girlfriend, says he's worried it will be too much for me. That the constant travel will be too much stress. That life on the move from city to city every night or the cramped, small spaces will be a trigger of some sort.

I know I worry him. I've been worrying him for nearly two years now. If I am honest with myself, I'm a little worried too, but I want to do this for him.

My brother's band is going on their first international tour. It all nearly came to a halt when Maddox, their vocalist and guitarist, broke his hand in some mugging. That's when they decided they needed Jake.

Jake was their bassist before the record contract. Then, suddenly, he was a single dad to a newborn baby girl, and the late nights on stage were replaced with late-night bottle feedings.

I was in Chicago for my first semester of college, but Dane told me about it. I felt terrible for all of them but especially Jake. I wasn't as close to him as Maddox and Ryder, the band's other guitarist, but I knew how much he loved the guys and playing music.

It's hard to believe it's been nearly three years. Lyra's next birthday will probably be celebrated in a bus or hotel room somewhere.

From what they've told me, the guys have been looking for every excuse to bring Jake back to the band. Not that Maddox intentionally got hurt, but it created the perfect reason. Of course, Jake's first concern was Lyra. I could see his desperation, though. Desperation they all shared. How badly they wanted this.

But Jake, no matter how much he wanted it, was wary. He wasn't fond of the idea of a stranger spending hours in the evenings and nights with Lyra. He had basically turned down their offer when an idea occurred to me. I didn't even think it over before it was spewing like vomit out of my mouth. I never let on that the second the words were out, I wanted to take them back. How could I when Jake accepted so quickly? He didn't take a second to think it over either.

So here I am. Packing to go on tour with a rock band to take care of a two-year-old and, hopefully, graduate with my degree in child development. I have a very strong feeling that someone with connections actually got *that* approved. When I made the comment about the fieldwork, I was talking out of my ass. No professor would agree to give credit for traveling and working with one child, but I got the dean's approval.

I lean my head against the shoulder of the most important man in my life. The man who voluntarily gave up most of his twenties to raise me. "I want to do this, big brother. I want to do this for you and the band."

"The band can wait," he nearly whispers. "You're more important than any of that. You know this."

"I know I am, but I need this. It's another step I need to take. I need to force myself to live my life again. And, if I'm completely honest, I'm a little afraid that I'll just crawl into myself again if I'm left here alone."

"Promise you'll tell me if it gets to be too much?"

I scoff. "So you can cancel the tour and drag me home? Absolutely not. *But* I do promise to call my therapist and work it out."

He chuckles with a shake of his head. "I'll take what I can get." He rises from the bed with a kiss to the top of my head. "Come on, brat. Our flight leaves soon."

He walks out of the room, and I let out a breath. I can do this. There is no reason for this to be a problem. I'll be with my brother and his friends, all of whom are *like* brothers to me. Camilla and Josephine will be there for most of the tour too.

I can do this. It will be fine.

Jake

"Lyra, come here, please," I find myself pleading with the love of my life and bane of my existence. "Let me brush your hair."

"No, Daddy," she stands ten feet from me with her feet spread and hands on her hips. "I bwush it."

I roll my eyes toward the ceiling with gritted teeth. It's a never-ending ordeal with her. She has to be stubborn and independent. I guess I should be grateful she at least wants to wear clothes without a fight. I have a very unlikely source to thank that I have one less battle to fight every day.

"We don't have time, princess," I try reasoning with her. Because, you know, two-year-olds totally care about time.

I really suck at this dad shit. I talk to my daughter more often than not like she's an adult, only to get frustrated that she responds in much the same way. It is very seldom she cooperates without a fight or a bribe. She is willful, independent, stubborn, and smart beyond reason. All traits that I should be thrilled for her to have. But once in a while, I wish she were a little less of those things because I already feel like I'm raising a teenager instead of a toddler. I'm not sure I'll survive when she actually becomes a teenager. Pretty sure I will die.

Also pretty sure I don't have a damn clue what I am doing.

She juts her bottom lip. A sure sign a terrible two meltdown is coming, and I'm just about to cave when a knock sounds at my door.

I open it to find my mom standing on the other side. I should've known she wouldn't let us go without coming by first, even though we just saw her last night.

"I was on my way to therapy," she tells me before I can scold her for coming all this way.

"Mom, your physical therapist is in the opposite direction," I tell her while kissing her cheek.

"Jakob Allen," she says in her *don't argue with me* voice, "I am not allowing my only son to traipse halfway across the world with my only grandchild without a goodbye. Judging by the veins in your forehead, I'm right on time."

"She wants to brush her own hair, but we're running out of time," I explain, the frustration evident in my tone.

Mom steps around me with a pat on my shoulder. "You go finish whatever you need to do while I finish getting Lyra ready. Maybe when you're done, you can tell me what's really bothering you."

I fight to keep the emotion off my face. I've always hated how well my mom can read me. I've never been able to hide anything from her. Absolutely nothing gets past her. Most of the time, that has been a good thing, but there have been occasions in my life I wished she couldn't see me quite so well.

With my tail essentially tucked between my legs because my *mommy* had to come save me from a tiny little girl, I go to my room to finish packing.

Mom is right. Lyra isn't why I am so on edge. It's this tour. Not the traveling part. Not the performing aspect. All of that is simple.

It's the part where I let my dick take over my brain and accepted Cara's offer to be Lyra's nanny. I guess that's what she'll be. But it doesn't matter. What matters is that I will be around her every single day, nearly all day for weeks.

It was a knee-jerk reaction to seeing her with that guy. Her boyfriend, I guess. She says they're just friends, but it seemed like more. Regardless, he is her *ex*-boyfriend. "Arrghh." I scrub my hand down my face and throw the shirt I just picked up across the room.

All these years, and I'm still hung up on the girl. Maybe we'd be together right now if Peyton hadn't shown up on my doorstep over three years ago. Perhaps we wouldn't be. But I wouldn't have these nagging, lingering feelings that I can't do anything about.

Why can't I do anything about it?

One, Cara does not see me that way, and I can't exactly pursue her. It wouldn't be fair, considering she wouldn't just be getting me. Lyra and I are a package deal. I can't expect a twenty-one-year-old woman to want to take on someone else's kid. She's got a lot more to experience in life.

The second reason is Dane. Three years ago, I was ready to risk his wrath because I knew he would get over it eventually. Today, I'm not sure he would. Cara has been through – something, and he's not going to let me waltz into her heart, possibly undoing all her progress.

I don't know what happened, but whatever it is, I know it's bad. I see it when those dark eyes get shadowed by memories of some sort. When she gets lost in thought, reliving whatever nightmare is haunting her.

That's all assuming I could convince her in the first place. I don't even know what her type is. Judging from the guy she's been spending time with her type isn't me.

That guy – *Daniel* – wore khakis and a polo. Very strait-laced and preppy. Nothing wrong with that. It's just the opposite of me.

I have a degree in mechanical engineering, but I work in my grandfather's garage. Music and motors are the only things I've ever really known. My grandfather taught me both. When I finished college, I came back home knowing I would do both of those things. I just hoped the music would take me places.

I guess it is now, even though it's been nearly three years since I was really part of the band. I couldn't work all day, stay out all night, and take care of a newborn.

I'm not complaining. Lyra is my heart. She is my entire world. From the moment I heard her heartbeat, she was my everything. I never knew just how powerful my capacity to love could be until I heard her cry. At that moment, nothing else in the world mattered.

At that moment, I understood Dane's fierce need to protect his sisters times ten. It was surreal, to say the least.

I never thought in a million years I'd be in this situation. A single dad. It's not something you plan for exactly. But I wouldn't take it back for anything.

Even when she makes me want to pull my hair out.

With a heavy sigh, I start shoving more clothes into a bag. Then move on to Lyra's things. She needs clothes, toys, books, pull-ups because we still haven't mastered the nighttime bathroom routine. Her stuffed elephant that she's slept with since she was born and her favorite blanket because all hell will break loose if we forget it.

These are all things I have to go over with Cara.

Cara. Always on my damn mind. Too much. When Dane went to River City to check on her, I invited myself. I'm pretty sure that's when I started making him suspicious. I couldn't help myself, though.

He'd been worried about her for so long. Every time he spoke of her and how closed off she seemed, my anxiety for her would spike. My need to see her again would surge.

I can't even explain why this girl has completely consumed my mind for five years now. It doesn't make sense. Just like it didn't make sense, the need I had when we saw her broken and defeated in River City, to take her in my arms and heal her. Make her whole again.

Ridiculous, I know. I can't heal her. I don't really have a relationship with her at all. I never have. For years I was away at school. When I came home, I kept my distance because of the urges she stirred within me. Desires that were more than a little inappropriate given I was twenty-one and she was sixteen.

Although I never stayed too far away. Just enough that she didn't notice me, but I noticed her. I always noticed her.

For the last few years, she's been away. To Chicago at first, until something happened. Something that Dane will not divulge, and quite frankly, it kind of pisses me off. I'm supposed to be his best friend. I was until Cami came along anyway.

I'm not bitter over that. The guy deserves to be happy. He deserved to find love. It took him a long damn time to find it, too.

After Chicago, Tori, Dane and Cara's sister, convinced them she should go to River City with her. Dane was on the road at the time and didn't want her alone. It didn't help, though. Whatever happened, it really messed Cara up.

When we walked into her apartment, I couldn't believe what I was seeing. It looked like she hadn't cleaned up in months. There were clothes everywhere. Food that looked like evolution was taking hold on the counters. Trash overflowing from the bins. Absolutely nowhere to sit. Barely anywhere to stand.

Then she walked in the door. I'm not sure if I contained my shock or not. The girl that walked in that door didn't look a thing like the girl I knew. Her face was sallow. Her eyes had circles deep and dark from not sleeping. Her hair looked like it hadn't been brushed in days. She wore clothes two sizes too big. The most disturbing part, though, was the look in her eyes. I will never forget that haunting look of hopelessness.

I was pissed. I was pissed that she was there. That Dane let her go there. I was pissed he hadn't brought her back. And I was pissed he wouldn't tell me what in the hell happened. Because that girl was hurt, tormented, and broken.

18

It seems like she's improving since she's been back. She is making an effort to get her life back. But that fire that once lived inside of her is still gone.

I'd give anything to help her find it again. To help her find that piece of herself.

"No, jackass," I chastise myself. "She's there to take care of Lyra. You cannot make a move."

I finish with the last of our packing and take the bags to the front door. In the living room, Lyra is sitting in my mom's lap with her two fingers in her mouth, hair neatly brushed and pulled into two ponytails on each side of her head, and her clothes actually match.

"Get everything done?" Mom asks with a warm smile.

I shove my hands in my pocket and shuffle over to where they sit. "She doesn't need to go to sleep yet," I nod toward Lyra. "She'll be a nightmare on the plane if she starts a nap she can't finish."

"She'll be fine, Jake. Now. Sit. Tell me what's got you so worked up. Everything about you is tense. I've told you before that Lyra will pick up on that and be more difficult to handle."

She has told me that. And she's right even if I hate that she's right. Lyra mimics my moods. Or maybe they just rub off on her. But it never fails; if I'm in a pissy mood, so is she.

"This was a bad idea, Mom," I tell her as I sit in the chair across from her, dropping my head into my hands.

"Jake, this is your dream, and it's being handed to you on a silver platter. How could it be a bad idea?"

"Just trust me on this, Mom. This was the worst thing I could've done."

"Jake, do you still have feelings for Cara?" she asks me softly.

My head snaps up. She might be able to read my expressions, but I *know* she can't read my mind. I've never told her about my attraction to Dane's little sister. I've never told anyone. "Why would you ask that?" I deflect.

"Son, you have never been very good at hiding your feelings about anything from me. I am your mother. For me, they are always written all over your face. I knew long ago you liked that girl. Lord knows I prayed you'd let it go since she was entirely too young for you at the time. I was relieved you never pursued her."

My mouth is slack. My mind is spinning as I realize just *how long* she's known. I wince just a bit because my mom knew her grown son had a thing for a sixteen-year-old girl. "I would never have gone after her while she was underage," I assure her.

"But you still have feelings." It's a statement. An observation. She's not judging. Mom would never do that.

"I don't know about *feelings*, Mom, but yes, I'm still attracted to her. Which is why this was a bad idea. I am going to be with her twenty-four hours a day for weeks. This will be the most miserable experience of my life." I lean back into my chair with a groan.

"I don't understand the problem. It seems like the perfect time to get to know her. To see if what you feel is more than skin deep."

I look at Lyra, who is still awake but just barely. "Dane is one reason. I'd be risking our friendship. He and the other guys have been more supportive than I could ever hope for with Lyra. I don't know if it would be worth the risk. Dane isn't the most reasonable when it comes to his sisters."

She gives me a knowing smile, but what she thinks she knows, I couldn't begin to guess. "What else?"

"Well, there's Cara herself. She's been through a lot. She's been broken somehow. I don't want to start something that doesn't work and hurt her more. Not to mention Lyra. What if Lyra got attached to her and things didn't work out?"

"I see. So you're telling me you're worried about Lyra, Cara, and Dane. What about how you feel, Jake? Where does what you want fit into any of that?"

I scoff. That's the most absurd thing she could ask. "What I want doesn't matter. You know that. I have to put Lyra first. If things went badly, she'd lose a lot of people she needs in her life. Besides, Cara doesn't look at me the way I look at her. I am just her brother's friend. Nothing more." Those last words leave a bitter taste in my mouth.

"Okay, Jake. Okay. Then go on this tour. You do your job, let Cara do hers, and just forget about the rest."

I narrow my eyes. I want to push her to tell me what she really thinks because I can see she has more on her mind. Another knock at the door stops that train in its track, however.

I stand to open it to find Angel and Josephine. "You look like hell," Angel remarks with a smirk.

"Still better looking than you," I quip, letting them in the door.

"Are you okay, Jake?" Josephine questions with concern lacing her feature. "You do look a little – wired."

I wave them off. "I'm fine. Just ready to get this show on the road."

"Osie," Lyra says from my mother's lap. Her bright blue eyes looking over where we stand.

"There's the princess," Josephine calls out with a bright smile of her own.

Lyra quickly wiggles her way from my mom to get to Josephine.

In all the years I've known Angel, I knew the guy was missing something – someone. He told me about Josephine. I honestly thought, at the time, he needed to move on (pot meet kettle), but it was apparent he wasn't just missing a person – he was missing part of himself. Since she reentered his life, he seems like a different man. Like he has peace and contentment. Like he's whole.

I never knew the day I called and asked him to come to New York and take my place in the band, it would eventually lead him back to her. It's funny how things can align like that. Like the universe had its plan despite the people who tried so hard to keep them apart.

Josephine squats down to Lyra, wrapping her arms around my little girl. For years, it was just us guys. With Angel reuniting with Josephine and Dane with Cami, my little girl has two more people to love her. Two more women in her life that she'll need one day.

My chest squeezes a bit. It's hard sometimes to look at her. She is so beautiful and sweet and loving, and she deserves to have a mother and a father. It hurts knowing she won't ever have that. Especially when I see how much she adores Josephine and Cami. Cara too. When we've been at Dane's, Cara spends every second with her. Although sometimes, I think it's so she can avoid the rest of us.

"We have to be out of here in ten," Angel tells me as he watches Josephine with Lyra.

"Got the bug, man?" I nod toward Lyra jokingly. He only shrugs without denying what I've said. My mouth falls open. "Seriously?" I ask with surprise.

"What?" he laughs. "I've wanted babies with her since I was old enough to know how to make them."

"You just got married. Don't you want to enjoy that first? Babies are a lot of work."

He laughs again. "You forget who lived here when Lyra was born?"

I didn't forget. All my friends stepped up when she was born, but Angel lived here with us for a while when he didn't have to. He even took turns with feedings and changings. It wasn't what he came out here to do, but it didn't stop him from doing it.

Lyra looks up from Josephine, finally catching sight of Angel. "Anel, Anel," she squeals. Angel winces at her mispronunciation of his name while I cover a laugh because it may be awkward, but it's funny as hell.

Josephine doesn't do quite as good of a job at covering her amusement. She catches sight of Angel's glare and covers her giggling mouth with her hand. "Ang-el," he pronounces slowly for her, picking her up. "Remember?'

"Dat's what I says. Anel." She looks at him with a stern seriousness that no one can hold back their laughter, except Angel, of course, who looks like he wants to stab us all.

"We've got to come up with something else for her to call me until she can say my name right," he grumbles.

"I says it wite," she says again, grabbing his face. "A-nel."

"Yep," he smiles through tightly closed lips, recognizing her no argument face. "That's my name."

He kisses her forehead before setting her back on the floor. She wastes no time returning to Josephine, who is sitting on the sofa with my mother.

"You ready for this?" Angel asks me with his usual seriousness.

"Yep. What's not to be ready for?" I shrug ambivalently.

"You forget this is me you're talking to," he chuckles quietly. "I mean, are you ready to be around Cara twenty-four/seven with big brother watching your every move."

"No, but it is what it is," I tell him honestly. "Not like anything would happen anyway. I've had this stupid crush for years. Proximity won't change anything." God, that sounds stupid. I'm twenty-six years old with a damn crush.

He laughs loudly this time. "If you say so. You know what they say about close quarters, though."

I give him a wry look. "Close quarters with a two-year-old. Yeah. Pretty sure we'll be fine. The most action I'll be seeing is with my hand."

"I did *not* need that visual, man," he looks at me disgusted, and it's my turn to laugh.

"Come on, princess. Time to go."

"Go," she looks up at me with sleep once again showing in those big eyes.

"Yeah, remember. We are going on a trip."

"Otay. Wets go," she walks over to me, still sucking on her fingers. I know I should break the habit, but I haven't figured out how. And I love watching her sleep so innocently with that comfort. She came into this world with those fingers in her mouth. I just don't have the heart to take it from her just yet.

She raises her arms for me to pick her up. *Lazy, spoiled little thing.* I do, of course, then she starts jerking her body. "Tome on, Daddy. We gots to go."

I laugh at her precociousness with a kiss on her cheek. I feel like I'm drowning in this most of the time, but I wouldn't change any of it.

An hour later, we're at the airport with everyone else. The other guys, Liam, Josephine, Camilla, and – Cara. I swallow hard when she walks in, looking as beautiful as ever.

I've avoided the hell out of Dane's place for the last several weeks. I've only seen her once since her offer, at Dane's birthday party. *That was a blast.* Watching her all night with her friend/boyfriend or whatever he is and Maddox and Ryder.

I watch as she stays close to Dane and Cami as they make their way to us. Her shoulders are practically to her ears as anxiety drips from her. A very different scene from Dane's party the other night at Lucky's, where she seemed a little more like the old Cara.

This is a smaller airport specifically for chartered and private flights, but a few people are still around. Apparently, it's enough for Cara to jump every time someone bumps into her.

"Fuck, this is going to be bad," I mutter to myself as I realize I should not have accepted her offer for entirely different reasons now.

25

She is dragging her bag behind her. Her eyes dart around the airport terminal nervously. She almost looks like a wild animal, and my heart clenches in my chest. I wonder, again, what happened to take that fire she once had.

"We goes on big pwane, Daddy," Lyra says from my side where she is holding my hand.

I look down at her, those big blue eyes curious and excited, one hand in mine, the other wrapped tightly around her elephant with her fingers in her mouth. Of course, she fell asleep on the car ride here. It was only half an hour, but that is all she needs to recharge. "Yeah, rugrat. We're going on the big plane."

"I wikes the big pwanes," she tells me from around her fingers.

She looks around at everyone, and I know the second she realizes Dane is here. She drops my hand and takes off running to him. I have no idea what it is about my best friend she loves so much, but she does. She loves all the guys, but something about Dane takes precedence in her tiny mind.

He grabs her up as she starts climbing him with a laugh. Maybe he's just got that fatherly thing going. Hell, the guy helped me in more ways than I can count.

I was a skinny thirteen-year-old little jerk when we met. I was headed for a world of trouble as the anger I felt from my dad dying consumed me. I got caught stealing from a local convenience store, but Dane kept me out of trouble. He paid for the stuff I swiped then took me home with him to his grandfather's house. He was eighteen at the time. The age he should've been chasing tail, not a thirteen-year-old asshole, but he took me under his wing.

He did the same for Cara in a sense. Twenty-three, barely out of college, but that didn't stop him from moving heaven and earth

26

to bring her to live with him when *she* was thirteen. The guy just cares. Too much sometimes.

"Let's get this show on the road," Maddox calls out to all of us as we make our way to the tarmac where the private plane awaits.

We boarded the plane, and a while later, we are in the air on our way to St. Petersburg. Lyra is cradled in my arms as she holds her ears, crying. She's only flown a handful of times, but this is the first time she's shown any discomfort. It worries me that she may be catching a cold. That would be perfect fucking timing, right?

When she cries like this, it breaks my heart. I hate to see my baby in pain. After her first set of vaccinations as a baby, my mom had to start taking her for the others. I couldn't handle it. It makes me feel helpless and out of control.

Finally, her sobs and tears subside, turning to quiet whimpers as she places her two middle fingers into her mouth. The whimpers get replaced by the soft sounds of her snoring, and I can finally relax.

"We need to go over the itinerary," Liam whispers about an hour into the flight.

"So, go over it," Ryder tells him with a yawn and a wave.

"Maybe we should go over there," he jerks his head with a roll of his eyes toward the front of the plane, still whispering.

"Why?" Dane questions him, leading Cami to smack him in the head. He looks at her with a grin. "What was that for?"

"For being dumb," she hisses with a roll of her eyes.

27

Cara begins giggling. I've been forcing myself to keep my attention off of her. Because every time I do, I lose myself in her. In that smile and in those eyes that, despite the demons swirling, are still like black diamonds.

I'll never understand this attraction to her. How, with one glance at her all those years ago, I became obsessed. But obsessed I am.

It's just physical, though, right? I mean, I don't really know her. Not anymore. I never really did. I was simply infatuated with her to the point that I noticed she always crinkles her nose when she thinks something is funny but is trying not to laugh. She always smiles with just her lips if she doesn't like something but doesn't want to say it. When she's pissed, and about to lose it, she will grab her hair at her neck and start twisting, like she's ready to throw down. And when she's fucking flirting with some dipshit, every tooth in her head is exposed while she twirls her hair around her finger.

So fucking sane and healthy for me to watch that closely, right? But that's what I've felt since the second I saw her – unstable, obsessed, and insane.

Josephine is laughing, now as well, at the dumbfounded expressions on the other guys' faces. I drag my attention away from Cara with effort to see Liam scrubbing his hand down his face in frustration. "Remind me again, why I came to work for you dumbasses?"

"We wondered the same thing a few times," Maddox returns his unique brand of smart ass.

"I am surrounded by goddamn clowns," he grumbles. "Go over there, so you don't wake the baby, you morons."

"How does that solve anything?" Angel quips. "Jake has to come with us."

It is taking everything in me not to die with laughter at how they are fucking with Liam and the girls. They are excited about this tour and showing it by acting like assholes. It's a good distraction for me. Until...

"I'll take Lyra, Jake," Cara says almost shyly, walking to me. "I'll stay in the bedroom with her."

I look up to see those dark eyes staring right at me. My eyes move over her face from her eyes to the lusciously plump lips, and my damn brain short circuits. I feel like a fucking prepubescent punk who's just discovered girls. I can't hear anything but the roaring of blood in my ears as it rushes like a tidal wave from my head to – well, my head.

My eyes drop in an attempt to get myself together. Big mistake. They fall straight to her chest, where those perky breasts sit high and proud. Not too big. Not too small. Probably a little less than a handful. I force them farther down, only to find myself staring at those long damn legs of her. Those legs I've pictured wrapped around me more times than is probably normal. Those legs that go on for miles. And miles. And. Miles.

"Shit," I mutter under my breath at the damn semi that is quickly becoming a steel pipe in my pants.

"Excuse me?" Cara looks at me nervously, clearly not understanding what the problem is. She looks upset, but I can't tell if it's *rip me a new one* upset, or if it's *I just made her very uncomfortable* upset. I don't want either.

"I – uh – she's – I don't know...." I stutter like a fool because I cannot form a complete thought when I'm still picturing those legs wrapped around me while I dri....

29

Get it together, you dumb fuck.

Her eyes narrow. Those eyes spark with a fierceness I recognize that is not helping my situation because she's sexy as hell.

"Jake, I am here to help you with Lyra. I can't do that if you don't let me." I watch her mouth move as she speaks. Her bottom lip is a little fuller than her top, I notice, not for the first time. Then my mind takes the worst path possible as I wonder what those lips would feel like wrapped around my -.

"No," I quietly reprimand myself.

The way Cara flinches and her face falls tells me she heard that too. My stomach plummets like a piano shoved off the Empire State Building. I need to fix this fast, but I don't know how. I can't explain I wasn't talking to her. Not without explaining why I'm talking to myself or risk sounding insane.

"What's your problem, man?" Dane demands through narrowed eyes.

I close my eyes. If I'm not looking at her, maybe I can form a complete thought that isn't straight from the gutter. "No problem," I say as I work to come up with a rational explanation for why I said what I did. "I just don't want to wake her up." Yeah, that sounds logical, right?

Damn, I'm having to question myself a lot lately.

Cara looks at me doubtfully, and it guts me. She thinks I don't trust her with Lyra. That couldn't be farther from the truth. But she doesn't let on. "Then why don't you go lay her in the bed?" she offers.

But the word 'bed' coming from her mouth sends my brain straight back to the filthy, dirty slums of my mind. Images of her beneath me, my body pressing hers into the mattress, fill my head.

I stifle a groan with a hard swallow, then nod. I stand, praying no one notices the issues I'm having down under, and make my way to the bedroom. I try my best not to jostle my tiny princess as I work my way into the narrow room.

I lay Lyra in the center of the bed, placing a kiss on her forehead. When I turn to leave the room, I bump into Cara, making her stumble back. I quickly wrap an arm around her waist to stop her fall, bringing her flush against my chest.

"I – I'm sorry," she pants, catching her breath from the shock. "I thought you knew I was behind you."

"I didn't." My voice is gruff and deep as I try to keep my composure. My earlier problem hasn't fully deflated, and her soft body being pressed into mine is not helping, but, by God, I don't want to let go. I do, though. Quickly. Before she notices my dilemma.

"I'm – uh – just going to go out there," I stammer, averting my eyes to the space behind her so I can concentrate. "Get me if you need me."

I sidestep her, doing everything I can to keep our bodies apart. A feat considering the amount of space to do so.

"Hey, Jake," she calls me before I make it out the door.

I turn to face her with a breath to keep myself under control. It is a wasted breath because when I turn to see her curled up next to Lyra, a whole other set of emotions and impossible possibilities fly through my mind, taking my breath away. I grab the doorframe to stop myself from going to her and kissing the hell out of her. "Yeah," I say with a strained voice.

"I'll take good care of her," she says softly, her nervous eyes darting between mine.

Another breath lost. "I know you will," I rasp weakly.

That's actually part of the problem.

Cara

Jake stares at me with some indecipherable look for a few more seconds before he finally leaves the tiny room. I'm not sure what just happened. When he grabbed me to keep me from falling, a weird feeling comes over me. I don't know what it means, but my mind went to places it has never been when it comes to him for a split second. It unnerved me a bit.

But I decide that I must just be feeding off the weirdness he's been putting off. I'm not sure what to make of his reactions today. I know we don't know each other very well. Well, not as well as I know Ryder and Maddox anyway. Or even Stitch and Jasper, the guys who run Dane's tattoo shop.

But he's definitely been acting strange since we got on the plane. I've caught him more than once staring at me with a frustrated, uncomfortable look on his face. I've wondered if he thinks he made a mistake accepting my offer. Maybe he doesn't trust me with Lyra. Which is why I wanted to assure him I would take care of her.

He must trust me on some level, though. He said he would only come on tour if I were the one to keep Lyra. Why else would he have agreed so quickly when he was initially so reluctant?

It makes me wish I'd taken the time to get to know him better, but I was just a kid when he returned from California. My relationship with Maddox and Ryder had long been established at that point. They are my brothers and best friends. When Dane was an overbearing jerk, Maddox and Ryder were who I went to until Tori came long. And even then, I still went to them for some things, often afraid she'd tell Dane.

While I knew of Jake, knew he was Dane's best friend, even if they were several years apart, when he returned, he was just my brother's friend. And I was his friend's little sister. I only exchanged small talk with him here or there, and he never seemed too interested in me either. There were a few times, I remember, that forced proximity required more than a passing pleasantry. It was those moments that he seemed like it physically pained him to be near me.

I never took it personally. I was just a teenage girl. His best friend's baby sister. He was fresh out of college and very much grown. He probably didn't think we had anything to talk about.

Though I will admit he was – is nice to look at. My sixteen-year-old self drooled when I saw him the first time. The first thing I noticed was his eyes. Not blue, not green, but so damn sexy. The second thing I noticed was his mouth. Those lips looked like they knew how to kiss a girl – everywhere. He was always dressed in low-slung jeans and vintage band tees that molded to his broad shoulders, showing off a well-defined physique, and his

34

brown hair was often shaggy and curling around his ears. He always looked in need of a haircut, and it just made him hotter.

My girlfriends and I would spend hours giggling about him. Of course, they often included Dane, Maddox, and Ryder in the same context, and that was horrifying. As an adult, I can objectively say they are all beautiful men, but if I think about my brother and Maddox and Ryder like that too long, my stomach turns.

Considering my relationship with Jake, or lack thereof, it was surprising to see him in my apartment with Dane those months ago. Even more surprising was the way he comforted me while I sobbed in his arms.

"I can't do it anymore," I sob into his chest, clinging like he's my lifeline. "They won't stop. The nightmares won't stop. Every single night, it replays over and over and over on a loop."

"Shh," he soothes. "Do you want to tell me about the nightmares?" I nod rapidly because all I've wanted to do is talk about it. To tell someone who isn't close to the situation. Someone who doesn't trigger the overwhelming guilt on top of everything else. "Then tell me, sweetheart."

"I – I can't." My words come out hysterically. "I can't tell anyone."

His arms tighten around me, his body suddenly tense. "You can tell me anything, sweetheart. Absolutely anything."

"Not this, I can't." My chest tightens as the weight I've been carrying presses down.

I feel him inhale sharply as he continues to stroke my hair. He presses his lips to the crown of my head and just lingers there. He doesn't say anything for a while, allowing me to release my tears.

35

"Why are you here, Cara?" he asks when my sobs turn to soft hiccups, never stopping the gentle caress of my hair. "You don't belong here."

"I didn't want to be a burden on Dane anymore," I admit. "I've disrupted his life long enough. I've been a brat. I know that now."

Another sharp breath comes from him. I can hear his heart pounding like a drum inside his chest. I'm not sure if I'm making him uncomfortable or angry, but I just don't have it in me to move at the moment.

Dane walks back into the apartment after taking a call in the hallway. He is looking between us, his brows furrowing in his typical big brother fashion. I move away from Jake, not wanting Dane to be upset with him. I look at my brother as I consider Jake's question.

Why am I here?

Initially, it was to be closer to my sister, but she is the reason behind so much of my guilt.

It was also so Dane wouldn't worry about me. So he wouldn't put his life – his dreams on hold for me again. I knew he would do exactly that if I went home with him.

But being here has hurt far more than it has helped. I'm a shell of myself. The anxiety that I feel every day has become unbearable. I barely leave my apartment because the fear and worry and guilt just presses down so hard that I can't breathe.

"I want to go home, Dane," I cry. "I want to come home with you."

I must've fallen asleep at some point because I'm awakened by the cutest little face surrounded by a mess of blond curls falling out of her ponytails while her tiny body sits on my chest. She bends over, pressing her forehead against mine. "Tawa, yous wakes up?"

I laugh at her little expression. So serious, with her brows furrowed into a V between her eyes. "Cara," I tell her.

"Dats what I says. Tawa." Her brows go impossibly lower as her nose scrunches and her eyes narrow.

"K," I sound it out, "ar – a. Say 'k'."

She studies me for a second. She tries but fails to say it correctly. "I tant does it," she pouts, folding her arms across her chest.

I laugh again. "Okay. How about you growl like this," I growl at her with the back of my throat only. I know she can make the sound. She has plenty of words in her abnormally large vocabulary with c's and k's. I just need to coax it out of her.

She does the growl with a giggle. "I does it."

"Good girl," I praise. "Can you do it again?"

Her tiny head bobs as she does it again, giggling louder. It's a beautiful sound and one she does often.

"Okay. Now say 'k'," I encourage.

When she finally makes the sound, she starts bouncing proudly. I rest my hands on her little waist to still her before she cracks a rib. "Now, say Cara."

Her pale brows scrunch again. "Car-a," she says slowly. Her little eyes light up with recognition and pride when she makes each sound. "Cara. Cara, Cara, Cara."

37

She scrambles off me faster than someone that small should be able to do. Before I can get to her, she is out the door. She moves like lightning to the guys, who are all seated around a table near the plane's cockpit. "Daddy, Daddy," she squeals loudly. "I tan says Car-a," she beams as she climbs in his lap.

Everyone at the table looks at her with amusement. "What?" Jake asks, trying to get her to sit still.

"Cara, Cara, Cara," she sing-songs loudly.

"That's good, princess. Maybe next time, she'll do a better job of watching you, too."

"Excuse me?" I gasp in shock.

"You knew we were having a discussion, but let her fly out of the room anyway," he says sharply. "You're supposed to be watching her."

My mouth falls open. I may not know Jake as well as the others, but he's *never* spoken to me like this. He's never been rude.

Dane's face turns beet red as his eyes flame with anger. Maddox and Ryder don't look much happier while Angel and Liam look at Jake like he's grown horns. He doesn't seem to notice. His eyes fixed firmly on me.

Dane starts to say something, but I stop him with a raised hand. "I was obviously watching her, or she wouldn't have been so excited to show you what she learned. But next time, I'll be sure to tell your two-year-old that her daddy is too busy to share in the excitement of her accomplishments."

And *that,* ladies and gentlemen, is how I earned the nickname, brat.

Jake winces at my words, looking properly chastised. His eyes drop as he starts to say something. An apology, I'm assuming. I hold my hand up again. "Save it. I don't want or need your apology."

I reach for Lyra without another word or look at him and make my way to Josephine and Cami.

Lyra sits on the floor in front of us with a book as I sit next to Cami, who looks at me with a wide grin. "You did good," she tells me with a nod.

"What's up with him?" Josephine whispers to the two of us.

I shake my head. "I have no idea unless he's having second thoughts about me watching her."

"It's a little late for that," Josephine shakes her head. "That was completely uncalled for. Just so you know, he's not usually like that."

I wave it off like it doesn't matter. Truthfully, it does matter to me. It pissed me off, but it also stresses me out. I don't want him to be uncomfortable or doubtful about my abilities to take care of Lyra.

Cami pats me on the knee. "You're okay, Cara. Jake is probably just stressed out over this. It's his first time on tour. It's perhaps a little different when you have a kid to consider."

I nod then look in the direction of the guys. Jake is looking this way but not at Lyra. He's looking at me. His eyes show remorse, but something else also that sends a shiver down my spine and makes me gulp a little too loudly.

I quickly drop my eyes to Lyra before his intense gaze burns a hole in me.

Whatever is going on with him, I hope he gets over it soon, or this trip will be very uncomfortable for both of us.

Jake

Shit!

I don't know why I snapped at Cara like that. She didn't do a damn thing to deserve my harsh words. Words I didn't even mean.

But when I look up to see her, hair messy, eyes still slightly hazy, all my synapses misfired. I wanted to wrap that blond bird's nest around my fist and kiss the fuck out of that pouty mouth. Then I wanted to take her back to the bedroom and fuck the hell out of her. It irritated me that I couldn't do just that, and my irritation was taken out on her.

I mean, it's not her fault that I can't think clearly around her. Just like it's not her fault that I am, and have been, attracted to her for so damn long that no one else has even come close to

41

taking my mind off of her. It most definitely isn't her fault that she doesn't know any of this.

Nope. All of this lies squarely on my shoulders.

At this rate, I'm more likely to make her hate me. It would make things easier, maybe, but the thought of her hating me makes me sick.

I glance over to her again, begging her to forgive me with my eyes. Trying to convey that I was an ass. All I get in return are daggers from her black eyes. Her harsh words still sting my chest, but she was right. I totally deserved what she said and more.

With my proverbial tail tucked between my legs for the second time today, I turn my attention back to the guys.

I should've kept my attention on Cara. She may be shooting daggers, but they don't seem quite as deadly as the glares I'm receiving from her brother's eerily similar eyes right now. Thank God they're different colors, or it would be weird. But I am reasonably certain he's plotting my death right now.

I look to Maddox and Ryder and finally flinch. They are both glaring at me just as hard as Dane. I am getting no sympathy from them.

Angel and Liam's expressions both say they think I've lost my mind.

I have news for them. I'm pretty sure that ship sailed the moment I agreed to Cara's offer. I am sailing on the S.S. Straight Jacket straight to *Shutter Island*. Because keeping these feelings bottled up is driving me insane.

And to think, I'm the one who convinced Dane he needed to bring Cara home.

"What the hell was that?" Dane basically growls like a momma bear protecting her cub.

I scrub my hand down my face with a sigh. "That was me being an asshole," I openly admit. "I'm sorry. This whole tour thing has me on edge."

"Keep it up, man, and you'll be eating through a straw, and I will send her back home. She doesn't need that. My mom, Rachel, and Daniel can keep an eye on her."

My jaw clenches involuntarily when he mentions her ex-boyfriend, who she is still very friendly with. For the briefest of moments, I swear he smirks at me, but he's up and moving toward the girls before I can be sure of anything.

"That wasn't cool, Jake," Maddox grunts with his arms crossed.

"The brat didn't deserve that," Ryder, as usual, agrees with Maddox. Although it would be more unusual if he didn't since they're right.

"You're right," I sigh again. "I'll apologize."

"It's not her fault she makes you sexually frustrated," Ryder continues with a raised brow, daring me to deny it.

I open my mouth to do just that, then snap it shut when the words don't come. They smirk at me, which irritates the hell out of me.

"Hold up," Liam lifts his hand. "You have a thing for Cara. Dane's little sister, Cara."

I can feel the guilt written all over my face. Again, I want to deny it, but who would believe it.

"That's just fucking fantastic," Liam grunts. "Do I need to worry about bloodshed?"

"If Maddox and Ryder's faces after they fucked Tori are any indication, then I'd say you can definitely expect some," Angel cackles. I groan.

"Man, you just need to get laid," Maddox tells me with a laugh. "How long has it been anyway?"

I wince again because the only action I've seen lately has been with my hand. "Sex isn't the solution to everything."

"That long?" Ryder smirks.

I give him a middle finger. "I'm not interested in fucking everyone that looks my way." The grumble in my tone is probably less than convincing. The truth is, even if I had time lately, I haven't wanted to. Not since Cara came back. It's weird, too, because I didn't have any problems when she was too young for me. And I haven't had any issues in the nearly three years she's been gone.

Maybe it was better when she was unattainable. She's still unattainable, but not for the same reasons. Now it's just my worries that are stopping me and maybe a slight fear of rejection. Which is also strange as hell since I've never worried about being rejected in my life.

"Don't knock it 'til you try it, mate," Ryder's grin spreads while Angel and Maddox chuckle.

"I don't think fucking anything with a pulse ever solved a problem for you three," I challenge.

"We're not saying it will solve your crush. Aren't you a little old for that, by the way?" Angel mocks with that damn straight face he manages all the time. Broody fucker.

"It's a bandaid, but at least you'll feel better for a little while," Maddox shrugs.

"Always looking for that escape, huh, Mads?" I remark acidicly.

His brows furrow a bit. He presses his palms to the table, leaning forward to look at me. "Better than wallowing."

"You sure about that?" I grit out through my teeth, getting pissed that they're pushing this.

This is definitely going to be a long few weeks if I'm already at people's throats. Especially Maddox. He's a good guy whose only crime is caring too much for everyone else and not enough for himself. He's so damn self-destructive. The most self-destructive person I know, and he doesn't need me digging at his wounds. They're deep enough without my help.

I scrub my hands down my face again. "Sorry, man. I didn't mean that."

"Look, I don't care who any of you fuck," Liam finally chimes in. "Just don't kill each other. I quit my job for this dysfunctional family, and I'd rather not go back begging for them to take me back."

With that, we laugh. Ryder slaps him on the back. "Mate, we have been a dysfunctional family for far too long to let the dysfunction break us now."

"And you became a part of this family the minute you took the job," Maddox adds. My point proven. Maddox cares too much and feels too hard.

"God help me," Liam laughs with a huff.

Lyra's laugh cuts through the entire space. I look toward her, and my throat catches. I have no idea what they are doing, but she and Cara are entirely in their own bubble. Already.

"Why don't you tell her how you feel?" Maddox asks quietly.

45

"I planned on it once," I confess. "Or, at least, I planned on asking her out."

"What stopped you?" Angel asks curiously.

"I've wondered the same," Ryder ponders. "God knows you've had a thing for her since you met her."

My mouth falls open. "Your face gives it away," Maddox laughs. "Every time she is around, you never take your eyes off of her. Not to mention the way you looked like you wanted to kill Daniel." I growl at his name. "That. That right there is what I mean."

"Well, at least everyone couldn't tell," I chuckle. "Best friend for not, Dane would kick my ass if he knew I was perving over his sixteen-year-old sister."

"Brother, I would've kicked your ass if you'd made a move on her then," Maddox smirks.

"You've had a thing for her that long," Liam blinks in surprise.

I shrug. "I don't know what it is I feel. I don't know if it's sexual or what."

"I hate to tell you this, but it's more than sexual attraction or an infatuation if it's gone on for that long," Liam tells me. "You'd have gotten over her by now. Unless you're an obsessed stalker."

"I sometimes wonder," I grumble. "I feel like an obsessive stalker."

"You're not a stalker," Ryder laughs. "Cara is an amazing girl. She's funny and sweet with a huge heart. Hopefully, one day, she'll be back to that firecracker I watched her grow into, but even if she doesn't, Cara is beautiful, inside and out."

"You wouldn't get so fucking jealous if it were just a crush," Angel nods toward Josephine. "Something just takes over you. It's like you need to mark your territory because down in your bones, you just know they belong to you, and it eats you alive to think of anyone else touching what's yours."

"Fuck me," I grunt because everything he just said is exactly how I feel. How I have felt for a long damn time. "I'm just totally fucked."

"So, what stopped you?" Angel asks. I tilt my head a bit, letting my confusion show. "You said you started to tell her once. What stopped you?"

"Peyton," I say with a sigh.

His brows shoot to his hair. "Fuck, man." All I know to do is nod. Not much more can be said about that.

"What's stopping you now?" Ryder quirks a challenging brow at me. I look at him with surprise. My mouth opens to reply, then snaps shut.

"Dane won't care," Maddox tells me as he turns up a drink our attendant brought him. I snort my disbelief. "He won't, Jake. Your not a manwhore like Ryder and I are. You're not the fuck up I am."

My jaw tightens at his self-deprecating remark. Maddox has a lot of demons, but the guy is not a fuck up. He is a fucking musical genius. He and Ryder used what they've learned from their families to ensure the band is always taken care of business wise. Not to mention he graduated Summa Cum Laude from NYU. "You should, at least, try," Ryder says, ignoring Maddox.

47

"It's not that easy now," I laugh mirthlessly. "She's been through something. I don't know what but she's a little bit broken now."

"So that means she's suddenly not worth the risk?" Maddox bites.

"What? No! That's not what I meant. I don't want to make it worse. I don't want to put any extra pressure on her. I also have Lyra to think about. Besides, what twenty-one-year-old girl wants to be strapped down to someone else's baby." I say the last part a little bitterly, then instantly feel ashamed.

"The right one. A fucking special one," Maddox says with such conviction it shakes me to my core.

"Learn from Dane," Angel says as he stands from the table. "There will be someone, and she might be right in front of you."

The rest of them nod in agreement as they leave me at the table with my thoughts.

Cara

I walk behind Jake, holding Lyra while he carries our bags into the hotel suite. Dane told me before we left that there wouldn't be many nights on a bus during the European leg of the tour. It's not as spread out as things can be back in the States, and they have more than one night in most cities, so there also won't be hours upon hours of riding on the buses either.

Because of that, staying in hotels is easier. I was shocked the label was willing to pay for that kind of expense. That's when Dane let it slip that the label wasn't paying. They wanted Jake and Lyra comfortable, so Maddox and Ryder decided to take care of the bill.

Jake has no idea.

The suite is beautiful and cannot possibly be cheap, but I don't know much about the cost of things in Russia. There are three

49

bedrooms. One for each of us. It seems excessive because what two-year-old needs a king-sized bed. But that's Madsy and Ry for you. They spare no expense for their friends.

There is also a beautiful kitchen that leads to a formal dining area with a table large enough for the band and the crew. To the left is a living room with two navy-colored velvet sofas and matching wingback chairs that are a stunning contrast against the cream-colored walls.

I nearly laugh at how very non-kid-friendly the space is, but it doesn't matter. We're only here for two nights, then off to Moscow, which they've chartered a plane for as well. Another expense the guys are paying. I just wonder what they've said to Jake to convince him the record label was paying.

I stand awkwardly in the middle of the overly luxurious space. The jet lag is very real, and the time difference is throwing me off. It's just after midnight in New York. It's breakfast time here.

I'm so tired, I feel it in my bones. I need my medicine, and I need sleep. It's one thing I promised Dane and Maddox when they agreed to let me do this. I would do what I must to avoid a setback in my therapy and recovery. Although, I'm not sure they realize I may never fully recover. This is part of me forever. I'm just learning a better way to deal with it.

I look at Lyra, who lets out a yawn so big I'm not sure how it comes from such a tiny body. "Come on, pretty girl," I tell her. "Let's go get you changed for bed."

"I'll do that, Cara," Jake tells me. I press my lips together firmly. For all intents and purposes, I have been hired to be Lyra's nanny. I have a job to do, and I can't do it if he won't let me. But he is her dad, so I can't argue.

"Don't go anywhere," he tells me with stern eyes as he takes her from me. "She'll be asleep in five minutes, and I want to talk to you."

I stand there for a second, debating his request. No. Not a request. A demand.

I decide I'm too tired and too disgusting to deal with him. Not after his little outburst on the plane. The audacity he had to accuse me of not taking care of her. He may have looked apologetic, but I'm not feeling especially forgiving right now.

Whatever he has to say can wait until I've had a shower and sleep. Not necessarily in that order.

He took Lyra to the middle room, so I choose the room to the right of that. I don't even take the time to appreciate the massive bed with the fluffy, oversized duvet or the spa-like bathroom with its huge, sunken whirlpool tub or the shower with a dozen showerheads to hit you from every angle.

My shower lasts just long enough to scrub the grime off my body and hair and brush my teeth. I step into the room and drop the towel on the floor. I've barely got my pink panties pulled over my hips when the door opens.

"Cara, I told you ...." Jake starts, but his words fall away as he realizes I'm not dressed. His eyes widen and flare as his adam's apple bobs in his throat. He just stands there, staring.

I turn around from him with a huff. "Jake, could you get out?" I yell as I grab my pink tank off the bed. I am pissed that he just walked into my space without an invitation or even an announcement. My stomach is also tightening from the way he is reacting to my naked body. The feeling is not welcome.

I pull the shirt over my head before searching through my bag for something to cover my lower half since my underwear covers nothing. I find a pair of soft gray shorts and quickly pull them up my body since he seems to be frozen in place.

I finally turn to face him again, his hands braced on either side of the door frame, gripping so tightly his knuckles are white. His blue-green eyes are hazy and full of heat that it starts a fire of my own in my belly. I am incredibly uncomfortable with the lust in his eyes. And turned on. I cross my arms across my chest to hide my hard nipples poking through my shirt.

Why am I so turned on? It's Jake! I've never felt anything for him before. Not like this. What I felt was a teenage infatuation.

I get a grip on my emotions. It's Jake. Just Jake. I have no reason to feel weird. It is not my fault he walked into my room without knocking. And he's sexy as hell, so of course, that look of lust in his eyes is doing crazy things to my insides. It's a normal, physical response.

The most surprising thing here is Jake's reaction. If I were just any other girl, I would completely get it. I'm not the same kid he met five years ago, but I'm still me. His best friend's little sister. He has never spent more than a few minutes around me before finding somewhere else to be. The same guy that was an asshole this morning.

I know if Maddox or Ryder were standing there, I would not get this reaction. I understand the relationships are a bit different but still.

Gathering my wits, I move forward until I'm standing directly in front of him. I place a hand on the door and another on his chest so that I can push him out of my room. Sparks ignite when my hand connects with his chest. Sparks I choose to ignore.

I push against him. When he doesn't budge, I try to use my body only to gasp at the very prominent bulge between us. I look down then back up to him with surprise on my face. Lust is one thing, but *that* is more than just a little lust.

His irises are nearly wholly swallowed by his pupils. His jaw is clenched tightly, the muscles there flexing under the strain. "I told you to wait for me," he grits.

I swallow down the nerves that threaten to bubble. "I'm jet-lagged and tired, Jake," I tell him, praying my voice doesn't give away those nerves.

I push him again, trying to ignore the heat radiating off his very hard body without any luck.

Before I can register what is happening, he grabs my wrists, pulling me even closer. Electricity is not sparking. No. Lightning has struck. My body has erupted into flames.

Where the hell is all of this coming from?

With another quick, unexpected movement, he spins me. My arms are pinned across my chest by his while his other hand presses against my belly. Lightning flashes and thunder rumbles as the storm we just missed moves in. My back to his front, he drops his mouth to my ear. "I just wanted five minutes," he growls.

But his words barely register. The heat of arousal is replaced with the icy, cold tendrils of panic. My already racing heart picks up speed for entirely other reasons. My entire body feels frozen in place. My mind has gone to a place I hate. To a place I wish didn't exist. Images – memories flash. I can't breathe; my lungs seized with my fear.

Arms wrapped around me, hold me in place with bruising force forcing my back to press against his erection. A hot, wet tongue slides its way up my neck causing bile to rise in my throat.

"Watch," a hot breath demands in my ear.

Breathe, Cara. It's not really happening.

I smell expensive cigars. The taste of blood fills my mouth. I hear screaming; pleas for help assault my ears. I feel teeth biting into my shoulder as I try to close my eyes. "I said watch," the man demands again.

I'm not there. I'm not there.

Lightning flashes from the high windows. Thunder rumbles in the distance. More screaming fills the air. Another rumble. This one much louder.

I want to scream. I want to fight. I can't find the ability to do either. All I can do is watch.

"Cara, come on, baby. I'm right here. Listen to me," I hear repeated over and over in my ear. "Listen to my voice, Cara. Please, just breathe."

Jake. That's Jake's voice. Jake wasn't there that night.

I feel myself eased to the floor, and I hear shushing sounds. That didn't happen either. I'm not there. I'm with Jake. I'm with Jake.

My body practically convulses as sobs violently wrack my body. His arms wrapped tightly around me, no longer from behind but cradled like a child in his arms. It feels safe.

I choke on my sobs as I remind myself it's only a memory. It's in the past. It cannot hurt me today unless I let it.

Usually, these episodes have warnings. Signs that I've become aware of, thanks to my therapist, and I start working through it. Latching on to what is real. I use the techniques I've learned to keep me in the present.

There are still triggers I'm not aware of, though. I had no idea Jake was going to do that, much less that it was a trigger. I'm not even sure if it's what he did or if it was the way I was pinned against his body, or if it is the weather. I know the weather is a trigger for me, but so much happened so quickly that I can't be sure.

I have no idea how long this episode lasted; how long I was reliving that nightmare. It was completely real for me until my mind was finally released from that dissociative state. I am suddenly aware that the screams I was hearing were my own, thanks to my incredibly raw throat. My face is wet from the tears that have fallen like a river.

Jake, is rubbing my back while making shushing sounds. He rocks me from side to side with his chin propped on my head. Warmth unfurls within me from his gentle comfort before the heat of embarrassment floods my cheeks.

I try to remove myself from this very intimate position, much more intimate than those months ago, in my apartment. He doesn't allow it, though. His arms only get tighter when I try. "I'm okay now, Jake," I tell him. I'm not okay. It will be a bit before I feel less unsettled. Hopefully, it will be hours and not days, but a call to my therapist is probably warranted. "Really. I'm fine."

I look up to see so many emotions flitting through his blue-green eyes. Concern and care are clearly displayed. I'm more than a little stunned at the affection I see. It's unhidden and unbridled and so powerful, I forget to breathe. "Just let me keep you here for a minute, okay? You may be fine, which I don't believe you are, but I'm not. Let me just have one more minute."

I nod my head, still pressed against his chest, in agreement. He is sending me all kinds of odd signals that I don't understand. Frustration and agitation earlier. Then absolute lust and desire a few moments ago. Now, it's absolute care and concern.

His heart is racing so fast; it's like a stampede in his chest. And it occurs to me, maybe he's worried about Lyra's safety with me. Perhaps that was why he was so reserved this morning and why he snapped at me. Because he saw my breakdown in River City. Maybe all this worry and fear isn't for me but for Lyra.

We may have gotten off to a rough start this morning — or yesterday — but I need him to know I would never let anything happen to Lyra. "I would never hurt Lyra, Jake. I swear I won't let this happen when she's with me."

I feel him go rigid around me. He doesn't say anything for a bit which is murder on my nerves. He finally pulls me away to look at me. His jaw is set, but his eyes are soft. "Cara, that never crossed my mind. I know you would never hurt anyone. I was worried about you."

"I — I just assumed, maybe that was why you were so hesitant this morning and why you look so scared right now."

"You assumed wrong," he sighs. "You assumed very, very wrong. I'm so-."

"No. It's fine," I cut him off. I'm still a little bitter over this morning, regardless of why, and I don't want his apology.

"You're not going to let me apologize for that, are you?"

"I just don't want it, Jake. It stung, but you have every right to voice your concerns about your daughter."

"I wasn't really concerned, Cara. I was an asshole because I ...." he stops for a second, then shakes his head.

"Because you what?" I ask, now wanting the answer. I've always been nosey.

He smiles at me, brushing his fingers over my cheek. He has a look in his eyes I've seen every time on the handful of occasions we've been alone. One I've never been able to decipher. One that makes me a little nervous with its intensity. "Cara, what happened to you?"

Just like before, I want to tell him. I want to reveal all my secrets to him. The ones that no one else knows. It's a desire I can't indulge. A desire I do not understand.

Jake is Dane's friend, not mine. We don't really know each other. We've never tried. Dane, Maddox, and Ryder are our only connections.

But this strange pull I have felt for him since that day in my apartment won't go away. It makes no sense, making me uncomfortable because I don't want to feel this way.

I feel another bubble of panic. Panic that I am in his lap. Panic that his arms are around me, cradling me, comforting me. Alarm that I am ready to tell him everything. Panic that I trust him.

Trust is what started this entire thing. Trusting a man.

"Don't do that, Cara," he says as he brushes my hair from my face. "Don't pull away. Let me in."

I push against his chest, detangling myself. I throw my walls back up. Walls that aren't just meant to protect me but him too. Then quickly reinforce them. "I need to go to bed now. I need to rest for Lyra tonight."

His eyes get tight, and his mouth sets into a firm line. I turn my eyes away from him, not wanting to see his displeasure. I push it far away. "I'm sorry about all of this," my voice quakes with nerves.

He lets me go without a fight. I stand up, going to the bed to pull the covers down. I feel rather than see when he is standing right behind me. My entire body goes on alert. An undercurrent of tension fills the space between us. My mind wars between my need to put distance between us and my desire to share everything.

He gently grips my upper arm, coaxing me to turn toward him. My eyes go wide when he trails a finger down my cheek again. I struggle to keep my breathing even and not flinch from the intimate gesture. "Do not apologize, Cara. Not for that. Not to me."

I suck in a sharp breath but nod. Every other muscle in my body is paralyzed from the torrent of emotions the sweet gesture causes. Sensing my discomfort, he puts space between us. Sadness fills his eyes. I'm not sure if he is sad about me or for me. I hope not the latter. I don't want his sadness or pity.

He turns to leave when I remember he wanted to talk. "Jake," I call out, surprising myself. I want him to go. I want to get my emotions under control, and I can't do that with him confusing me. Yet, I call out to him. I mentally shake myself when he turns to me with a raised brow. "What did you want to say to me?"

"I just want to say I was sorry about the plane," he tells me over his shoulder. "Guess it would've been a waste of breath." He doesn't say anything else as he pulls the door shut behind him.

I exhale, then climb into the wonderful bed between the soft sheets and pray for sleep. Sleep I know won't come when my mind is too overwhelmed with – everything.

I lay there quietly, trying to figure out why I suddenly feel such a pull to Jake. Trying to figure out his reaction to me. What those looks mean. Why he seems so concerned. Then decide none of it matters. It doesn't matter how I react to him. It's just a physical reaction. Nothing more. I won't let it be more. I won't bring anyone down into my darkness, and that's precisely what being with me would involve.

I'm not the same girl I was. I've seen things that no one should see. Worse, those things are my fault and will haunt me forever. So I shove it all down and away. I lay there inhaling deeply, holding it, then exhaling slowly. I clear my mind and focus my attention on the here and now. On sleep. Trying to think of anything but the memories that threaten to invade my newly found peace.

Jake

I should be sleeping. God knows I've tried. For at least an hour, I tossed and turned, replaying the events of the hour before over and over in my mind.

When I came out after putting Lyra to bed, I was going to apologize. I had a speech planned that I worked on the rest of the flight. But she wasn't there waiting like I asked.

Okay. So maybe I didn't ask. It was really a demand. When she wasn't there waiting, it pissed me off for some reason.

I know the reason. No. It's not because I'm bossy, although I'm that too. It is because I am and have been absolutely obsessed with this girl for years. I finally have her, all but to myself, and I can't do a damn thing about it. That she went to her room after I told her to wait for me is like she just put two thousand miles between us again.

It irritates me that everyone can see how I feel about her but her. Or they can see that I'm very much attracted to her anyway because I'm not entirely sure how I feel about her.

I know I feel very protective of her. I want to take her pain away – go back to whatever happened to take that constant sparkle in her eyes away and stop it. I know it drives me insane when I think of her with someone else. I can't stand the thought of another man's hands on her or inside her body. I know I worry about her all the time. I've been concerned for a long time, even without knowing what happened to her. I care.

That's what this is. Care. I care about Cara. I've cared about her for a long time. Even Dane can see. I know he can. He just hasn't said anything.

But being highly frustrated that Cara can't see how I feel isn't fair to her. Two of those years, I watched her from a distance. I felt like a horrible person, wanting her when she was still so young. Young, impressionable and naïve. There was no way she could've known I always noticed her. I saw the way her face would be so animated when she was excited. The way her eyes would get wide and her smile would stretch across her face. The way her hands flailed around while she spoke.

There is no way she would've seen that I was watching her like a damn creep. Even now, when I think about it, I cringe.

Then she finally turned eighteen. At last, I could ask her out. Let her know I was interested. Finally, I could put it out there and let the chips fall where they may, except I didn't even make it to the buy-in.

Peyton showed up. Cara left for college, and another nearly three years have passed.

And since she's been back, I've kept my distance again because being around her is hard. Especially since I thought I was hiding my feelings. I thought I was burying it deep down, but apparently, I suck at it. It shouldn't be surprising. I've always been a lousy liar.

I'm such an idiot. Of course, she has no idea how I feel. Has no idea how ridiculously attracted to her I am. I'm honestly afraid it would scare the hell out of her if she did know. I think it just did a little while ago.

What I do know is that my mom was right. Ryder and Maddox are right. I've waited forever. It's time to go after what I want. I might as well do it now. Because Lyra is going to get attached regardless because of the time they will be spending together. That makes this the perfect opportunity.

I need to try. But I can't rush it. I have to move slow. But, at least, I'll be moving forward instead of stuck in this stagnant stalemate.

I can move slow for her. Give her a chance to get to know me. Let her see the chemistry between us because I know she felt it earlier.

I could see it in her eyes. Could tell by the way her breathing picked up and her cheeks flushed. It was electric. The attraction and spark were undeniable. For a split second, I thought we would fly right past the get to know you phase straight to the bed.

Then it all went to hell. She crumbled before my eyes. A piece of me crumbled right there with her. She practically convulsed in my arms. Her sobs were heartbreaking, much like that day in River City. Her mutterings, almost indecipherable.

Except for one phrase.

Please stop.

Those two words stopped my heart. When I think about what happened right before she fell apart, my blood boils. Dark thoughts filter through my mind, sending bile to my throat.

I wanted to keep her wrapped in my arms, protected and safe. It was instinctual. And for a minute, she allowed it. She sunk deep into my chest once again. She clung to the comfort I offered. We were in a bubble. A bubble I wanted forever, it seems. Although under different circumstances.

I knew the minute the bubble burst. There was a physical shift in the air, like a bucket of ice water doused over our heads. Her body, which had finally relaxed, was tense again. Her breathing increased. The hope that maybe I had a shot evaporated. When she pulled away, I let her. It killed me, but I let her.

Now on my third glass of whiskey, I need answers. I have no right to ask her. When I did, I could practically hear her walls erecting around her with steel reinforcements. She doesn't trust me, but I think she wanted to. Or maybe she does trust me and doesn't want to. I just know, I felt her hesitation.

But I know who does have answers. This time I'm not leaving until I get them. I'm tired of being told they can't tell me. We're supposed to be best friends. Well, it's time for my best friend to spill.

I text Dane, telling him to meet me in Maddox and Ryder's room in five minutes. Then inform Maddox and Ryder that I'm on my way.

I get to their room just as the door opens. A petite brunette walks out with Maddox and Ryder behind her. She turns to kiss Maddox first, then Ryder, before walking past me.

I tilt my head with a bit of a smirk as I try to figure out how the hell they work so fast.

"Don't knock it 'til you try it," Maddox repeats his earlier remark.

I just shake my head at them, walking into the room. Dane grumbles behind me. "What the hell is going on, man?" he scrubs a hand through his hair. "Can't a guy make love to his girl without some kind of emergency?"

"Can't you three go twenty-four hours without sex?" I snap.

"Jealous?" Ryder taunts with a wide grin.

"No," I lie. I lie so damn hard.

"Come on, let's get this over with," Dane says, stalking past me to the identical living room that my suite has.

"You two," I point at Dane and Maddox, "are going to tell me what the hell happened in Chicago, and you are going to tell me right now. No bullshit."

Dane starts shaking his head while Maddox looks at Ryder. "Don't look at me, mate. I want to know, too. I've been asking as long as he has."

"We can't tell you," Maddox tells us both, sitting on the long blue sofa. "It's as simple as that."

"I don't like secrets, Mads," Ryder's brows drop to a deep V. His mouth presses into a thin line. I imagine if I looked in a mirror right now, I'd have a matching expression. "We don't have them, remember?"

Maybe they don't.

"It's not that simple, Ry," Maddox tells him.

Ryder's green eyes turn cold as he levels Maddox with a stern gaze.

"Look," Dane says with a sigh, "Cara was targeted by some guy because they wanted Tori."

"Dane," Maddox leans forward with his elbows on his knees. His eyes narrow, and his jaw tightens. His body language both threatening and warning in equal measure.

My worry and fear amplify in reaction to their sketchy behavior. This isn't like Maddox at all. He's often quiet and thoughtful. Easy-going to the outsider. He only radiates this much tension over his family or when he gets in over his head with something.

"We trust them," Dane says, not reacting to Maddox at all. "They are family, remember?" He gestures to both of us.

"Which is why we agreed to protect them from any fallout. Just knowing puts them at risk," Maddox grits through clenched teeth.

Dane looks to me, then to Ryder. "It doesn't leave this room. *Do not* bring it up to Cara."

"Shouldn't Angel and Liam be here?" Ryder asks. "They're family too."

Dane nods while Maddox leans back on the sofa with a huff. "Text them," Dane nods toward the phone on the coffee table in front of him.

Five minutes later, Angel sits next to me on the sofa opposite Maddox and Ryder. "What's going on? I just want to be with my girl," he whines.

"Good grief," I mutter at the ridiculousness of all of them.

"I was sleeping damn good, guys. This better be important," Liam tells us with a yawn.

"The reason we asked you two to come is that you're family," Maddox tells Angel and Liam. "Liam, you weren't around when this happened, but we're not telling the story again. You need to hear it."

"A year and a half ago, Mads and I left the tour for Chicago." Angel, Ryder, and I nod, remembering they disappeared and wouldn't tell us why. I wasn't there, but I talked to one of them every day.

"I've heard," Liam acknowledges.

"All you told us was that Tori and Cara needed you," Ryder nods.

"Zoey called me," Maddox explains. "She didn't think it was right for Dane to be kept in the dark."

"About what?" I grit out, tired of what feels like the runaround. "Just tell us what the hell happened."

"Cara started seeing this guy in Chicago and started dodging me. I sent Tori to go check on her. Apparently, this guy knew all about me from Cara, I assume, and knew if she avoided me long enough, I'd send Tori. They wanted Tori for underground fighting and threatened Cara if Tori didn't play along. When she finally told Zane, he somehow connected them to a human trafficking ring. They weren't just using Tori for fighting. They planned on selling them both."

"Jesus," I mutter, hearing my fears confirmed.

"Zane and his brothers did what they had to to get them out before they had a chance, but it got hairy," Maddox tells us.

66

"How did that *not* make the news?" Angel asks quietly.

"Let's just say they have some really good connections and leave it at that," Maddox tells us, definitively ending that line of questioning.

Dane nods. "The rest isn't important."

"It feels like you're leaving huge chunks out. Important chunks," Ryder tells them both.

Icy tendrils of disgust and fear snake their way down my spine as lava builds in my chest from absolute, unfettered rage. An odd combination that makes for a volatile cocktail.

"Was she raped?" I ask, my voice low and threatening.

Dane's eyes snap to mine, wide and surprised. "What?"

"Was. Cara. Raped?" I repeat, slowly, with barely contained fury.

"No!" he yells, leaping from his seat. "She didn't even want a doctor."

"And that's supposed to mean what exactly?" I hiss. "You are not stupid. I know you've seen her flashbacks."

Maddox's eyes dart between the two of us. He's gone pale. I know this is a rough subject for him, and because of that, I know he should know something too. "Did she tell you?" I wonder.

He shakes his head. "She's never said a word. What flashbacks?"

"Cara wasn't fucking raped. She would've told us," Dane continues to insist. "A lot of shit went down that night. Most people would be affected."

67

I stand up, shaking my head. I hope to God he's right and not just in denial. But I know something else happened besides what he's saying. Something, I guess, Cara hasn't told him, but I know that's all I'm getting out of them.

I leave without another word as they murmur amongst themselves. When I'm in the hallway, a hand to my shoulder stops me. "What was that about?"

I turn to my best friend. His jaw is tightly clenched, and his lips pressed firmly together.

"You didn't see what I just saw, Dane. You didn't see how completely shattered she was."

"So, this inquisition – all the demands for answers – it was just because she freaked out on you?" I keep my face as straight as possible. I know what he's really asking, but I'm not in the mood to deal with his freak out right now. I nod without a word. His face grows harder. "Bull-fucking-shit, Jake."

I raise a brow in challenge. "What else would it be? I was worried about her. She is here to take care of Lyra. I need to know she can do that."

"Don't do that," he scoffs. "Don't use Lyra as your scapegoat. You're better than that."

"I'm not using Lyra," I snarl at his accusation.

"You were with me when I brought her home. If this were about that little girl, you wouldn't have been so quick to accept Cara's offer."

I need to walk away because right now, I am so pissed. I am pissed at what she's been through. I'm pissed that she's still going through it. And part of me blames Dane.

Logically, I know it's not his fault. Hell, I've told him as much when I could see the guilt eating at him. But he's the one who confronted me in this hallway, knowing I'm already pissed. I inhale sharply, getting my mouth in check before I say something I don't mean. "Then you tell me, Dane. Tell me what this is all about."

I wait, knowing what he's going to say before he says. I want to hit something, and he is priming himself to be that something. Because I swear, when he loses his shit, I will punch him in the face, and right now, I will enjoy it. I'll save the guilt and remorse for later.

"How about you answer a question first. How long have you had a thing for my sister?"

And there it is. What he's been dying to ask me for months, probably, and what I've wanted to tell him for years. My fists clench at my sides as the corner of my mouth tips up. "Long enough," I sneer. "Too goddamn long. Longer than I should."

Anger flares in his eyes. Lines forms around his blue eyes, and his nostrils flare. I'm ready for whatever he brings. "You still haven't answered my question, Jake," he grinds out.

"For years, Dane. For fucking years," I yell.

The door to Maddox's room opens. They all come out. They stand there watching, ready to jump in at any minute but won't interfere before it's necessary.

"Since you haven't seen her in *years* until a few months ago, I'm guessing longer than it's been appropriate," he accuses, daring me to deny it.

Except, I'm not in the mood to deny anything right now. "Since the first time I saw her," I grin without the slightest bit of mirth.

"You pissed, Dane?" I taunt. "You pissed that your best friend wants your baby sister? You want to kick my ass?"

"Jake," I hear Maddox warn.

"You think I'm pissed because you like her?" He jerks back. Incredulity and shock line his face and voice. "Jake, I'm fucking pissed because you never said anything. We're best friends and you didn't tell me."

I scoff, "Come on, Dane. It's not a secret that you don't want anyone with your sisters, much less your friends. Mads and Ry are proof of that."

"Maddox and Ryder didn't like Tori. They just fucked her. I didn't want her to get hurt. And those two are a heartbreak waiting to happen." He looks over his shoulder at them, daring them. "Am I wrong?".

"I have a past, too, Dane," I remind him, knowing full well that's what he really means about Maddox and Ryder. "And a fuckton of baggage."

"Man, if you've been hung up on Cara this long, she is your past and baggage," he says, the tension in his shoulders and eyes falling away. "I'm just saying that she can and has done a lot worse."

I shake my head, trying to wrap my head around what he's saying. I look behind him to the guys who look just as disbelieving as I feel. Either I'm in an alternate universe right now, or Dane has been taken over by pod people. I still don't trust it.

"It doesn't matter how I feel," I tell him firmly. "Cara doesn't see me the same way."

Even as I say it, I remember the moment earlier. The moment before it went to hell. The energy between us charged the whole room. It was not one-sided or imagined. She may not feel the same as I do, but the attraction was there.

"Then make her see you that way." My jaw hits the floor.

"Holy shit."

"What the fuck?"

"What the hell?"

"I'll be damned."

The guys all mutter my exact thoughts while I try to scrape my jaw off the floor. He's not just telling me he's cool with how I feel. He's encouraging me to go after her. To go after the little sister he's protected like a momma bear for – well, forever.

He laughs for the first time since this conversation started. "I'm not that bad," he mutters.

"You really are, brother," Maddox tells him.

"Well, not this time. You'd be good for her, man. You should know, though, you have your work cut out for you. She doesn't trust her own judgment anymore. Not since that bastard in Chicago betrayed her, so it will take a lot to get her to open up."

I nod, not knowing what to say to him at the moment. I'm trying to process how up became down and left became right. I turn away from all of them to go back to my room.

"Oh, and Jake," he calls just as my hand grips the handle to my door. I stop without looking back at him, "if you hurt her, you die."

And with those words, I feel like the world is right again. Almost.

71

Cara

I wake to soft knocking on my door. My eyes flutter for a moment in an attempt to adjust to the light streaming into the room. Momentary panic sets in when I don't recognize where I'm at.

The door begins to open slowly. My heart begins to pound in my chest. My breathing speeds up.

"Cara," I hear from the cracked door.

My lungs fill with relief as I exhale. Familiarity courses through me as my panic recedes. "Come in," I say, my voice slightly strangled.

Jake pushes the door open a bit further so that he's standing just inside. He stares at me for a moment. I wonder if he sees the fear I felt only moments ago. If he does, he says nothing. For which I am grateful.

"I have to leave for the venue in a little bit. Thought you'd want time to get yourself together." His eyes dart back and forth between mine as he assesses me. I assume he's trying to decide if I'm okay after my epic meltdown.

"I'm okay, Jake." I try to assuage his obvious nervousness.

He gives a short nod but doesn't look convinced. "Just take your time. I'll let you know when I need to get ready."

"Thank you." I force a smile, hoping it's convincing because the last thing I want is for him to worry about Lyra or feel sorry for me. The truth is, though, I do need a few minutes. I'm still feeling a bit drained.

He flashes me a small smile, his eyes still searching mine for something. I'm not sure what, but it does strange things to my stomach. Things I've never felt for anyone. Things I don't entirely understand, and I'm not sure I want to feel now. Then he finally turns, leaving the room.

I drag myself out of bed. The truth is, I would rather stay there all day. Stay buried under the weight of the pillows and blankets until this weight I feel pressing on my chest subsides.

It's not an option, though. So I have no other choice than to drag my tail from this bed and do what I need to do to get through the rest of this day.

I go to the bathroom to relieve the pressure on my bladder. I quickly wash my hands, brush my teeth, and run a brush through my hair. It's three in the afternoon here, and it seems a little ridiculous to get dressed now, but it's part of my therapy. To get up, get dressed, and face the world even when I don't want to.

It's been a month since my last flashback. That one wasn't as bad as today. I wonder as I sort through my bag if that means I'm allowed a pass. If it would be too much to let getting dressed slide. I'm up and out of bed. I'm moving. I'll be taking care of Lyra, so I can't spend too much time in my own mind.

But what happens when I put her to bed? When it's just me in this ridiculously large suite, alone with only my thoughts? Not thoughts. Memories. What was triggered was a memory, and I'm still not sure what triggered it.

I shake my head. I need to call my therapist.

I walk to the nightstand where I left my phone. Picking it up, I quickly pull up the number and click the call button. He picks up on the third ring.

"Cara, how are you?" No awkward pleasantries are ever exchanged when I call, and he always answers.

"Not as great as I'd like to be." A sigh escapes me. One day away, and I'm already on the phone with him. It feels like I've made no progress at all as I break down the events of that morning.

"What memories did you remember when this happened?"

I swallow hard against voicing them. I hate talking about that night. "I remembered being held against him. My arms pinned so I couldn't move as he licked down my neck, telling me to watch."

"How did you come out of the memory? What brought you back?"

"I'm not sure anything did. I didn't think it was ever going to stop." I squeeze my eyes shut against the threat of tears. "I kept hearing that word over and over. *Watch.* And I did. I couldn't stop it, just like that day. I had to watch. I tried to close my eyes. I didn't want to see."

My breathing begins to pick up as everything tries to invade my mind. "But that wasn't really happening, was it? You were really there."

"No." The word comes out as a whisper.

"Because that was a long time ago. It's a part of your past, and the past can't hurt you now."

"It hurts me," I admit. "It hurts so much. The guilt and the shame feel like they will bury me."

"Have you journaled any of this? Did you do your worksheet?"

"No. I just went to bed," I confess.

He chuckles lightly. "And tossed and turned, no doubt."

"Yes, but not entirely for the reasons you're thinking." The words are out before I can stop them, but who else would I confess this to?

"Oh really? What else caused the restlessness?" Genuine curiosity blooms in his tone. I can almost see his brow quirked high.

"Jake. We had a moment before *and* after. It was strange."

"And when you say moment, you mean -?" He leaves the statement open-ended, waiting on me to fill in the blanks.

"Sparks. I've never felt anything for Jake. In all the years I've known him, he's just been my brother's friend. But today, it was like a strange pull."

"Just suddenly?"

I feel myself heat at the admission bubbling to the surface. "No. Not entirely. I've – I don't know, since that day in my apartment, I've felt this pull toward him. I can't explain it. I just know I don't want it."

"I see."

"Do you?" I ask indignantly.

"Back to earlier. Have you identified the trigger so you can prevent it?"

I exhale, glad he's not going to push about Jake. "No. Everything happened so fast. I didn't even have a chance to prepare myself or stave it off."

"Cara, while you have the tools to help yourself, you know I did not recommend you going on this trip. You need more sessions here."

"But you agreed we could do this over video," I argue.

"No. I told you we could continue over video after you insisted."

"We'll make it work," I nod definitively.

"We will definitely try, Cara. Like I said, you have the tools, but you cannot rush this. You have certainly made wonderful progress. Don't push yourself into a setback. Travel like you'll be doing can be stressful under the best of circumstances."

"I won't get stressed," I promise. All the while wondering how I will keep that promise.

"Okay, Cara," he sighs. "We'll talk again next week unless you need me beforehand."

"Thank you," I say, then end the call.

76

I am not helpless. I am safe. It is not my fault.

I inhale sharply, then hold it for a count of five before releasing it through my mouth with my tongue pressed against the top of my front teeth. I repeat the process twice more before exiting the room.

When I walk out, I turn into a pile of mush. Warmth unfurls in my belly almost immediately at the sight in front of me. It nearly brings tears to my eyes.

Jake has Lyra in his lap, reading her a story. Her two middle fingers in her mouth, she smiles widely as he changes his voice for each character.

I stand back, letting the adorable scene wash over me. I commit it to memory because it's the type of image that will be useful during my breathing exercises.

I've never seen a kid cuter than Lyra, except maybe my nephew, Dax, who is also all blond ringlets like his parents but has ultra pale blue eyes like his father's twin sister. Lyra's eyes aren't ice-blue. More of a sky blue with a smokey center. So big and full of intelligence. Expressive and happy.

"You can come sit with us," Jake says without looking up. I wonder how he knew I was there.

I suppose it would be weird to continue to stand here and watch. I walk toward them until I'm standing just to the side of the sofa. Lyra's eyes light up when she sees me.

My heart skitters and skips that those eyes light up for me.

"Cara." She whispers around her fingers.

Jake jerks his head to the seat next to him. I look at the spot. Hesitation fills me. "I didn't mean to interrupt."

"You're not. I'm just doing this now because she'll be asleep when I get back tonight."

Warmth spreads further, filling me to the brim with feelings I don't want. I swallow it down, refusing to let it surface or take hold.

I wouldn't be a woman if seeing him with his daughter didn't evoke some kind of emotion. There's just something about watching a man with a child – a father with his child – that always pulls at my heart. Maybe it's because I never knew mine.

Dane has always assured me that my father wasn't worth knowing. Deep down, I know he's right. I never laid eyes on my father. He knocked my mom up even though he was married to Dane's mom at the time. My mom didn't know that. It was just a fling, I suppose. She didn't live long enough for me to really find out. I just know she said she never regretted it because she got me. The same thing happened with our sister Tori. Unfortunately, she didn't even get a great mom out of the deal.

Dane found me when I was eleven. Just showed up one day. He said he didn't even know I existed until then. His mom told him about me.

My mom immediately let him in. I suppose she could see the goodness that is my brother. Saw how he just wanted that connection. How he wanted to protect me.

I don't know where I would be today if he hadn't. When mom died, I landed in foster care for a bit. My brother did everything he could to get custody of me. His grandfather helped. Then, finally, it was done. I came home with my brother, the only family I had left. Or so I thought. A few years later, completely by chance, Tori stumbled into our lives.

Watching Jake with Lyra makes me wonder what it would have been like to have that bond. That beautiful connection that only a daddy and his daughter can have. It's not worth lingering over. I'll never know, but every time I see him with her, my heart squeezes. He is such a good dad.

He's still waiting on me to sit, so I do. I keep space between us, but I sit and listen while he continues to read to her from a huge book of fairytales. I watch as she nestles in tighter to her dad, listening intently. Contentment and innocence fill her tiny face.

I don't miss the way he keeps looking at me from the corner of his eye. I don't miss the sizzle in the air either. Like if I got any closer, that zap would strike me again. It makes me scoot away a little more because the last thing I need is any kind of spark between Jake and me.

He finishes the story, his eyes firmly attached to me as Lyra takes the book, crawling to the floor. I fight the urge to squirm under his intense stare. "Cara, I...." he starts.

"I've got her," I interrupt, not knowing what he was about to say but also not sure I want to know. "You can go take a shower now."

His lips press into a firm line before he nods. He walks out of the room with a shake of his head, mumbling something about never having a chance.

When he is in his room, I move to where Lyra is sprawled across the carpets floor with her book. I watch as she turns the pages with such gentle regard. More than I thought would be possible from a child her age.

"What do you have there, pretty girl?" I crawl to the floor, stretching myself beside her.

"My faiwytales," she grins. "My daddy weads to me." She shoves the book closer to me and flips the pages. "I wuv Sweeping Booty," she tells me with wide eyes. I can help but grin at her enunciation.

"I like Sleeping Beauty, too. Can you say Sleeping Beauty?" I ask, emphasizing each syllable.

She taps her chin thoughtfully. "Sweeping Booty," she says, only this time emphasizing the 'oo' sounds even more. I giggle, and she pouts.

"Don't worry, pretty girl," I tug her hair. "You've got plenty of time to learn."

"But I wants to does it now." Her arms fold across her chest as that bottom lip juts out.

"We'll practice later, okay?" I offer, hoping it will get that lip back in place.

"O-k-ay," she says with determination and purpose.

I giggle again. She is almost too smart and definitely too cute.

I get to my feet to go to the kitchen. I grab a bottle of water from the fridge and then grab my pills from my hoodie pocket. I take two, quickly chasing them with water.

"What's that?" I hear behind me making me squeal a little too loudly.

I look over to Lyra, making sure I didn't scare her, then turn my attention to Jake. "You scared the hell out of me," I spit.

"I'm sorry." His eyes show concern and worry. He hands me a sheet of paper. "I just wanted to give this to you. It's a list of her favorite movies and such."

I take the list, shoving it into my pocket. "I'll use this later. We won't need it today. I'm taking her to a puppet show."

"You can't take her out," he tells me with an absolutely stunned look.

"What? Why?" I demand.

"Because you don't know anything about this place. You can't speak the language. It's not safe."

"Everywhere we go on this tour will be unfamiliar," I tell him sharply. "You don't expect to keep her locked away in hotel rooms the entire time, do you?"

His shoulders slump. "I didn't think about that."

"Liam has hired security detail so we can venture out safely. We'll be fine."

"Are you going to answer my question?" I look at him, confused. When I don't answer, he elaborates. "The pills."

"They're from my doctor. For my anxiety," I grit out, a little pissed at whatever he's insinuating.

His eyes move between mine. "Are you okay?" I open my mouth for another snarky remark. My natural reaction is to be defensive but swallow it down when I see the genuine concern in his eyes.

"I'm fine, Jake. I swear I won't let anything happen to Lyra," I tell him, assuming that's what his real concern is.

"I'm not *just* worried about Lyra. I'm worried about you too."

"If this is about this morning, Jake...." I begin, but he is quick to cut me off.

81

"It's not about this morning. Or, at least, not in the way you're thinking."

"Look, Jake, I know you feel some kind of obligation to Dane or something to watch out for me, but I really am fine."

"It's not about that either." Frustration lines his face and fills his tone as he roughly scrapes a hand down his face then through his hair.

I give him a curt smile and nod, then begin to move around him when he grabs my elbow. The electric tingles start again. "Cara, " he starts.

It's obvious he wants to say something. But it's the way he's looking at me that makes my stomach flip. He reaches up, brushing the hair from my face. I can't stop my gasp when his fingers brush my cheek. If touching me through my clothes gives me tingles, the touch of his skin touching mine feels like an electrical storm, just like this morning.

I am utterly frozen to the spot, unable to breathe.

"I have wanted to tell you something for a while now." He is watching me closely. Too closely. Close enough, I feel like he can see inside my soul. When I still don't say anything because I can't even form a complete thought with his hand still lingering on my cheek. "Cara, I…." He gets cut off by a knock on the suite door. "Of fucking course," he mumbles.

The conversation seemingly ends when he goes to answer the door, and I can finally breathe again. I'm not sure what that was. It felt like a panic attack but different. And the different part scares me more than if it had actually been a panic attack.

I return to the living area with Lyra again. I need to get my mind off of whatever just happened between Jake and me, so I start talking to her. "Lyra, how would you like to go to a fairytale house?"

I remember reading about the Skazkin House when I researched things to do in the different countries on the guys' schedule. It is perfect for a little girl in love with fairytales. I also make a mental note to check out the ballets while we are traveling.

"Faiwytale house?" she looks at me with wonder.

"What's the fairytale house?" Jake asks as he walks in with Liam and a huge, intimidating blond guy. I feel a bout of nerves flutter at the sight of him.

I turn my attention to Jake instead so I can answer his question. "I told you about it earlier."

"You said a puppet show." His head tilts as he tries to figure out the connection.

I nod with a sigh. "It's called Skazkin House. It's also referred to as the Fairytale House."

"Oh," is his only response. He's still not comfortable with us going out.

"Looks like I'll be starting to work right now," the blond guy chuckles. It's a warm, friendly sound that is at odds with his physique and stature.

I finally allow myself to make eye contact with him. His green eyes shine with a warmth that matches his laugh. Tiny lines crinkle around the corners of those green eyes. He seems nice.

But I've been wrong about that before. Which is why I keep my distance from strangers. Why I don't let people get too close anymore. Why I can't trust my own judgment.

"Cara, this is my friend Henry. He agreed to be your security detail. He's well-traveled, knows many of the areas we will be traveling and will act as a translator too," Liam explains to me.

I breathe out a sigh of relief. He's Liam's friend. Liam is Dane's friend. All the guys' friend. If they trust him, then I know I can too.

"Translator for where exactly?" I ask curiously because we'll be traveling to lots of places. How many languages can one person possibly speak?

"Nearly everywhere we go. He speaks most European languages," Liam tells me bluntly.

"I speak fourteen languages, ma'am. Spent a lot of years working as a translator while I served," he explains. I finally take a good look at him. From the way he holds himself to his hair, I'm surprised I didn't realize before that he is military. More proof that my judgment sucks.

The nervous bubble in my stomach begins to dissipate at the revelation. "When did you retire?"

"A few years ago. Medical discharge. I'm good as new, now, though," he grins. I notice that severe expression softens when he does. "I'll make a pretty good tour guide."

I smile shyly at his teasing. Jake scowls for some strange reason. I would think he'd feel better with someone like Henry watching after Lyra and me.

"So we good here?" Liam's eyes fall to Jake and me.

"I'm good," I nod. Jake's lips are pressed into a tight, thin line, but he nods as well.

84

"Good," he says with a clap, "now you and I have somewhere to be," he tells Jake.

Jake sighs, looking at Liam. "I need another minute with Cara."

A silent message passes between the two of them. "You don't have a minute," he answers with a shake of his head. I'm glad because I don't think I want another minute with Jake alone.

He looks back at me. I quickly avert my eyes. Looking anywhere but at him. "Fine," he says with a heavy sigh.

"Give me a minute to change Lyra and pack her a bag," I tell Henry once he and Liam exit. My voice is thick with nerves at being left alone with the strange man. I know he is there for my protection. He won't hurt me, but, for a moment, that discomfort from earlier returns.

He chuckles again, those lines crinkling his eyes. "You don't have to be nervous, ma'am. I won't bite."

I give another grin with a shake of my head. "I'm sorry. I didn't mean to offend you."

"None taken, ma'am."

"Cara."

He nods with a grin then I head to Lyra's room to get her ready to go.

Half an hour later, we are surrounded by people in costumes and miniature houses that could be straight out of a fairytale. Lyra's eyes sparkle with delight, and she wiggles around dancing to the music. We watch *The Tale of the Silly Mouse*, Henry by our sides the entire time taking it all in stride.

We leave Stazkin House in search of food a two-year-old will eat.

"Pizza is always a good choice, right? That's what my sister's kid lives on," Henry suggests with an easy smile.

"They have pizza in Russia?" I ask, surprised. Then immediately feel my face flush for asking such a stupid question.

He graciously ignores it. "I know the perfect place. How about it, Lyra? Want some pizza?"

"I yikes pizza," she tells him with her own wide, smiling face.

A little while later, Henry and I are sipping coffee while Lyra devours ice cream.

"How long did you serve?" I ask to make small talk. I may as well get to know the man that will be my shadow of sorts for the foreseeable future.

"Straight out of high school. Served my full eight years. Signed a new contract. I was coming up on my twelfth year when I was injured."

I give him an apologetic nod. "What happened?"

The funniest thing happens. This large, intimidating man who looks positively lethal turns several shades of red with a deep, rumbling chuckle. "I've been through a lot of shit. I won't go into details, but I'm sure you can guess. But a fu – freaking slip in the shower got me." I cover my mouth to stop my laugh from showing, but he knows what I'm doing. "Go ahead, kid, laugh it up," he chuckles. "So, yeah, a year in rehab wasn't enough to let the government keep me on. A buddy of mine got me a job doing personal security for punk-ass rock stars a couple of years back."

"Liam?" I asked, a bit surprised because Liam and Henry are so different from each other.

"We've known each other since we were kids. That guy saved my life, and I think I may have saved his," he says, his eyes getting the haze of memories.

"No wife and kids?"

Regret fills his expression for a split second before it's gone. "No woman wants a man like me, kid." He doesn't say anything else, telling me that part of the conversation is over. But it leaves me more than a little curious. "What's your story?"

"I was raised by my mom until she died when I was eleven," I tell him. "My dad was scum, according to my brother, but Dane – he was amazing. He didn't hesitate to do everything he could to make sure I got to live with him after my mom died."

Henry leans back in his seat. His eyes scan my face as he studies me. "I'm sorry about your mom. You're very lucky to have a brother to step up. But I want to know what put that look in your eye."

I fight the flush of embarrassment that threatens. "I don't know what you mean." I hope my voice doesn't belie my words.

"Don't bullshit a bullshitter, kid. I recognize the look," he levels me with a hard stare. "Your eyes always darting around. The way you clench your fist to stop a fidget."

I didn't even realize I was doing these things. "I – uh – really can't talk about it."

"All right, kid. I'm here if you need me, though. I'm your shadow until this thing is over. And I'm a pretty good listener too." His eyes exude warmth and concern. I feel like I've just obtained another brother.

Like I needed another one of those.

After we finish dinner, it is nearly seven. The guys will probably be going on soon. I hope their first show goes well.

I look over to Lyra. Her little head is bobbing as she begins to doze. A small laugh escapes me as I watch her. Her belly is full, and she's had an exciting adventure today.

"I suppose it's time to get this little cutie to – uh," I pause, not wanting her to have a meltdown over bedtime. I've seen it happen. It's not pretty. And she's since learned that b – e – d spells bed.

"Krovat'," Henry offers.

I tilt my head a bit, attempting to mimic what he just said. I laugh at myself, wondering if this is what Lyra feels like trying to repeat me. I butcher the word.

"Close enough," Henry laughs.

"Careful, or she'll know it in every language."

I'm surprised Lyra doesn't fight me once we're back in the suite. She has her bath, her teeth brushed, and is nearly asleep before I have her dressed.

Now the hard part. Sitting in this huge hotel suite with nothing but my thoughts. I grab my pills from my bag, then move to the kitchen for some water to chase them down. When the quiet becomes too much, I pull out my laptop to turn on a movie. I scroll through a few options before settling on reruns of *The Big Bang Theory*.

After a few episodes, my mind hasn't quietened at all. I'm jumpy at the shadows dancing across the room. My heart races every time I hear a noise. I think back over events that happened and choices I made that led to those events.

I've got to use the tools given to me before I spiral.

I sit on the floor, stretching a few times before crossing my legs. I breathe in slowly, holding it, then release it. I pull up a calming memory like I've been taught to do. The first memory that comes to mind is earlier today when Jake was reading to Lyra. The sound of Jake's voice spreads warmth through me while images of Lyra curled into him in absolute contentment dance behind my eyes.

My body finally begins to relax as my mind focuses on the here and now.

I am alive. I can't change the past. I am not responsible for the actions of others. I have my family. What happened in the past can't hurt me in the present.

Over and over, I repeat these things to myself until I finally find myself calm and collected. I'm not sure how long I do this, but soon enough, I feel sleep tickling the edges of my mind.

I look to the room Lyra is sleeping in. I worry if she wakes in a strange place, she'll be afraid. I worry I won't hear her.

I decide to stay on the sofa. I find another blanket covering myself. Finally satisfied, I settle in for the rest of the night.

Jake

It's after midnight when I roll into the suite, completely wired and exhausted all at once. I could've gone out with the guys afterward, but I wanted to get back to my girls.

Girl. I remind myself. Only one is mine. The other is not.

I want to finish the conversation I tried to have with her earlier. The conversation that was interrupted. I wasn't sure what I was going to tell her. Not exactly. But I had to tell her something. I need her to know, at the very least, that I'm interested in her.

Interested? What a shit word. A shit way to explain that I was borderline obsessed with her. That's a whole other area I need to be careful about knowing what I now know.

But what else would explain five years of wanting her when two of these years she was off-limits and nearly three more, she was across the country? I am living proof that out of sight, out of mind does not always work.

Yep. Totally obsessed.

My body burns with lust and desire at the thought of those near ebony eyes. My heart races and stops and races again with affection like I never felt for any other woman. At the inexplicable need and want for her to smile and laugh. At the need to be the one to put that smile on her face. Although, I will admit I've done a shit job of that so far.

All of that must make me insane, right?

I walk through the foyer of the suite, following the sounds of Sheldon Cooper, hopeful I will be able to talk to her. Uninterrupted.

It only takes a second to realize that conversation isn't happening. I watch her as she sleeps on the deep blue sofa. I want to say she looks peaceful, but she doesn't. Her body jerks, and her eyelids flicker rapidly.

What does it say that I want to climb into her dreams and slay those demons I know are chasing her? That I want to go back in time, to the day Peyton showed up at my door, and go to that party to tell her how I feel?

At the time, I thought I was doing the right thing. If I knew then what I know now, I would go. Peyton being pregnant didn't have to stop me from going after the girl. It didn't have to change anything. Did it?

It doesn't matter, though. I can't go back. And I still don't know that Cara would've accepted me.

What I do know is that she is definitely attracted to me. We have chemistry. I've seen it and felt it. Like a living, breathing

thing buzzing around us and between us, and that is something I can work with.

I squat beside her on the sofa and brush her hair from her face. I would pick her up and carry her to bed, but I don't know how she'll react. It's better to let her be aware of my presence first.

"Cara," I whisper.

Her flickering eyes fly open as she jumps up. I watch as she pulls her knees to her chest and scoots away from me. Hurt and anger fill my chest. It's not her fault. But the bastards that hurt her, that took that spark out of her need to pay. I know Dane says they have, but it doesn't feel like enough.

"It's okay, baby. It's just me," I tell her, then silently reprimand myself for calling her 'baby'.

Even sitting here, curled into herself, she is beautiful. Never have I seen anything like her. Wide eyes and flushed cheeks, panic at the edge of her mind, and she is gorgeous. Honestly, it hurts to look at her.

"I just wanted to get you to bed," I tell her, moving slowly to her with a smile that's killing me to wear because she looks like a scared, wild animal in the corner of that sofa. I reach out, offering my hand. "You with me, Cara?"

I watch as she begins to realize where she is. That she's safe. "Jake," she whispers.

The way my name sounds from her mouth right now is something I want to keep there. It's reverence and trust. I nod and then ask again, "You with me, Cara?"

She nods, slipping her hand in mine. The vice that gripped my heart when she threw herself into that corner loosens.

92

I pull her to her feet. She wobbles on her sleepy legs, but she doesn't try to move. She's too disoriented.

I reach for her, hooking my arm behind her knees, and carry her to her room. She doesn't even hesitate to lay her head on my chest. That does crazy things to my insides, but I try to tamp it down. She probably won't remember this in the morning. She won't remember the way she trusted me without thinking. The way she curled into me and found security.

I lay her in her bed, pulling the covers up to her chin. I place a kiss to her forehead, then turn to leave the room. I'm more than a little surprised when she grabs my wrist.

"Can you stay with me? Just for a minute?" Even in the dark room, I can see her pleading eyes. I can hear the fear in her choked voice.

And, again, I feel like an ass for accepting her offer to come here so quickly instead of realizing she probably needed more time. More time to deal with what is obviously PTSD. More time readjusting to her life.

I should tell her no. I should tell her it's not a good idea. But she has no idea why it would be bad. She has no clue that being that close to her sends my mind to dirty places. That it will be torture.

But I won't tell her no. While I hope someday soon I can do this with her all the time, I'm not going to take a chance that this will be the only time I get to lay beside her. Hold her in my arms.

"Let me check on Lyra, and I'll be right back," I whisper.

She nods, releasing my arm. I go to my little princess. She's snoring softly in the middle of the big bed. I bend over her,

93

kissing her forehead, and take a second to inhale her sweet baby scent. "Love you, princess," I whisper into her hair.

"Love yous, Daddy," she mumbles in her sleep. I can't stop the smile that spreads across my face or the way my heart fills to overflowing. Many hard and fast decisions had to be made where she's concerned, and I wouldn't change a single thing. I wouldn't give her up for anything or anyone. She's my baby girl, my princess, and no one will ever take that from me.

I return to Cara's room. She's curled on her side. I wonder if maybe she has fallen back to sleep. I stand over her, brushing the hair from her face. "You still want me here?" I whisper softly.

"Please," her strangled voice breaks through the darkness.

I slide in behind her, pulling her to my chest. I kiss the back of her head softly. "Go to sleep, Cara. I'm not going anywhere."

She nods, and in minutes, we're both asleep.

I woke up later that morning in Cara's bed alone. I heaved a sigh. Then dragged myself out of her room. I didn't miss the way she wouldn't look at me as she helped Lyra with breakfast.

Not gonna lie. It stung like a bitch, but I didn't regret it. I could never regret having her in my arms. Even if it was just to be some sort of comfort through whatever was tormenting her dreams.

I realized that night that I definitely had feelings. Feeling so far beyond a simple crush or attraction. I knew the minute she curled into my chest, I wanted everything from that girl.

That was three weeks ago. Three weeks and she's barely looked at me. Before the shows, her sole focus is Lyra. After the shows, she's been asleep in her own bed, usually with Lyra.

94

Three weeks of her giving me perfunctory nods and answers only as it regards Lyra. The rest of the time, she avoids me. Whenever I've tried to talk to her about anything that doesn't concern Lyra, she changes the subject. Even just small talk.

All I can really do is sit back and watch her with Lyra. That has proven to be another problem. For me anyway. It has filled me with a longing to give Lyra something she's never had – a mother. A position that I've been envisioning Cara filling which isn't the best place for my head to go considering I can't even get her to talk to me as a friend. Hell, she acts more like my employee than someone who's known me for years.

I am frustrated in every sense of the word and in more ways than one, and there isn't a damn thing I can do about it. Not until I can stop her from running away or avoiding me.

My mood has become irritable and prickly. The guys are in hysterics. They have no sympathy for me at all.

"You should've been thinking with your head and not your dick before you jumped on her proposition," Angel ragged me.

He's not wrong, but that's not the point. The point is I'm teetering on the razor-sharp edge of completely losing my shit. I have to remind myself every day that it would not be a good idea to throw her over my shoulder, tie her to my bed, and force her to talk to me right before I dive in between those long legs. I have a strong feeling that all of that would be the worst possible thing I could do, and there would be no coming back from that.

I walk off the stage in Prime Hall. Another sold-out show has my adrenaline pumping fast and hard. It only amplifies the irritation I'm feeling. Yes, it's with Cara but more with myself.

I am instantly crowded by several half-dressed women. They push their tits in my face, groping me in a way that's more than a little irritating. I don't even acknowledge them as I follow behind Ryder and Maddox to our dressing room.

"Can't people keep their hands to themselves?" I thunder when I walk in the door. Josephine and Camilla laugh as the women following behind me jump in shock.

Maddox and Ryder pull a couple of the women to their sides with boisterous laughs that make me want to slug 'em. "Man, you so *need* to get laid," Maddox cackles as he turns to do a line of coke off one of the girls' chest.

I turn away from that with a shake of my head. I've done it a few times when I was younger. It's fun while it lasts but to be in constant *need* of it so you can cope with life is not how I want to live life. It's sad as hell, honestly.

That is not the Maddox I've known for years. That is a man that has spiraled so far away from who he is, I doubt he recognizes himself most days. Of course, when you spend most of your days and nights high or drunk, it would be hard for anyone to recognize themselves. He's trying too hard to silence his demons, but I have a feeling it won't be long until he is face to face with all of them.

It's hard to watch, and I'm not just watching one friend fall down that slippery slope. Although, Ryder does seem to be capable of pulling back when he needs to. I'm just glad Josephine and Angel found each other again before he was spiraling right next to them.

"As long as he's hoping to get with my sister, he does not need to get laid," Dane grunts, pulling Cami to his chest. She isn't even paying attention to him. She is deep in conversation with Josephine. He buries his face in her hair, inhaling her like she's the calm he needs to bring him down from the high of being on stage.

"I meant he needed to get laid by…." Maddox grins widely, his aquamarine eyes already glazed.

Dane cuts him off with a look that promises violence. *"DO NOT* finish that sentence," he orders while turning an interesting shade of green. "God, I might get sick."

"Mate, Cara is a grown woman. You already know she's not a virgin," Ryder taunts him.

Dane makes a face while my inner caveman growls at the thought of anyone else touching her. "Could you *not* say that shit? How can you even think it?"

"Because we're fucking grown-ups," Maddox laughs. "She is a gorgeous girl on top of being an amazing person. There was no avoiding it."

"Well, doesn't mean I have to hear or think about it," he grumbles. Cami pulls out of his arms, and she and Josephine begin gathering our clothes. When they're out of the room, he turns to me. "Why haven't you talked to her yet? Then maybe this dickish attitude wouldn't be so bad."

"Because I haven't had a chance," I groan.

"You're with her all day, every day until we have an interview or have to be at the venue. There are a lot of hours between daylight and six p.m." Maddox gives me a doubtful look. It takes real talent to be a smart ass without sounding like one. Must be a southern thing because I don't know anyone else with that skill.

He's right, mate," Ryder smirks. "You've had plenty of time to lock that shit down."

97

Dane groans, sticking his fingers in his ears like a child.

"You all assume I'm the only thing holding us back. You do realize Cara may not have any interest in me, right?" Even as I say it, my gut tells me that's not entirely true. I can tell Cara is, at least, attracted to me. "Besides, she's avoiding me, man," I tell them honestly.

"Why? What did you do?" Dane looks like he's ready to pummel me.

"I did exactly what she asked. First night, I came in, and she was asleep on the sofa. I carried her to her room, and she asked me to stay with her. I did. I stayed with her all night. Didn't do anything but sleep. Next day, she won't even look me in the eye."

"Wonder what's up with that?" Maddox's brow furrows into a deep V.

"I have no clue. Not like it's the first time I've comforted her."

"For some reason, she's not comfortable with you now," Dane tells me simply. He may not realize that his simple statement felt like he just stabbed me in the heart. I rub absently at my chest, trying to soothe the ache. "She's never done well in situations if she's uncomfortable. She has always shut down. You have to force her to deal with that discomfort."

"You sure that's a good idea?" Maddox looks at him with worry.

"No, but it's the only choice he has." Dane pushes from the wall he's leaning against and walks to me. He puts his hands on my shoulders. "She may not feel the same, brother, but you won't know until you try."

I nod with a heavy sigh. I know he's right. Guess it's time to man up.

An hour later, I walk into our room in Minsk. I fully expect to find her asleep like every other night. Imagine my surprise when I see her on the sofa with her bodyguard laughing and throwing popcorn at each other.

My jaw snaps so hard I swear I hear a crack. They look entirely too comfortable together. I can't get her to give me more than a few obligatory words, but she's here laughing with him like they're best friends.

Or something else.

"Having fun?" I ask with a snarl.

Cara jumps ten feet then clutches her chest. She looks over at me with a guilty expression. That's definitely interesting and makes me wonder what the fuck else is going on here.

Henry, on the other hand, smirks in my direction. That smirk really pisses me off.

"I'm gonna head back to my room, kid. You'll be good here," he tells her with a kiss to the top of her head then ruffles her hair.

That gesture tells me that there is absolutely nothing sexual or anywhere close to that going on here. He is looking at her just like Dane looks at her. Like all the guys look at her.

But I've never been the most logical person. I'm a jealous, possessive asshole, and logic doesn't go well with those two attributes.

Henry walks past me with another smirk, and I clench my fist.

Cara doesn't say a word to me. She won't even look at me. I can't figure out for the life of me what the hell is going on.

She gets up from the sofa, takes the popcorn container to the kitchen, and makes her way to her room. All without looking at me once.

My mouth has disconnected from my brain. It is being fueled by my jealousy, frustration, and anger. "You fucking the bodyguard?" I growl.

She spins on her heels. Her mouth hanging open. She's damn sure looking at me now. Her face turns red, at first with embarrassment, but then it morphs. "What did you say to me?"

I move until there's less than a foot between us. "I asked if you're fucking the bodyguard?"

"Who in the hell do you think you are?" she hisses.

"I think I'm the guy who just asked you a question," I smirk. I am getting way too much pleasure out of seeing her so pissed. And I'm so damn turned on my dick could cut glass.

"You're asking questions that are none of your business."

"I just made it my business." I close a little more of the space between us. We are nearly touching.

"I've got enough big brothers. I don't need another." She is almost yelling. I should be worried about Lyra waking up, but this is the most I've gotten out of her in weeks.

"You're being paid to watch Lyra, not fuck the guy being paid to watch you." She raises her hand to slap me, but I catch her by the wrist. "And I have *never* considered myself a brother to you."

Her face distorts in anger, but I see it. I see the lust and desire, and I snap.

In what could probably be the dumbest thing I've ever done, I slam my mouth to hers. It's all frustration and aggression and not how I wanted the first time I kissed her to be, but reasoning and logic have evaporated completely. Now I am burning with unbridled flames of rage, lust, desire, and need.

I nip and bite at her lip, causing her to gasp. I take advantage by slipping my tongue into her sweet mouth because, my God, it is a sweet mouth. Her hands move up my chest, and I continue to take from her deliciousness while preparing for her to push me away.

Except she doesn't. She grips my shirt, trying to pull me closer. I reach up, gripping her hair, and pull her hair to force her head back to give me deeper access to her strawberries and mint taste. My other hand travels down her body until I'm gripping her ass.

I lift her, her legs automatically circling my waist. She moans into my mouth as she rocks against my rigid length. Our tongues collide and crash like a train wreck, I'm sure this will prove to be. I swipe the roof of her mouth. She bites my lip. She sucks my tongue. I bite hers.

I move from her mouth across her jaw and down her neck. I nip at the tender flesh at her collarbone, causing another deep, raspy moan to escape her. I pull back to look at her lust-filled eyes. I'm at the end of my restraint. She's got to stop this before we go too far. Cause I'm headed there at light speed.

"Tell me to stop," I growl against her neck. "If you don't tell me to stop, I won't be able to."

"Don't fucking stop," she groans.

"Fuck, Cara," I grunt as I push my way through her door.

I lay her in the middle of her bed, watching her breasts rise and fall with her rapid breathing. I quickly pull her shirt off, my mouth drops to her peaked nipple. She writhes and moans beneath me as I work her shorts off her long legs.

My hand slips between her thighs. "Goddamn, you're fucking soaked," I mumble. "You turned on by me, Cara?"

"Yes," she mewls as my fingers slide through her folds.

"You're fucking beautiful, you know that?"

"Don't talk, Jake. Just fuck me."

Abort! Abort!

That's what I should do. That would be the smart thing to do. Because I know she will regret this tomorrow.

I look at her. Her pupils are blown wide. She is twisting and grinding beneath me, chasing the physical release she wants.

"Cara," I say softly, moving my hand across her face gingerly. "Open your eyes and look at me."

Her eyes fly open. Her pupils are completely blown with lust and desire. I want to satisfy her, bring her the pleasure she seeks, but...

"Are you sure this is what you want? I don't want you to regret this tomorrow."

She looks at me. Her eyes jump all across my face. I watch as the lust evaporates and reason returns. She shakes her head, her throat bobbing with a hard swallow. I drop my forehead to her with a hard exhale.

"I'm sorry," she whispers.

"Don't be. I'm the one who slammed the brakes." I kiss her forehead then turn to leave the room.

Cara

I roll over with a groan at the sounds of the alarm. I feel like I only just fell asleep. The truth is, I probably did.

I bury my face into the pillow and scream. I have no idea what happened last night. One minute Jake is insulting me, and I am yelling at him. The next, our lips are tangled in a kiss that struck like lightning from my head to my toes. When he laid me on the bed and stripped me bare, I nearly exploded right then. It was a fire blazing across my needy body.

Then he pulled back. He hesitated when I told him to fuck me. He asked me if I was sure.

I was until he asked that. I was completely gone in the moment. I was a writhing mess of need. I needed his mouth and his hands and so much more.

The spark between us wasn't just contained to us. It was like a heavy presence that filled the entire room. It licked and lapped at our flesh, but it was more than that.

I figured out a few weeks ago, when I woke up to Jake in my bed and liked it a little too much, that I felt something for him. I remembered him waking me, and I remembered my initial panic. I'd been sleeping restlessly as nightmares haunted my sleep. When he went to leave the room, I asked him to stay.

When he climbed in behind me and pulled me tight against his chest, I felt safe. When he kissed my head, I felt cared for. Every time I watch him with Lyra, I melt. Every time I catch him watching me with Lyra, my stomach flips.

When I think about all of it, I feel panic bubbling to the surface. It feels like all of this just came out of nowhere, and it's suffocating me. I don't want to feel anything for him. I can't.

I can't trust my judgment. Last time I thought a guy cared about me, would take care of me, he betrayed me. That betrayal got the people I love hurt. I won't do that again.

And Jake doesn't need someone like me. He needs someone strong. Not someone that has to medicate so she can leave the house. He doesn't need someone that has nightmares and gets triggered with flashbacks to the point she is completely paralyzed by her fear.

I'm not arrogant in my assumptions. I saw it last night. I saw the jealousy in his eyes, in the way his jaw clenched and the tone of his voice, over Henry. I heard it when he spat out his offensive question. I *felt* it in his kiss and the touch of his hands.

Then I saw it in his eyes.

It was all there in those beautiful blue-green eyes of his when he pulled back. After I told him to shut up and fuck me. He wasn't just there for some quick fun.

I'm glad he stopped it. It would've been messy. I can't give him what he wants. I can only do sex. I don't want the emotions. Emotions are what get you hurt. In my case, in every sense of the word.

I stay in my room all morning, waiting on time to leave for the bus. Until this point, all our travel has been by plane. Liam said that now most of it will be on the bus, although we'll still stay in hotels a lot.

A knock sounds at my door that I ignore. I've been ignoring it all morning. I know it's Jake. I know he wants to talk about last night. I don't, and I'm not.

"Cara," he calls out. "Maddox said we're leaving in ten minutes."

I don't respond. I'll leave this room in ten minutes and not a minute before. I don't want to talk about last night. I don't want him to tell me what I know he's been trying to tell me for a few weeks. This trip was supposed to be about helping out Jake and the band. I wanted it to be at least a little fun. This has turned out to be anything but fun, and it's only been a few weeks.

"Cara, come out of the room. I won't bring it up."

I ignore him. I will keep ignoring him until I can't.

Am I being immature and childish? Probably. I'm not proud of it. No. I just don't know how to deal with him right now or his feelings right now. Or deal with what I'm feeling. I'm not even sure what it is I'm feeling. I do know it scares me, and I know I don't want it or need it.

Ten minutes pass, and I hear Maddox and Dane's voices outside my room. I grab my bags and pull the door open. The guys are standing in the suite's entryway, huddled together while Lyra sits on the couch with her elephant, looking ready to go back to sleep.

I walk to my brother and Maddox, giving them each a hug, but I can't look at Jake. Being near him is bad enough. The chemistry and attraction between us are tangible.

A look passes between the three of them. Dane's eyebrows scrunch while Maddox smirks. Jake answers their silent question with a slight shake of his head and a huff. My brother shakes his head in response.

What the hell? Do they know?

I know Jake and Dane are best friends, but I never thought he'd tell *my overprotective brother* that he is attracted to me. And I never thought he'd live through the day if he did. Dane can't seriously be okay with this. Can he?

And Maddox knows? Which can only mean Ryder knows. And, of course, Angel knows because he's Jake's other best friend. I *expected* him to know.

Dane looks at me. His furrowed brow quirks in question. I duck my head, turning my attention to Lyra. I hear Maddox cover a laugh with a cough, making me secretly smile. Madsy has my back even if my traitorous brother doesn't.

"Ready to go, pretty girl?" I ask Lyra, ignoring the stupid male species in the room.

"Uh-huh," she tells me with a big toothy smile. "We goes on a bus."

"We sure are." I rub her head with a smile. I wonder if it looks as forced as it feels because I suddenly feel sick knowing that now I'm going to be stuck in a tiny space with Jake for hours at a time.

"Ready?" Dane is watching me with a strange look. I'm not sure if it's disapproval or worry, but it's pissing me off.

"Ready." I give my most saccharine smile. One I know he'll know is fake. The same one he knows brings out my wrath if pushed.

I reach to grab my bag just as Jake grabs it. "I've got it." I look up and see those blue-green eyes boring holes in me. I know I've probably frustrated him these past weeks by avoiding him. He's probably wondered what he did wrong other than staying with me that night when I asked. But today, I know he saw it coming. It's why he slammed the brakes and why he's tried so hard to talk to me this morning.

In the parking lot of the hotel sit several buses. The guys all grin when they see the solid black entertainer buses with *Sons of Sin* written across them in glowing red and white letters. It's not a fancy design, but it's theirs. Dane designed it for them years ago.

Three of them, I'm told, belong to the band. There is the bachelors' bus where Maddox, Ryder, and Liam will stay. When Maddox and Ryder are done in there, the whole thing will need to be sterilized. There's the couples' bus that is for Dane and Angel along with Cami and Josephine.

Then there's what they've all decided to call the baby bus. It's for Jake and Lyra and completely set up to make them as comfortable as possible.

The bus door opens, and Jake lifts Lyra to the top step. She takes off without a word, ready to explore. He gestures with his hand for me to go first. I bite my lip and shake my head. He blows out a hard breath and scrubs a hand, roughly, over his hair. He turns, grumbling under his breath, to go inside.

I move behind him with my head down. Which is why I run right into his broad back. "Holy shit," he gasps as he drags that large hand over his day-old scruff.

The physical contact with him has heat blazing a path into my belly until it reaches between my thighs. Moisture pools at my center, causing me to stifle a groan.

"What?" I snap, irritated at my reaction to touching him.

He looks over his shoulder at me, his brows falling between his eyes. He's getting pissed with my childish behavior. That much is exceedingly clear.

He moves a few inches so I can get by him but not without brushing against him. I repress the shiver that wants to escape as well as the groan at the energy and heat between us.

I step around him to see what had him frozen in place. It doesn't take a genius to figure it out. According to Dane, Jake has led a pretty simple life. His dad was a police officer, and his mom managed the office of his grandfather's auto shop. He didn't grow up in the lap of luxury like the rest of these guys. He's seen plenty of luxuries, but none he could consider his own, even if for a little while.

And this bus is luxurious. A beige leather sofa sits on one side. Across from it are two reclining captain chairs in the same buttery material. Lighter beige tile adorns the floors, and light, gray-washed wood accents the dining and kitchen area that is equipped with stainless steel appliances. Built-in televisions hang over the captain chairs and the dining table, as well.

"There are two bunks, both with built-in TVs and headsets as well as a bedroom in the back," Liam says, coming in behind us. "Fridge is fully stocked with water, juice, and snacks for the munchkin."

"I's not a munchkin. I's a pwincess." Lyra looks up from where she has just dumped her bag in the middle of the floor with an absolutely serious expression. I cover my mouth to keep the laugh from escaping.

"Is that right?" Liam chuckles.

"Yep." She tilts her head and narrows her eyes like she is daring him to challenge her.

"All right then, princess, you be sure to tell your dad and Cara that there are movies and toys for you too."

I look at Liam with a gaping mouth. These buses, well, they're not cheap. I know this is not coming from Mads or Ry or any of the other guys. Not that they can't afford it, but this isn't an expense they would carry. Liam must have a lot of pull with the label.

"Time to pull out," the driver tells us.

Liam nods and exits the bus. Leaving just Jake, Lyra, and me.

"Cara," he whispers as the bus begins to move.

I shake my head. "Nope. Not doing it," I tell him, heading to the bunks as quickly as I can.

I fall into the first one, pulling the curtain shut. Seconds later, a tiny blond head pops in.

"I's can watch movies with you?" she asks sweetly.

I swear on everything, no one could look at that face and say no. Those big blue eyes are just too cute. I cackle when she proceeds to bat those long lashes at me. "Pwease."

"Come on, pretty girl. We'll find a princess movie."

Her grin splits her face as she climbs into the bunk with me. She snuggles into my side while I press the button that brings the TV down. I'm surprised to see Disney is already there. Though, at this point, I'm not sure why. Everything on this tour has been meticulously arranged to benefit Lyra as much as possible. To make her comfortable, so her daddy is comfortable.

I scroll until I find Lyra's favorite fairytale and queue it up. Her face is pure delight when the music starts and the pretty colors dance across the screen.

As she watches the television with rapt attention, I watch her. She has so many people in her life – that love her. Would tear down Heaven and walk through Hell for her. Jake, in her short life, has already sacrificed so much without a second thought. Much like Dane did for me. He adores his little girl, and she adores her daddy.

Jake *is* a good dad. He's a good man. Under different circumstances, he's the exact type of man I could love. But too much has happened to me. Too much has left me broken. I pretend I'm getting better, and I have learned to use tools to help me function, but the part of me that was good died a long time ago. I have blood on my hands, and it can't ever be erased. But no one knows that. I intend to keep it that way.

Moments like this with Lyra make my heart ache. As she snuggles deeper into my side, two middle fingers in her mouth, it is apparent that she craves female affection. A mother's affection. It reminds me of what I once dreamed about having once I was older.

It also reminds me of what I've lost.

My mother died ten years ago. The hole she left behind is still gaping, even if a little less painful. I was completely devastated when she died. I knew it was coming. She was so very sick for so very long, but that didn't soften the blow of watching her fade away. How do you prepare for that? Especially when you're just a little girl.

I had panic attacks frequently for the first couple of years after her death. They lessened over time, but once in a while, it would sneak up on me. I never told Dane or Tori.

Right now? I've never been more grateful for the time I had with her. I wish I could give that to Lyra. I wish she could experience the unending, unconditional love of a mother.

I drift off thinking of my mom. Flashes, not full-blown dreams, of my childhood filter behind my closed lids, drifting endlessly through my subconscious. My mom's beautiful green eyes and that long dark hair that always framed her delicate features are just as clear as ever. Birthdays, holidays, and every other cherished moment skip through my mind until I'm suddenly looking into dark eyes so cold it chills me to the bone.

"No," I beg.

A slimy, wicked grin full of sharp, too-perfect teeth flash at me, moving closer. Behind him, I hear the crying. I close my eyes, not wanting to see what I know is there. I start moving away when he grabs me, spinning me quickly, so my back is pressed against his chest. One arm holds my arms tight across my chest while the hand of his free arm grips my face.

112

"Watch." His hot breath growls into my ear.

"No," I scream. *I thrash against his restraint, trying to free myself. Trying to break free.*

"Cara."

A whimper escapes me. "No," I whisper. "Don't make me. Please, stop."

"Cara, open your eyes."

I shake my head back and forth in refusal. I don't want to open my eyes. I don't want to watch. I don't want to see.

"Cara, sweetheart, open your eyes. Wake up."

My eyes fly open. My heart races like a stampede in my chest. Sweat runs down my temples, and tears stream down my cheeks. I gasp for air and struggle against the arms wrapped around me.

"Shh." A hand strokes my hair, rocking back and forth. "I've got you, baby. Nothing can hurt you here."

I tilt my head up, looking into his blue-green eyes, swirling with worry. "Jake," I breathe out, then bury my face into his chest.

"I've got you," he whispers.

After another minute, he pulls me back, resting his forehead against mine. "You were having a bad dream, yeah?"

I give a little nod, breathing in deeply. His scent of mint, orange blossom, and a hint of cedar are comforting. It has a heady effect on me. Warmth envelops me. Affection and concern fill the small space.

I pull back, looking into his eyes again. I swallow hard at the genuine care I see.

113

It makes no sense to me. Why, after all these years, does he have this effect on me now? Why does he suddenly seem so interested in me?

It's ridiculous. Feelings don't just appear out of nowhere. Attraction maybe, but not feelings. Even though I swear, that's what I see when he looks at me. If it were just attraction, it wouldn't scare me so badly.

I drop my eyes quickly. I try to pull away, but he doesn't let go. I feel my heart that hasn't slowed since my dream speed even more. "I'm not going to hurt you, Cara." He tips my chin, so I have no choice but to look at him. "I will never hurt you."

"I – uh – I didn't mean to scare Lyra," I say, changing the subject.

His jaw muscles go taut. "You didn't scare her. She just told me you needed me to sing."

"I needed you to what?" I laugh. Genuinely this time.

He smiles too. God, why does he have to look so sexy when he smiles?

"When she has bad dreams, I sing until she feels better," he shrugs.

"I think my ovaries just exploded," I mutter under my breath, looking away from him.

"What was that?" he questions, but the way his eyebrow quirks tells me he heard me.

I feel flush with embarrassment. "I said that's sweet," I lie anyway.

He keeps smiling, but he doesn't acknowledge that he knows I'm lying. "Anything to stop her pain or fear," he tells me. Except

I get the feeling he's not talking about Lyra anymore. "Cara, about last night."

I pull in his grip again. This time he lets me go. I can't exactly get away from him, though. "I don't want to talk about any of that, Jake."

He nods. "Then, at least, let me apologize for being an ass."

"No big deal." I wave him off.

"It is a big deal. You didn't deserve that."

"Okay. It's over. Let's just drop it." I start to squirm because we are getting awfully close to talking about it.

"If you ever need to talk, Cara, I'm here," he whispers.

I feel my entire body heat. I hate the way I'm jumpy and scared when I say I'm not. When I say I'm fine. I hate the nightmares and flashbacks that paralyze me. But more than any of that, I hate that Jake has seen me, three times now, at my most vulnerable.

"You're not weak," he tells me. My eyes snap to his, wondering how he could possibly know what I'm thinking. "You've always worn your heart on your sleeve."

Unreasonable anger surfaces. "How could you possibly know that? You don't know me. We're not even friends. I'm just your friend's little sister."

Hurt flashes for a second, but it's quickly gone. In its place is a rock-hard façade. I immediately regret being a bitch. I hate my occasional volatility more than anything. "I'm sorry, Jake."

"It's fine," he tells me as he moves off the bed.

"I really am sorry," I grab his hand. Sparks ripple and flames slash across my skin. It takes every effort not to pull away.

His eyes drop to our joined hands. A smirk plays on his lips, briefly. "It really is fine, Cara, but for the record? I know you better than you think I do. You won't let me say it, but you're not stupid. Got news for you. I know you feel it too."

He leaves the bunk without giving me a chance to deny anything.

I sit there for the rest of the ride. I don't even leave the bunk for something to drink or eat. I sit there like a coward because I don't want to deal with how he does or doesn't feel. I damn sure don't want to deal with how I feel. I know if I ignore it long enough that this tour will be over. Then we'll be back home, and I won't have to see him every day.

Because that's all this is. It's just proximity. Forced proximity. Okay, maybe not forced exactly since I volunteered for this, but that was before I found myself ridiculously attracted to him.

Except I've always been attracted to him. It just wasn't something I had to face every day.

A few hours later, the bus stops. We're in Kyiv, Ukraine, for the UPark Festival, but they aren't playing until tomorrow night. Everyone has the night off. Which means Jake has nowhere to go.

I can't stay stuck on this small bus with him any longer. I am suffocating. Suffocating because all I can think about is what he keeps saying. Little things that seem like big things. I think about this crazy chemistry — explosive chemistry we seem to have. I think about the way my body reacts when he's anywhere near me. I think about how good his mouth felt on my mouth. On my breasts.

116

Nope. Don't want it.

Before the engine is off, I am opening the door and running as fast as my feet will carry me, telling him I'm going for a walk as I leave.

"Cara, wait," he calls out, but I pretend I don't hear him.

I make a beeline for Dane's bus. Then I remember the looks shared between him and Jake and think better of it. I want girl time, but I won't get that with him and Angel on the bus.

I change directions, going to Maddox and Ryder instead. I've always been able to go to them with anything. Even if they like to embarrass me a bit. And they will let me just hang around without expecting me to talk if I don't want to.

I don't even knock. I just open the door, darting in breathlessly. I am completely aware that I look slightly unhinged. I feel it too.

Liam and Henry's eyes snap to me from the captain chairs they sit in with beers and video game controllers, taking in my disheveled appearance. I completely forgot Henry was on this bus too.

His brow creases with worry. "Everything okay, kid?"

"Fine," I snap, my anxiety growing by the second. "I need Maddox and Ryder."

"They're in the back lounge." Liam nods toward the back of the bus, confusion marring his face.

I start that way, then pause. "What are they doing?" I ask cautiously. I learned my lesson about walking in on those two without asking questions a long time ago. Too bad they've never figured out what locks on doors are for.

"I don't know," Liam chuckles. "What do you think they're doing?"

My brows raise, wondering if he really needs me to spell it out.

"There are no girls on the bus, Cara," he laughs again.

Oh Lord, Liam doesn't know. I shake my head a bit. "That's not telling me much," I counter, raising both eyebrows, hoping he gets my meaning without me spelling it out.

His eyes widen before he shakes his head with another chuckle. "Why am I even surprised at this point? Okay, I'm going with the assumption they are too quiet to be doing each other, as well, but they may have their party favors out."

I nod, turning on my heels to the rear of the bus. I knock on the door, just in case, then open it a crack to peek inside. "Hey guys," I call out as I push it open a bit more to find them sitting across from each other on the floor. They each have a guitar in hand, but Maddox seems to be struggling a bit. I suppose that's to be expected since his cast only came off a week or so before we left New York.

They both look up to me with a smile that seems to fall quickly. "What's going on, brat? You look like you're on the verge of a panic attack," Ryder comments.

A tear slides down my face that I wipe away angrily. "That's because I am."

Maddox sets his guitar to the side and opens his arms. It only takes me a second to fall into them. Ryder goes to the door to make sure it's closed, then sits on the opposite side of me, rubbing my back while Maddox rubs my hair.

"Talk to us, brat," Maddox says softly. "Tell us what's going on in that head of yours."

I blow out a breath I didn't know I was holding. I fill them in on the last few weeks. "Logically, I know I don't really like him. It's just the whole close quarters thing."

"I don't think that's it, baby girl," Maddox tells me. "If it were, you wouldn't have been feeling it from the first day."

I look at him with panic. "I don't want it, Maddox. I can't."

"Slow down, love," Ryder tells me.

"I can't," I wheeze out, my tight chest refusing to let air pass.

"Why?" Maddox asks, resting his cheek against my head.

"Because I can't trust my judgment to know the good guys from the bad guys. I can't trust a guy not to hurt my family or me." My voice breaks on the last word.

"Cara, what happened was not your fault. You know that, right?" Maddox tells me firmly.

"I know what happened wasn't my fault, but it was also my inability to see through the lies – through the charade that led up to everything," I sob. This is where therapy hasn't helped at all. No one will ever convince me my poor judgment isn't, at least partially, to blame for everything.

My therapist keeps telling me that I've got to accept the past for what it is and learn to forgive myself. He doesn't think I have anything to feel guilty about either, but he said it's not about that. It's about my ability to forgive myself and let go.

I can't get him to understand that it doesn't have anything to do with forgiveness of myself or anyone else. It's about the fact that I can't trust myself anymore. If I can't trust myself, then how am I supposed to trust someone else?

"So the issue is that you don't trust your own judgment. Do you trust ours?" Ryder asks me. I give a weak nod. He looks over me to Maddox with a lift of his chin.

Without more warning than that, Maddox pulls me into his lap. Ryder scoots to my vacated spot and pulls my legs into hap. "Then how about you trust us when we tell you that you can trust Jake too. Maybe more than anyone else."

I toss him a disparaging glare. "I know that. I know that Jake is a good guy. Of course, he is. But that doesn't mean that he wouldn't shatter what's left of my heart and, trust me, there isn't much left. You can't guarantee he wouldn't break it either." My voice rises with each word until my throat nearly closes.

"Okay. Okay," Maddox appeases. "You don't have to deal with it right now."

"Ever, Madsy," I curl into his chest. "Ever."

"So, Jake gives the brat the tingles, huh?" Ryder teases.

"Shut up, asshole," I laugh softly. "I think you two are hot, but I don't want to jump your bones."

I feel Maddox flinch beneath me. I look up to catch his grimace. "Never thought I'd say this, but please never call me hot again, okay?"

A grin spreads across my face. I look to Ryder, who's wearing a similar expression. "I agree with him, brat. Don't say that again. Ever. Coming from you, it's just wrong."

"Should I say sexy instead?" I taunt, mischievously. "Or maybe fine as hell. Oohhh, I know. Fuckable."

Maddox's hand claps over my mouth. "That's it," he growls, moving so quickly I don't have time to register the movement until he has me on my back.

"No!" I scream, knowing what's coming.

Ryder climbs over to straddle my legs while Maddox holds my arms in place. "Aren't we a little old to be tormenting her with loogies?"

"Yes!" I yell. "We are all too old."

"Then just tickle her until she swears to never utter those words again," Maddox shrugs.

"Come on, brat. Last chance. You know I have to do what he says," Ryder grins like the devil he is.

"Liar," I accuse. "You don't do anything you don't want to do."

"You're right. You gonna swear?"

"No way," I yell again, refusing to give in to terrorism.

"Remember you asked for it."

His fingers quickly dig into my ribs, then my feet and back. I am screaming at the top of my lungs but refusing to accept defeat. Tears run down my face as I laugh uncontrollably.

"Ryder, stop," I shout as the door opens.

"What the actual fuck?" Jake bellows, fury swirling in those blue-green depths.

Dane walks in beside him. He looks to the three of us on the floor with a roll of his eyes. "Let her go, guys. People are actually threatening to call the police."

Maddox looks down to me. "Truce?"

121

I nod, still trying to catch my breath. They release me from their tortuous grip while helping me to my feet.

"What are you doing here? Jake said you just took off," Dane questions in that overdramatic, big brother/dad way he has.

My mind struggles for an explanation, coming up blank.

Fortunately, Ryder comes to my rescue. "We asked if she wanted to hang out for a bit. Look at another face beside that sorry sod."

Dane shakes his head with a laugh. "Why didn't you just tell him that?" He nods toward Jake. "Then he wouldn't have come to my door in a panic."

Guilt churns in my belly. Knocks the air right out of my lungs. But as I've done more often than not in recent months, I deflect with anger. "Didn't know I had a warden."

Jake winces, and Dane sighs. "You don't, Cara. Just people who are concerned."

More guilt for my harsh words and poor attitude weighs down on me. "Right," I nod, swallowing another pushback.

I start to leave, unable to stand under Jake's intense gaze any longer.

"Where are you going now?" Dane asks suspiciously.

"Um – I – I have an appointment with my therapist soon," I tell them.

Jake grips me by the wrist when I move past him. "Stop running from me," he whispers.

"Sorry, I can't be late. I've already missed a couple of appointments," I tell them.

"What do you mean you've missed a *couple* of appointments?" Maddox demands, his playful demeanor from earlier replaced by the voice he uses when he's in boss mode. I've always meant to ask him where that voice came from.

"We had an agreement, Cara," Dane adds just as sternly.

"Which is why I need to go." I smile, refusing to meet Jake's eyes.

He lets me go with a sigh. I seem to make him do that a lot.

I get out of there as quickly as I can without looking back.

Jake

I burst into the back lounge of Maddox and Ryder's bus at the sounds of Cara's screams. Remembering how she screamed and sobbed a few weeks ago and again only this morning play on repeat in my head.

Rage roars in my ears as I take in the scene. Cara's helpless form being held in place by two men I consider friends. My hands clench at my sides. I'm two seconds from killing them both.

Until Dane strolls in beside me, telling them to let her go. Minutes later, I watch her retreating form running from me for the second time in less than an hour. And I have no doubt it's me she's running from.

"Close the goddamn door, Jake," Maddox bellows behind me.

I inwardly flinch at the anger in his voice. Now that I can think clearly, I know I crossed a line. Even without saying a word, what I thought was happening was written clearly in my body language and expression.

I do as he asks – orders – knowing an argument is about to ensue. Hell, the way I burst into that room, I deserve nothing less than a punch to the face.

"I should knock the holy hell out of you," Maddox grunts, echoing my thoughts.

"It's my turn when he's done." Ryder's eyes narrow in disgust.

"I deserve that." I hang my head in shame.

"Whoa! Hold on." Dane steps between the three of us. "First, no one is hitting anyone. Second, why the hell would anyone want to? What the hell happened?"

"You didn't see his reaction when he walked in here?" Ryder jerks his head toward me.

Dane turns to me, confusion blatant on his face. He didn't catch anything but Cara, Maddox, and Ryder. "What reaction?"

"Let's just forget about it." I grimace as I recall what I just thought.

"Oh no, you don't." Maddox moves a few steps closer to me. "You don't get to look at us like we're attacking her then say forget about it. Really, Jake? You don't know us better than that?"

"Fuck," I hiss. Of course, I know they would never hurt her. They love her. Which sends my mind in another direction now. I bite back the coals of jealousy beginning to ignite in my belly. I've got to get my shit together. "I know you'd never hurt her."

125

Dane's eyes grow wide with disbelief and shock. "Wait. You thought...seriously?" I wince again, knowing exactly how out of line and ridiculous it was. "Are you crazy?"

"Maybe." I scrub my hand over my unshaven face. The truth is I am absolutely losing my mind over this girl. Because every day I want her more. Watching her with Lyra is just making it worse. But there was a reason I reacted the way I did, as irrational as it may have been. "You weren't there this morning when she was flailing and fighting in her sleep. You weren't there when she sobbed over and over, 'No. Please stop.'"

"Shit." His hand moves to his hair. It's always been his go-to move when he gets stressed. "I thought those stopped."

"As far as I know, this is the first one." I try to reassure him. Last thing I want is him to feel guilty.

"Wonder what's causing them?" He says it aloud, but you can tell he's really questioning himself.

"It's stress," Ryder tells us with hesitation.

"All she was doing was watching *Sleeping Beauty* with Lyra in the bunk." Why would that stress her?

"It's the tour. I knew it would be too much for her." Dane worries his lip. His guilt over his sister pours out like a flood.

"It's the tour." Ryder nods. Then he gives me a strange, knowing look that I don't completely understand. And I have a feeling I'm not going to want to hear it.

Then realization strikes. I don't need to hear it. I know exactly why he's pointed that look at me. My stomach clenches because the reason the tour is stressing her out is me. I'm the reason she's here, and I'm the reason for her stress.

"Or rather, it's not the tour itself but the reason she's here." He smirks at me like the jackass he is.

"Ryder, I love you, man, but keep your mouth shut for once." My mouth falls open at the reprimand from Maddox. Not just the reprimand but the complete look of irritation that is never directed toward his best friend.

"I keep my mouth shut about plenty. You know that." His jaw clenches as he shoots daggers at Maddox.

"Too late for sealed lips," Dane grunts. "You know something about my sister, you spill."

"Fuck. You two can't mind your own business for shit, can you?" More shock filters through the room at Maddox's demeanor. This is not his typical behavior. I'm not sure what to make of it. It feels like something else is going on here.

"Cara is my damn business." It feels like a challenge has been issued from Dane, and Maddox is not backing down.

"No. Not everything, Dane. If she wants you to know, she will tell you herself. What is it about brothers, huh? Can't just back the fuck off and let a girl live her life." Maddox steps forward until he and Dane are nearly chest to chest. This went from me being pissed and pissing Mads off to Dane being pissed and pissing Mads off.

Tension and anger fill the air. This escalated quickly. Dane's hot head and Maddox's waning patience are about to meet head-to-head. That never results in anything pretty.

And Maddox has been a time bomb for a while now. He pushes everything down. He never deals with his feeling, problems, or life in general. He bottles it up and shoves it as far back into a corner as he can. Or he drowns himself in sex, drugs, and alcohol.

People think it's the rock star lifestyle that becomes too much. That the fast pace life is what becomes too much to handle. Maybe for some, that's the truth. For Maddox, it couldn't be further from the truth. He's been trying to bury his demons any way he can for years. In fact, I think if it weren't for the music, he would've crashed a long time ago.

Unfortunately, it's catching up with him. We all see it. We're waiting for the fall. We'll all be here to pick him up when he does. Just wish he'd let us hold him so he didn't have to fall.

I move the same time Ryder does. He reaches for Maddox, who, despite the anger that is dripping off him, continues to wear his typical cool, calm façade. I grab Dane, who couldn't be described as calm or cool if you threw him in the Arctic Ocean.

"The can's been open. Might as well share what's in it," I tell them while keeping a firm hold on Dane.

"You know what the fuck is in it." Maddox points at me.

"I don't," I deny.

"He needs to know, Mads, before he makes her run for the hills. Or the first flight back to New York," Ryder says only to Maddox, their foreheads pressed together like they do often when they disagree or need to talk to the other down.

"Fine. But when she asks, this was all you."

"You can't protect everyone's secrets, mate."

"I can when it's not my place to tell."

"And that has cost you your own nightmares." Ryder's lips pull into a grimace. Dane and I both suck in a breath when Maddox pushes Ryder out of his space then leaves out the door.

"Did you have to say that?" Dane growls.

Ryder casts him a hard look. "It's not his job to carry everyone's burdens all the time. He can't keep going like he's going for much longer."

Dane's face distorts into frustration and sadness. I'm pretty sure mine looks the same.

"You have room to talk?" Dane accuses. "It's what we fucking do. All of us. We carry everything."

"Not like he does. And he's not listening to me anymore." He exhales a heavy breath. "You think you know, Dane, but you have no idea."

"Maybe I would if you'd talk to me instead of getting high all the time."

"Man, open your bloody eyes. I don't get high nearly as much as you think I do. I'm just there to watch out for him."

Dane jerks back. This is obviously new news to him. It's new to me too. I always assumed they were enabling and influencing each other. Of course, I haven't partied with them much in the last couple of years, but it always looked like whatever one was doing, the other was right there.

"Enough about this for now." I change the subject because it would take weeks to muck our way through the shit of Maddox and Ryder. Cara is what I want to focus on. Maybe that makes me a shit friend, but I don't care. "Tell us about Cara."

"Don't think this conversation is over." Dane levels him with a glare. Dane makes it his responsibility to take of the people he loves. The list isn't very long, but anyone on that list can consider themselves loved, sometimes to the point of suffocation. "Now tell me, what has my sister stressed."

Ryder gives me that pointed look once again. I can't stop the sigh that escapes me. She told them something. A lot, judging by his face. I wonder just how much.

"I don't think, mate, I know. Jake has her stressed."

I rub my chest at the strong ache that forms. I hate that I'm the cause of her stress. It's not what I've tried to do. Even though I know, last night probably did just that. And this morning because all I want to do is talk to her.

"What have you done to her?" Dane turns those accusatory eyes on me. "I told you if you hurt her, your ass was dead."

I open my mouth to say something. Then snap it shut when I can't come up with a single thing to say. Fortunately, I don't have to.

"He didn't *do* anything. It's because she likes him."

My head drops. I should be ecstatic. Except, I already knew Cara was attracted to me, but it's more than that. It's a connection. Like electricity running down the wire.

"Why would that stress her out? Why would that cause nightmares?" Dane still watches me from the corner of his eyes, but his demeanor has relaxed slightly.

Ryder looks at me sympathetically. My heart plummets because I know what he's going to say. I've already figured it out. Kind of hard not to when she's done nothing but avoid me.

130

"Because she doesn't want to like him. She doesn't want to be attracted to him. She doesn't want to feel anything. She doesn't trust herself anymore, so she doesn't trust anyone else either."

Exactly what I thought.

"Why the hell doesn't she trust herself? What the hell has been the point of all the therapy if she is still living with all this guilt?" Dane is clearly frustrated. He can't stand it that this isn't something he can fix.

I think it goes deeper than that for her, though. I'm not sure why, but I get the feeling therapy isn't helping Cara with all her issues because she's not telling them about all of her issues. She is keeping things locked up. For what reason, I don't know.

She shuts down when anything gets too personal. She closes herself off when she starts to feel too much. I don't know if her therapy hasn't given her the tools or if she's not using them, but it's become apparent to me after watching her the last few weeks that she doesn't want to feel.

Considering how we found her in River City, I get it. She was feeling too much there. She didn't know how to process what happened to her or her feelings. She was broken.

She's still broken. But she's built walls around the pieces to stop them from breaking even more. The problem with that is those pieces can't be put back together with a fortress guarding them.

Before, I liked Cara. I felt an intense attraction to her like I've never felt for anyone. The girl climbed into my head and under my skin, and I've never been able to get her out.

These last few weeks, I've found myself falling for her fast. It's been those moments when I watch her with Lyra when those walls seem to come down. It's in moments when she thinks I'm not watching as she sings while writing in that journal of hers. It's the way her face lights up when she sees her brother or talks to her sister. I've seen glimpses of her heart.

And I want to be the one to carry that weight on her shoulders. I want to heal those broken pieces. I want to dry the tears I caught falling a time or two. I want to show her that the past doesn't define her but mold her into someone who rises above it all.

Is that crazy? Does it make me insane that I am so completely wrapped up in a girl that won't even stay in the same room with me? Probably no crazier than having an obsessive crush over that same girl for five years.

"Dane, it's going to take more than a few months of therapy for her to really be better," Ryder tells him. "What we see is an act. She puts it on so we won't worry and to make her feel like she has some control."

"I can't stand it." His shoulders slump.

"She was seduced and manipulated by her first adult boyfriend. He betrayed her in the worst possible way by handing her over to be sold like a piece of cattle. She watched her sister get hurt, and in her mind, it was because of her decisions. Is it really that surprising that she doesn't trust herself or anyone else? Three months of therapy is not going to undo all of that damage."

"Speaking from experience?" Dane questions, but it's not condescending. It's genuine curiosity.

"Years of therapy didn't help me," Ryder laughs.

They continue to banter back and forth, but my mind is elsewhere. It makes me sick what that douche bag did to her. I *know* something else happened too. Something Dane and Maddox don't know about and what that could be scares the hell out of me.

It makes me sad and angry to know she doesn't trust me. I wish I would've let her get to know me years ago instead of watching her like a creep from a safe distance because I knew my attraction was wrong at the time. If I'd taken the time to talk to her, maybe she'd trust me now. She'd know I would never hurt her.

"Get out of your head, Jake. She knows you're not like that sick fuck. It's not you specifically she doesn't trust." Ryder's eyes are firmly latched on mine. His tone is determined to make me understand.

"What then?" I don't mean for it to come out angrily, but damn. When you've wanted a girl for this long only to find out that some other bastard has done so much damage you may never get a chance, it's hard not to be angry. I don't know what I'm supposed to do. She won't even have a simple conversation with me. I don't want to be the cause of her anxiety and stress.

"You're not," Dane tells me with a hand to my shoulder.

"What?" I tilt my head in confusion.

"You not the cause of anything, Jake." I don't respond. I didn't realize I said any of that out loud. "It's how you make her feel that is causing her panic. And that's not a bad thing. She needs to feel. She has gone from one extreme to the other. From feeling overwhelmed with her guilt and sorrow to trying to feel nothing at all. Whatever it is that you've been doing, you need to keep doing it."

"I haven't done anything." It's hard to do something when she's gone out of her way to avoid me.

133

"The reason she doesn't trust you is that she doesn't trust herself. She knows this logically, but it doesn't change anything. She's terrified, I think, of making any real decisions on her own. I think it's why she wanted to come on the tour. She's afraid of being left alone to make her own decisions." I shake my head at how much Ryder got from her in such a short period. That jealousy bubbles again because I want to be the person she tells all of this to.

"She basically said that to me the day we left," Dane nods in agreement.

"So, are you trying to tell me I shouldn't tell her how I feel?"

"For now. Show her instead. They say actions speak louder than words. Then show her how you feel. Show her you're safe. Somewhere inside of her, she already knows this."

"Why the hell not," I throw my hands up in resignation. "I've wanted her for years. I can wait until she sees. I just wonder how much longer that will be?"

"If she's the one, as long as it takes." I turn to see Angel standing in the door I never heard open with his arms folded across his chest like he's been there a while.

"Dude, you were miserable," I remind him with a laugh.

His lips twitch at the smile that wants to spread. Broody fucker. "Josie was the only one who could make me happy. Is Cara that for you?"

"I don't know yet," I tell him, even knowing that it's not entirely true.

"Maybe that's something you need to figure out because the girl can't handle getting her heart broken. Try being her friend first."

I won't break her heart. If she'd give me half a chance, I would show her. I'd show her that I just want to be there for her and with her. Just like I want from her.

But I can't do the friends thing. "Nothing I feel for her is platonic. I've always stayed away from her because I can't just be friends with her. I want her too bad."

I watch Dane from the corner of my eye. He turns red for a second, his nostrils flaring before he closes his eyes with a sigh. "Try Jake. If Cara's the one, you'll know because it doesn't matter if it's five years or fifty, you'll only want her. If you can't have her, then no one else will do."

I consider what he says with a start. "Well, damn," I mutter. If that's what that means, then she's definitely the one. She's always been the one.

Cara

"You need a break from playing nanny," Cami declares as we wait for the polish on our toes to dry. Lyra sits at the table with a few crayons and her coloring sheets I printed off my portable printer. Her feet are stretched across the bench, waiting on her own toes to dry. It's so freaking cute.

I look into Cami's dark, mischievous eyes. "I'm not *playing* nanny. I am the nanny."

"But you need a break. You're so stressed. More than you were at home, and you promised it wouldn't happen."

I flinch. I did promise this trip wouldn't affect me. I meant it too. I had no idea that a certain blue-green-eyed man would have me tangled up in ways I don't want. In ways, I can't have. "I'm fine."

"You're not fine. Your shoulders are practically making out with your ears. You need to get laid." I choke on my water while she laughs at my reaction.

"That's not going to happen," I frown at her.

Josephine just sits in her seat watching the tennis match between us with an amused expression.

"What is it with you needing to play matchmaker?" She did the same with Dane, or she tried. It turned out the only person he wanted was her.

"It's not the same." Josephine points at me with her lagoon eyes sparkling. "She wanted Dane to find love. She just wants you to find some dick." My mouth falls open. Cami, I am well accustomed to speaking *exactly* what's on her mind. Josephine is usually more filtered. "Oh, close your mouth. I'm not a prude."

"Nope. She is definitely not that." A grin crosses Cami's face as she looks at Josephine. "A prude would never have sex on a bus with five other people."

"It wasn't my fault." Her grin is stretched all the way across her face.

"You didn't tell him no," Cami argues. "In fact, I do believe you specifically told him *not* to stop when he suggested it."

A slow blush rolls across Josephine's cheeks. My eyes are wide, but I'm grinning. "It was so worth it," she muses.

Cami turns her attention back to me with a grin. "Seriously, how long has it been?"

My own cheeks begin to heat as I think about what nearly happened last night. I don't tell her that. Instead, I continue to deflect and deny. "It hasn't been that long."

"But not since we've left New York." It's a statement. Not a question.

"Of course not. When exactly would I have been able to do that?"

"Exactly. Which is why you are going to go out to the festival tonight and find you a piece of ass."

"Cami!" I hiss, pointing to Lyra. "Little ears."

"Crap," she has the decency to look ashamed. "I forgot she was here. I don't think I've ever seen her so quiet."

"Which means she's probably listening." I look over to find her still intently focused on her picture, but I have learned that kid's nuances. She may be focused on her picture, but those ears never stop working. "I've been working with her on tracing lines. The worksheets keep her busy for hours, and she loves the coloring pages I've printed."

"Isn't she a little young for that?" Josephine asks.

My heart stutters, looking at the little towhead princess with her curls up in two ponytails. She is so engrossed in the pages. I love how eager she is to always learn. "No. She's not too young. She's really smart too."

I beam with pride over how much she's learned in just a few weeks. She absorbs everything like a sponge and loves every minute of it.

"You're falling for her." Josephine smiles sweetly at me.

"That probably makes me very stupid, huh?"

"Maybe not, but what about her dad?" Josephine asks casually

Her casual tone doesn't stop me from choking for the second time in a few minutes. "What about him?"

Both of their eyes light up like a dog with a brand new bone that it plans on chewing until it gets to the marrow. I manage to contain a groan at their excitement. Barely.

"That reaction actually said more than enough." Cami turns her drink up casually, but she's not fooling me. She is about to analyze everything I say and do.

I feel the panic rising. I managed to avoid him since I hauled ass off that bus. Well, except for those few minutes when he found me with Maddox and Ryder. I still have weeks of this tour left. It's not a good sign that I don't want to be anywhere near that bus.

And I want to be right there on that bus. That's the thought that makes me panic more.

"Are you falling for Jake?" Josephine gives me soft, warm eyes of understanding. She doesn't understand, though. She couldn't possibly understand.

She doesn't understand how utterly broken I am. She hasn't seen how I manage to hurt those I care about most with my reckless, foolish decisions. She doesn't know how I mess up everything.

Jake definitely feels something for me. I'm not sure why now all of a sudden, but it doesn't matter. I am not good for anyone, much less a single dad with a tiny little girl to think of. Yes, I may be her nanny, and I intend to protect her and make sure she is cared for. But I can't be a permanent fixture in her life. I would only cause her pain.

Besides, if he knew the truth, he wouldn't want me anyway. Maybe that's what I need to do. Tell him the deep, dirty secrets I've never told anyone, so he could see how toxic I really am.

"Absolutely not," I answer Josephine with conviction. I'm relieved there's not a hint of a lie in my voice. Even if doubt niggles my stomach.

"Jake is a good guy, you know?" Cami blows her wet fingernails while never taking her eye off me. "And he's sexy as sin."

"Throw in that daddy stuff, and he's a walking lady boner," Josephine adds.

"How would his two best friends like to know their women are checking him out." My brows raise in a challenge, hoping it will get them to change the subject. It doesn't, of course.

"Angel would get all growly and possessive and fuck me until I begged for mercy," Josephine whispers, so the little ears don't hear. "It's not my fault watching Jake with Lyra is so damn hot."

"Do not project your baby fever on her," Cami taunts. "Though, it's not a lie. Something about a man with a kid is just panty-melting. Every time I see Dane with her or Dax, my ovaries sing."

"Ahh! NO!" I cover my ears. "No. I do not want to hear about my brother making your ovaries sing. And I do not have feelings for Jake. At all."

"Pity," Cami sighs. "You wouldn't have to look very far to get laid."

I fight the blush that starts warming my face as I recall what *almost* happened last night. My thighs clench at the thought of his finger running through my dripping sex and his mouth on my begging nipple. I am so glad he stopped it.

140

I really am. I swear.

"Why are you so interested in my sex life or lack thereof?" I get suspicious.

She and Josie both giggle. "Because you look like you're about to snap," Josephine answers my question.

"I am a little tense," I admit. What I don't admit is that one sexy as hell, single dad musician is the cause of it and that, yes, sex would probably alleviate that tension for a minute or two. Until I'm pushed into his space again. Into that teeny, tiny bus where I can feel him in the air like an electrical current. There's simply not enough space on that bus.

"A few good orgasms would help that," Cami points out. "I have an idea."

I feel the first flutters of apprehension. Flutters in my belly at whatever idea this crazy, beautiful woman is concocting in that Lucy Ricardo brain of hers. "I'm afraid to ask, but what's your idea?"

"You go back to the bus. Put something that's rock festival sexy, and go out there. Go find you a hottie. Spend the rest of the evening talking or whatever. Bring him to watch one of the shows. Jacob's Ladder is playing tonight. Go see them. They've done a great job opening for the guys. When it's over, bring him back to the bus and let him fuck your brains out. Or you fuck his out."

My eyes are probably as wide as saucers. My jaw is sitting on the floor. Josephine tosses her head back in laughter. "Colorful as ever," she pats Cami's knee. Cami just grins like the Cheshire cat. "But I do agree with her."

All I can do is gape at both of them. Cami's 'colorful' suggestion doesn't surprise me nearly as much as Josephine's agreement.

"Did Dane really shelter you that much?" Josephine questions.

"Protected? Yes. Sheltered? No," I tell them both honestly.

"Then why do you look so freaked out?" she prods a little more.

"It's been a long time since I did something like that," I tell her without any real details. Cami knows. Cami knows everything because Dane told her. Which is why she's giving me a sympathetic look.

"You have – you know?" Cami says, waving her hand over me, suddenly shy about just saying what she's thinking.

"Just with Daniel," I tell them honestly.

"As in your best friend, Daniel?" Cami's brows shoot up to her hairline.

"Pay up?" Josephine laughs with her hand stretched toward Cami.

"I'll send it to you," Cami scowls while I watch, confused.

"What is all that about?"

"I told her you were fucking him, and she told me you were just friends." Josephine still laughs.

"We are just friends," I tell them. "But I'm comfortable with him. He has no expectations either. It's just easy."

I sigh. Easy is what I need. I can't handle emotions. Not anymore. And I need someone I'm comfortable with.

Once i left for college, I became very sexually adventurous. I was no longer under my slightly insane older brother's watchful eye. I just wanted to explore and experiment to discover what I liked. It's what drew me to Stephano in the first place.

I learned a lot about what I like. I also learned how all of that can be used against you. How trust can be broken.

There's still a part of me that wants those things I learned I like. There's another part of me that's ashamed. If not for those desires, I would never have been drawn to Stephano, and my life and so many others, wouldn't have been irrevocably changed.

I feel tears burn the back of my eyes as I think about the people hurt by my carelessness. I force it back.

"I'll go out to the festival," I tell them. I'll do anything to change the subject. "I don't know about finding a guy or anything, but I could use some time to just relax for a bit."

"Just promise you won't turn down a hottie," Cami waggles her brows.

"I can't bring someone back to the buses," I tell her with a chuckle.

"Why?"

"Because of my brother, my other brothers, and all of the rest of the guys." I roll my eyes at her obnoxious obtuseness.

"Are you afraid of the guys walking in?" Josephine smirks.

"Oh God," my cheeks flame at the thought. "Do you have any idea how absolutely traumatizing that would be for all of us?"

"We can keep the guys distracted," Josephine volunteers. "And we'll watch Lyra until Jake can come get her."

143

"Don't you guys want to enjoy the shows?" I ask, not wanting to selfishly monopolize their time.

They both wave me off. "We'll see plenty tomorrow."

"All right," I finally agree. "I'll go change."

A few hours later, I'm in line at a food stand. Another band tuning their instruments can be heard in the background. Henry stands off in the distance, watching me, but he's given me this time to myself. I suppose he can tell I just really need space right now. I think his presence is probably overkill, but I have to admit it does make me feel safer.

"American?" I hear a lovely, lightly-accented baritone voice ask behind me.

I turn to see a jaw-dropping six-foot-something Greek god standing behind me. His deep blue eyes are like sapphires reflected in the sun. His nearly black hair shines even though the sun has set. He's wearing a plain white t-shirt that stretches perfectly across his broad shoulders. Tattoos peek beneath both sleeves and from his collar.

Even though I haven't sought after any men, I can say that there have been plenty of mouth-watering eye candy to look at, especially around the pool area. But none looked quite like they belonged on the cover of a romance novel.

I give him a shy smile and nod in response to his question.

"Enjoying the festival?" he smiles, showing a beautiful set of teeth. Not perfectly straight, though. Just crooked enough to add character and make him more approachable. And his accent. I can't place it, though I've never had an ear for languages or accents. But it's so sexy, even if it is barely noticeable.

144

"I am enjoying it. Are you enjoying yourself?" I tilt my head a bit to look up at his tall form. I'm not short at five-foot-eight, but I'm used to looking up at the guys I'm around. Maddox and Ryder are the shortest amongst the guys, and they're both six feet. This guy has to be as tall as Dane's six-foot-four frame. If not taller.

"It just got a lot better." His smile widens, and his eyes crinkle a bit at the corners. Something about him seems vaguely familiar all of a sudden. I have a strange sense of déjà vu or something, though I can't put my finger on it. "Will you be here much longer?"

"I leave day after tomorrow," I tell him.

"Pity," he says with genuine disappointment. "I would like to get to know you better. I don't suppose you'd be interested in some company for a while?"

I think for half a second, casting my eyes over to Henry, knowing he's watching me. It makes me feel more comfortable, but I still shake my head no. His face falls pitifully. "But if you can find me during Jacob's Ladder's performance, I might enjoy the company.

"They go on soon," he muses. "I will do my best to find you. Shouldn't be too hard. I just need to find the most beautiful woman in the crowd.

I feel flush at his flattery. There's also this strange feeling of familiarity with him. I just wish I knew why.

Jake

After the big fallout on Maddox and Ryder's bus, I wanted nothing more than to find Cara and make her listen to me. She didn't have to talk, though I wish she would. But I remembered Ryder's words.

If I push her, then I won't be doing myself any favors. So I let her have her space.

Shortly after the conversation ended, we were brought to a press conference and then a podcast. By the time we made it back to the buses, we barely had time to change. We weren't technically supposed to perform tonight, but Dylan and Wyatt, the guitarist and vocalist from Jacob's Ladder, asked us to perform a couple of songs with them.

They were the latest up-and-coming band and had lots of promise. Dylan was actually a good friend of ours from our earliest club days. He was with a different band then. It was pretty obvious the fit was bad. Not to mention those guys just never seemed serious. It shouldn't have been a surprise, given how young they were. They just thought it was an easy way to meet girls. But Dylan was all about the music. I was glad he finally found his band.

I head inside my bus, expecting to find Lyra and Cara. I assumed Cara would've stopped hiding in her brother's bus by now, but they're still gone. I take a quick shower, change, and head to Dane and Angel's bus.

I knock on the bus door because that is what my mom taught me, only to hear Dane yell to stop knocking. I walk in to see Lyra sitting on Dane's back as he stretches across the narrow bus floor. His large frame looks ridiculous in the small space. I suppose mine does as well at six-foot-three, but I don't have the bulk he does.

Cami encourages Lyra to use him as a trampoline which my little girl has no problem doing. She stands on her feet, jumping all of two inches, landing with her butt in between Dane's shoulder blades. Josephine and Angel are just as bad as Camilla as they cheer Lyra on. It takes me less than a second to realize Cara isn't here.

For a second, I panic worried she did exactly what Ryder said. Hopped the first flight back to New York. Then I realize Dane is entirely too calm for his sister to be missing.

"Get your kid," Dane grunts as Lyra lands on him again with one of her exuberant, high-pitched squeals.

"Are you trying to tell me you can't handle a twenty-pound little girl?" I toss his words from months ago back at him.

"I don't want to hurt her, asshole," he grumbles.

"Yeah, sure," I smirk. I reach down, scooping Lyra up in my arms. "Uncle Dane says you're beating him up."

"I not beat him up, Daddy. Cami says he's my apoline."

I laugh loudly. "Of course, she did." I look over to Camilla, who just shrugs.

"He laid in the middle of the floor demanding a back rub." She crosses her arms and looks down at Dane with a wicked grin. "I thought Lyra could do a much better job than me."

Josephine and Angel both burst into raucous laughter while Dane grumbles. "Just help me up from here," he grunts.

"What's the matter, old man, can't get those achy bones to work?" Cami taunts him.

Another rumble slips from his chest. "I'll show you who's an old man."

Laughing, she begins to back up, but she's not quick enough. He is on his feet with her toss over his shoulder before she gets more than two steps away. I have no idea how he managed to do it in the tiny space. Cami squeals loudly while Dane slaps her ass hard.

"Daddy," Lyra whispers in my ear. At least, that's what she thinks she's doing, "Nane panked Cami."

I chuckle at her seriousness. "He didn't hurt her, princess."

"Nope, not hurt, Lyra," Cami calls from her upside-down position.

"I would never hurt her, Lyra," Dane reassures her.

"Okay, Nane." She's satisfied. And apparently tired since she is laying her head on my shoulder with those two fingers in her mouth.

"Where's Cara?" I ask, knowing it's nearly time to get her ready for bed.

"We gave her the night off," Josephine tells me. "She needs a minute for herself now and then. She hasn't had that in nearly three weeks."

"That didn't answer the question." Dane lowers Cami to her feet, giving her a suspicious look. "Where is Cara?"

Cami rolls her eyes. "I've told you to stop hovering over her, Big Boy."

"I'm not hovering. I'm curious and concerned."

"We sent her to enjoy the festival." Josephine answers.

I look at them both completely slack-jawed. What in the world would make them think it's a good idea for her to wander the festival alone. Dane voices my thought before I have a chance.

"Oh, relax," Cami tells him. "Henry is with her but keeping a respectable distance so she feels like she can enjoy herself."

"Cawagetwaid," Lyra says around her fingers.

My stomach clenches. Her words weren't clear, but I hope my toddler didn't just say what I think she did. I look at Dane first, who looks like he wants to explode, then to Angel, who drops his head in his hand.

I still want clarification, though, because I like the torture. I gently pull Lyra's fingers from her mouth. "What did you say, Lyra?"

149

"Cara get waid."

"Laid?" I question calmly. Though, I feel anything but calm. She nods her head, and I look back at Dane, who is glaring at Cami.

"Where would she have gotten that idea from?" he asks her with his arms crossed.

"Don't look at me like that," Cami returns his glare. "Let her have fun. She is a big ball of stress. Let her get some relief."

"I guess you were part of all of this, weren't you?" Angel asks Josephine with just as angry of a glare.

"Why do you guys look so pissed. She is a grown woman. Leave her alone," Josephine is now glaring as well.

Me? Well, if I didn't have my little girl in my arms right now, I'd put my fist through a wall. Actually, I want to run out there and find her. Drag her back to our bus and make sure she knows she's mine. She just doesn't know it yet.

"You guys can't protect her from everything. And you damn sure can't stop her from having sex if she wants," Cami says. "You have to let go and let her find herself again, big brother."

Dane grips his hair by the roots hard. Probably so he doesn't wrap his hand around Camilla. "I love you, Muñeca, but your matchmaking and meddling went too far this time."

Angel stands up and moves away from Josephine. She looks at him in total shock. "Are you seriously angry right now?" she demands.

"Josie, have neither of you noticed that Jake likes her?" Angel nearly yells.

"This has nothing to do with being an overprotective big brother. It has everything to do with my friend getting his heart broken," Dane spits.

"What are you talking about?" Cami demands, her own temper flaring. "I know we talked about Jake having a thing for her, but he would've made a move by now."

They all discuss me like I'm not standing right there. And I'm getting more and more pissed by the second. The thought of anyone else touching her is enough to make me commit murder. I feel my blood pressure rising by the second. In fact, I'm pretty sure I'm having a stroke.

"Daddy mad?" Lyra places her chubby little hands on my face, bringing me back to my senses.

I kiss her forehead then set her on the floor. "I'm not mad at you, baby girl."

"Good." She walks toward the back of the bus, and the buffer for my anger is gone.

"Jake, if you like her, why haven't you told her?" Cami asks me softly. I've missed whatever has been said for her tone to change. I look at Josephine, who looks guilt-ridden as well.

"Because she's been avoiding me," I tell them with my teeth clenched, so I don't say anything stupid.

"How can she avoid you when you're sharing the same space?"

"It's not as hard as it seems. Turns out she can just hide out with you guys then get told to go get laid," I hiss.

They both flinch. "She never said anything earlier. Maybe she doesn't know how you feel."

"She knows. I may not have said it, but she at least knows I'm attracted to her."

"If you didn't tell her…."

"Cami, I promise she *knows*. After last night, she definitely knows."

Dane snaps his head in my direction. His eyes telling me to not finish that story.

"Look, we just thought we were helping her. She's wound too tight. The stress isn't good for her, and she's going to crack. She said she hasn't had sex since Daniel back in New York and…." Josephine stops her sentence when I growl.

"I keep forgetting to kill that kid," Dane grunts.

"No," Cami's hands land on his chest, but her eyes don't leave mine. "He's just her friend, and she's comfortable with him."

The door to the bus swings open. Maddox steps in and Ryder behind him. "Time to – whoa, what did we walk in on?" Maddox asks as he takes all of us in.

"Just Lucy and Ethel here who thought it would be a good idea to encourage my sister to 'go get laid'," Dane tells them with air quotes.

"That's a horrible idea," Maddox declares with a hard glare at the girls.

"We know. I mean, we know it's a bad idea. We didn't know Jake liked Cara. Or we thought we were wrong because it's been months, and he still hasn't asked her out. We were just trying to help," Josephine rambles on. "We didn't mean to cause any problems. We just wanted Cara to have some fun."

"It's not a bad idea because Jake likes her. It's a bad idea because she likes him. And she's not ready for that." Ryder tells them with his arms crossed.

If it weren't for the fact they just sent *my girl* to go hook up with some rando, I'd feel bad for them. We're all ganging up on them, and they do look mildly apologetic.

"Look," Cami says, waving her hands in the air. "Cara never said she was going man hunting. She was just going to check out the festival. Even if she does, what's done is done. If any of you try to interfere, she's going to be pissed."

"Better pissed, then riddled with more fucking guilt." Maddox almost looks as pissed as me. Almost.

"I mean it, guys. Leave her alone. She needs to figure out how to live her life again without anyone holding her hand." Maddox and Ryder huff. Angel just keeps glaring at Josephine, who squirms under his glare.

Dane rakes another hand through his hair. "She's right," he says in defeat.

My eyes grow wide. "Are you serious?"

"Let her figure it out, Jake. If Ryder's right, then either she won't be able to go through with anything, or she'll regret it."

"And I'm just supposed to sit back and watch the girl that I've wanted for the last five years get it on with another guy."

"One, you won't be watching. Two, you've watched her have boyfriends for those five years."

"Remember what I told you," Angel looks at me with sympathy.

"I do," I swallow hard. "Doesn't mean I have to like it."

153

"No, you don't." He nods.

"Come on. We've got a stage to get to," Maddox tells us with a jerk of his head.

"Just because I said you're right doesn't mean I'm done with you," Dane whispers to Cami.

"You either, Ethel," Angel tells Josephine.

"Jake," Cami calls out as I step out of the bus. I turn to see her standing on the top step. "I am sorry."

I wave her off like it's no big deal. Like the thought of Cara being touched by another man, especially after I'm the one who slammed the brakes last night, doesn't feel like a knife in my heart. "It's fine, Cami. It will either work out, or it won't."

"I know this doesn't mean a lot, but I hope you do work out," she smiles.

I nod and follow the rest of the guys across the lot. We make it to side stage, where Dylan sees us with a wide grin on his face as he belts out some cover I don't recognize.

"I've got some friends of mine here to help us out on a couple songs," Dylan says in the microphone to the cheering crowd. "I've known these guys for a while, and it has been a huge honor being on tour with them. Why don't you guys help me welcome Sons of Sin."

We get on stage to huge cheering from the crowd that will probably be here tomorrow night for our show. Jacob's Ladder's drummer steps back from his kit, bowing at Dane, who can only shake his head. The guy doesn't see where he's just as important to the band as the rest. I walk to an amp plugging in my bass while Angel and Ryder do the same with their guitars.

154

Maddox flips whatever switch it is that is ingrained in him, and his stage persona appears. The guy has more personalities than the guy from *Split*. He banters easily with Dylan. They manage to get the already roaring crowd even more amped. The cheers and screams are so loud, I wonder how they hear anything Maddox and Dylan are saying.

We start the song with the sounds of Ryder and Wyatt in a guitar battle before Dylan takes the first line of the song. When Maddox comes in, the crowd goes absolutely insane. You'd think we were Led Zepplin out here instead of some band that only came about publicly a couple of years ago.

I close my eyes. I try to let the adrenaline from the crowd take over my mind. Only problem is, it's not working.

Every time my eyes catch a flash of blond, I wonder if it's her. I can only be grateful that I can play without a lot of thought. It's only because Dylan wanted to sing some of our really old stuff. Stuff that we haven't even recorded. Those songs are part of my muscle memory.

We've played two songs and are halfway through the third and final song when I see her.

She's standing in the crowd, not too close to the stage, but close enough I can see those dark eyes shine with excitement and pride. I watch as that long blond hair sways back and forth. My eyes rake over those long legs, noticing that the cut-off shorts she is wearing make them seem that much longer.

For the first time since this trip started, she appears light and free. A combination of guilt and ego fills me. Guilt because I know I'm part of the reason she's been so stressed. Ego because *I'm* part of the reason she's so stressed.

Then, some guy walks up to her, and every muscle in my body coils. When he dips his head low, whispering something in her ear, my blood boils. When she nods and begins to follow him out of the crowd, my head nearly explodes.

The song ends at just the right moment. I hope. Because my ass is off that stage, chasing her through the crowd. Not an easy feat, considering everyone feels the need to touch me, begging for a picture or autograph, though I'm not sure why. Sons of Sin fans don't really know me. When they finally hit big, I wasn't part of the band, but here they are grabbing and groping, and all I want to do is get to the girl.

By the time I'm through the audience, I can't see her anymore. I stand there for a second to catch my breath. I'm ready to take off running back toward the buses because I hope like hell she wouldn't be foolish enough to go off with this guy to his place when a hand on my shoulder holds me in place.

"Don't rush in there like a jealous boyfriend, man," Ryder tells me. "It will only piss her off."

"I don't care if it pisses her off. She's about to make a fucking mistake." I shrug his hand off a little harder than necessary.

"You've got to let her do whatever it is she wants or needs to do, or you'll only push her away."

'Ffuuucckkk," I yell out in the open space.

"Need to hit something?" Maddox voice chimes.

I turn to find him with two brunettes tucked under each of his arms. "I don't think hitting something would be enough," I growl at him.

He steps away from the girls until he's directly in front of me. "Then hit me, man. Hit me if you think it will make you feel better. But I can already tell you, it won't."

"No, but hitting that douche she just went off with might," I sneer.

He chuckles. "It might for a minute. Go back to the buses, Jake. Better yet, come back with us. Forget about Cara."

I grind my teeth. I don't *want* to forget about Cara. I don't think I could if I tried, but I can at least do something to take my mind off her for a bit. If she can go off with some rando knowing how I feel – because I have no doubt she knows, or she wouldn't be avoiding me – and knowing she might even feel a little bit of the same, then I can get my rocks off too. I nod at Maddox, following him and Ryder back to the bus.

I follow them to the back lounge and take a seat on one of the sofas with my knees spread wide, and my arms draped across the back. It probably looks like I'm calm and relaxed, but that isn't even close to what I feel. I feel like I'm about to lose my shit. And that's something I can't afford to do.

I watch as Ryder and Maddox waste no time getting the girls' clothes off, touching them as they do. The girls turn to begin undressing Maddox and Ryder, but Maddox stops the one at his side. He instead turns the girl to face Ryder.

In no time at all, they have Ryder stripped. He kisses one girl's neck and shoulder while she kisses the other girl. Maddox just stands there and watches for a minute.

All the while, I'm watching live porn, and there isn't a flicker of interest. Not even a twitch. And isn't that just about right.

Maddox looks over to where I'm sitting with a smirk. He leans into the taller girl's ear, whispering something to her. Both of their eyes on me, she smiles and makes her way to my side of the room.

Maddox then grabs Ryder by the hair, stopping his downward descent on the girl, and orders him to sit on the other sofa. Ryder smirks at him but does as he's told. Maddox walks to Ryder, kisses him hard then turns back to the girl. Their dynamic is nothing short of fascinating.

Maddox grabs the girl, kisses her just as hard, then he orders her to get between Ryder's legs. She does what he says without question.

The girl Maddox sent to me climbs onto my lap, running her hand up my chest. "I make you feel better," she tells me in a seductive voice with broken English.

She moves to kiss me, but I turn my head before our lips meet. She doesn't seem to care, though. She just moves her mouth to my neck. I still feel nothing.

Actually, that's not true. I actually feel kind of dirty. Which is stupid. I've had a thing for Cara for years, but it's not like I've been celibate all that time.

I try to shove it down. Swallow the bile that rises in my throat, but it's just not helping. When she reaches for my belt, I grab her by the wrist.

"I'm not feeling this," I tell her, shoving her off.

I'm up off the couch and heading out of the room. Maddox, who was leaning against the wall watching everything in the room, follows me out.

I stand at the door of his bus, allowing the fresh air to fill my lungs.

"Ready to admit it now?" Maddox asks behind me.

"Admit what? That I had a very beautiful, very naked woman in my lap and couldn't get it up?" I chuckle without mirth.

"Admit that at some point, you're feelings changed from infatuation and genuine care to more." I hear the humor in his voice. Why is this funny to him?

Then I realize. "You knew this would happen?" I turn with a finger pointed at him, my teeth clenching hard.

"Had a feeling," he shrugs. "I've known all these years you've had a thing for Cara, but I also watched you, on more than one occasion, take a girl home or wherever. When?"

"When what?" I hiss with frustration and anger.

"When did it turn from lust to love?"

I open my mouth to deny it, but the words won't come. I think about what he's just said. Do I love her?

I've always wanted her. I've always been concerned for her. That doesn't constitute love.

But then I think about how insane it's been driving me that she won't even look at me. When I've had her in my arms, even as she's breaking down, I think about how it feels right. It feels like home.

When I watch her with Lyra, all I can see is how I want that forever. Except I want it to be real. I want her in my home with me. I want to share my hopes and dreams and hurts and my secrets. I want to tell her things that no one knows.

I try to figure out the exact moment it happened. When what I feel became more. It was weeks ago in Dane's apartment. The night they asked me to come on this tour. I remember watching her with Lyra and thinking I'd give anything for her to be mine. For her to belong to Lyra and me. It's what spurred the jealousy over her *friend* and had me accepting her offer so quickly.

"Fuck me," I hiss.

Maddox chuckles with a slap to my shoulder. "Do you really think Dane would've been okay with you going after her if he didn't see how you felt?"

"Why the hell am I so damn transparent?" I grumble.

"It's who you are, Jake. You don't hide anything. You're as real as they get."

"So, aren't you missing out on all the fun in there?"

He chuckles. "Contrary to popular belief, I do not have to dip my dick in something every night. Besides, they'll be there when I'm ready."

"Dude, I am colossally screwed," I blow out a heavy sigh. "I'm not sure she'll ever be ready for me."

"Maybe you need to try things her way." We step out of the bus into the night air. The sounds of parties and chaos are still loud throughout the place.

"What way would that be?" I hope he doesn't say try to be friends because I can't be her friend. I've never been able to see her that way, and I know I damn sure can't now.

"I don't know. You'd have to talk to her and figure that out," he shrugs.

"Kind of har...." I'm cut off by a piercing scream. I look at Maddox with my heart ready to explode out of my chest. "That was Cara."

I start to take off for the bus when he grabs me by the shoulder. "You can't just barge in. You don't know why she was screaming."

I start to argue, but the bus door flies open, the guy runs out. "I have a good idea," I growl.

He stops me with a hand to my shoulder again, and I swear I'm about to break it again. "Go to her." His face is hard and stone-like. Anger written all over his face.

He takes off running, and I see Henry and Liam step from where they were standing to do the same.

I don't waste any more time. I am on the bus, making my way to the bedroom in less than five seconds. I open the door to find Cara in the corner on the floor, rocking back and forth. My heart completely shatters to see her so broken.

I move slowly, stooping where she sits. I tentatively reach a hand out, brushing her hair. "It's just me, baby," I soothe when she flinches away. She still doesn't look up. I want nothing more than to draw her into my arms, but I'm afraid it might make this flashback or panic attack worse.

I just continue to stroke her head, feeling absolutely helpless.

"What the hell is going on?" Dane's voice bellows behind me. I turn to see nearly everyone standing there with a mixture of worried and pissed off expressions on their faces

I ignore Dane and turn my attention to Maddox. "Did you catch up with him?"

He shakes his head. "Henry is still looking, but he vanished in the crowd."

"It was him," Cara says, looking up with tear-stained cheeks. She throws herself in my arms, surprising me, but now I feel like I can breathe. "It was him," she whispers in my ear again.

My blood turns to ice. My mind, again, wonders what happened to her that she hasn't told her brother about. I pull her back, placing a hand on each side of her face. "Did he hurt you?"

She shakes her head before burrowing back in my chest.

"What happened, Cara?" Dane demands again.

I turn to him with a stone face. "Leave her alone right now, Dane," I command, leaving no room for argument.

Maddox says something I don't catch because the roaring of rage and fury is too loud in my ears. A few seconds later, it's just Cara and me.

I rise to my feet, bringing her with me. I place her in the center of the bed then climb in behind her. She's still crying, but they're more soft whimpers than uncontrollable sobs.

"What happened, Cara?" I ask her softly as I stroke her arm gently.

She shakes her head. She starts to move away. My arms reflexively tighten, not wanting her to go anywhere.

"Let me hold you, Cara, please," my voice breaks.

She nods and relaxes in my hold. After a few minutes, her breathing slows. Her heart is no longer pounding.

And I just hold her. I won't be sleeping any time soon. But I'd rather enjoy the feel of her in my arms than lose this moment to sleep.

Cara

An arm like steel holds mine firmly to my sides. He has one of his long legs wrapped around me, so I can't fight against him no matter how hard I try. His hand grips my face, forcing me to watch the brutality in front of me.

"Watch," he demands, his hot breath in my ear sends chills down my spine. "See what happens when you don't cooperate."

A whimper escapes my throat. I want to scream, but his tightly clasped hand prevents much more than muffled sound to escape. I close my eyes against the gruesome sight before me. A sight that is my fault.

His grip becomes unbearably tighter as his fingers dig into my jaw. "I said watch," his deep voice rumbles.

Tears pools in my eyes and stream down my face as I watch Jasmine being brutally violated by the other man. She wouldn't even be here if not for me. She doesn't even struggle anymore. Her eyes are completely blank, and her tears have dried. She has completely shut down.

I want to shut down. I am trying to shut down. To block out everything I've seen, but my mind won't allow it.

Lightning flashes outside, and thunder roars loudly as the other man pushes off my best friend with a grunt. At least, he's finally stopped.

He drops the knife he used to carve into Jasmine's flesh on the bed as he pulls his pants up. I see her eyes dart to it

That's it, Jas. Stab him in his black heart.

She grabs the knife, but she doesn't stab him. Muffled screams followed by uncontrollable sobs wrack my body as I watch the life disappear from my friend's eyes.

"Cazzo," the man growls. "We paid good money for her."

"You're the one who dropped the knife on the bed. Zasraný debil."

My entire body shakes violently as I'm thrown to the ground. "Time for your audition, malá kurva."

One man grips my hair, forcing me to look up. I close my eyes, not wanting to see the face of the man about to hurt me. I hear the sound of a zipper being lowered as a hand grips my face again. "Open up, little bitch," the man demands of me.

I shake my head. I'm not going to just do what he says even if he kills me. I'd rather die.

A sharp, biting blow lands across my cheek with a string of curses. I suck in a breath as pain shoots through my face. I hear more thunder in the background. It grows louder with each blast, almost sounding like it's right outside.

"You hear that?" one of the men asks.

"Ignore it," the other demands. "DeLuca is probably dealing with another problem. Hold her still so I can put my cock down her throat."

The hands gripping my hair and face pull me until I'm pressed against the owner. He releases my jaw but then grips my throat until I am forced to open my mouth.

Oh, God. No.

More thunder blasts. Blasts so loudly my ears ring. I wait for the violation only to realize the hands holding me are no longer there. Through tears, I vaguely realize the man in front of me is now lying face down on the concrete floor.

I reach up with shaky hands to wipe tears from my face. When I pull them back, they are covered in red.

I begin to scream. I scream even louder when arms wrap around me.

"Cara, wake up."

I struggle against the arms, fighting with everything I have left in me.

"Cara, wake up," I hear again.

My eyes flicker as thunder booms. Jake is hovering over me, looking completely enraged and terrified all at once. I reach for him, throwing myself into his arms. I hold him tightly.

"It was just a dream," he soothes my hair with a kiss to my temple.

"Not a dream," I whimper. "I wish that's all it was."

"You can tell me, baby," he says softly. I close my eyes at the emotion in his voice. In the way, he's holding me. In another life, maybe Jake and I could have been something together.

"I can't tell anyone." It comes out so low, I'm not sure if he hears me.

"Let me carry it, Cara. I can hold some of it, so it's not so heavy for you."

I shake my head. "No one can hold this but me. I deserve to carry it."

I feel his entire body tense. He pulls away from me, looking down with a contrasting combination of ferocity and softness. "You only deserve to be happy. Let me heal your hurt." Tears slip down my face again.

"You don't want me, Jake. I know you think you do. I see how you look at me, but I'm not good. I would only hurt you and Lyra."

"It'd be worth it, baby. It would be worth all of it. Do you think you're the only person with secrets, Cara? Do you think you're the only person that's been broken or has baggage? We've all got scars. It's what's under those scars that I love."

"Jake," I sob, "you can't love me. Please don't love me."

"Too late for that, Cara."

I shake my head, not understanding. How can he love me? He doesn't *know me.* It's only been a few weeks since this tour started. There is no way he's fallen in love with me. Especially considering I've avoided him every chance I get.

He laughs a sad chuckle as my reaction. "Cara, I've wanted you for a lot longer than you realize, but things got in the way of me doing anything about it. That doesn't matter, though. What matters is that you know I'm not going anywhere."

"I can't, Jake," I shake my head. "I can't be what you need."

"Then let me be what you need. Let me carry your pain. Let me hold your broken heart until it's whole again."

"I can't do that to you. You have Lyra to think about." I bite my lip at the thought of anything hurting that little girl.

He runs a gentle finger under my eye, catching the still pooling tears. "Tell me what happened to you, Cara."

I hesitate. I've never told anyone. Not even my therapist. No one knows how much damage I've caused. How much blood is on my hands.

But it's the only way for Jake to see that he doesn't want me. He's not going to believe me otherwise.

"When I got to Chicago, I went a little wild. I was no longer under Dane's watchful eye, and I wanted to discover who I was and what I liked without worrying about him losing his crap. Part of that was the desire to know what I liked sexually. It's how I ended up with Stephano. He was handsome and rich, and he catered to me. He was the adventure I needed.

"I don't think I ever loved him. I liked him a lot, though. I also knew Dane wouldn't have like him. He was a few years older than me, and I just knew Dane would lose it. So, I found myself cutting off contact with my brother.

168

"It turned out he wasn't a good person. On the night everything happened, I was supposed to meet him at his brother's underground club. He told me to bring my friend too. That evening, dressed to kill, Jasmine and I climbed into the car he sent for us.

"I knew. God, I fucking knew the minute we were in that car something was off. It wasn't his usual driver. It was his brother's driver. Before we got to the club, we picked up his friend, James. That was another red flag."

I take a deep breath, working hard to keep my voice from cracking as I get to the part no one knows about. "When we got there, James escorted us to a room, telling us that Stephano would be there soon. I knew the second that door closed, Stephano wasn't coming. The room was set up like a sex dungeon, but there was just something off about it.

"The minute the door locked, two men stepped out. I don't even know what they looked like. They stayed in the shadows enough to keep their faces concealed. I'm not even sure how long we were in there. But I was forced to watch while one brutalized and raped Jasmine, and then I watched Jasmine kill herself."

Another sob escapes my throat at the memory. At knowing my friend was attacked so viciously that she ended her life and that it's my fault. Jake's arms tighten around me. I can feel the vibrations of his body as anger pours off of him. "Did they – were you ...." he can't even finish his sentence. Violence and rage infiltrate his every cell to the point it's palpable.

"They never got a chance. One of Zane's friends burst into the room. I thought the sounds I heard was the thunder from the storm outside, but it was gunfire. I didn't even know until I wiped the blood from my face. They carried me out of that room. I don't remember much afterward, but Tori was shot. She nearly

169

died. What's worse is she was pregnant with Dax and didn't know it. If they'd died...." a painful, grueling sound escapes my throat.

"Shh," Jake tells me. "None of that was your fault, Cara. You can't change what happened, but you need to see it wasn't your fault. It was the asshole that took advantage of you. The fault lies with him."

"Don't you see now? Don't you see why you shouldn't love me?" I'm in near hysterics, pleading with him to change his mind. At the same time, in the recesses of my mind, I hope he doesn't.

"All I see is a girl that's been hurt. A girl that is carrying a lot of blame for something she couldn't control. If your heart weren't so fucking big, this wouldn't hurt you so much. You wouldn't hold this blame inside yourself."

"Oh, Jake," I whimper with sympathy and pity.

"I can carry it, Cara," he says in my hair. We stay like that for several minutes. Maybe it's even hours. I'm not sure. Then he starts talking again, breaking the silence. "Want to know my secret?" he whispers.

"You have a secret?" I ask incredulously because Jake, according to Dane, has always been an open book.

"I've got two, actually. One everyone knows about but you. The other I've never told anyone."

I sit up to face him. "You don't have to tell me, Jake. I didn't tell you all of that, so you'd share a secret too," I inhale deeply before I admit to him my reason, but I never get the chance.

"You told me that, hoping I would change my mind," he stroke my face with a sad smile. "Unfortunately, even if you'd told me you killed someone in cold blood, I don't think my mind would change. I've wanted you so long. It's ingrained in me."

170

"That's twice you've said something about how long you've wanted me. It didn't start with the trip?"

He chuckles with a shake of his head. Even in the darkness, I swear I see him blush. "Not even close beautiful. It all started when I came home from college. It was a party for me, and there was this gorgeous girl there. I couldn't take my eyes off of her. The problem was she was only sixteen, and I was twenty-one. She also happened to be my best friend's baby sister."

I gasp as I realize he's talking about the day we met. "All this time," surprise lines my whispered tone.

"The day of your eighteenth birthday, I planned on asking you out, but things change in an instant. Peyton was standing at my door when I opened it to leave."

"Oh my god," I gasp. "You've kept it a secret all this time."

He shakes his head. "I thought I was, but apparently, the only one that didn't see was you. Even Dane called me out on it," he laughs with disbelief.

"But you said there was a secret no one else knows."

"There is," he reaches for my hand, bringing it to his mouth, kissing each of my fingers. "When Peyton showed up, claiming to be pregnant with my baby, I knew it was impossible. But she claimed it was at a party we both attended where I got blackout drunk. I demanded a paternity test, of course. We went to the doctor together the next week for her checkup and to ask for the blood work. By the time we left, I didn't care what the results showed. After I heard the heartbeat, I was done. The next week when the results came, I pretended they said I was the baby's dad. Peyton knew she was lying, and she knew I knew. We just kept pretending. After Lyra was born, Peyton signed my name on

171

her birth certificate. Later that afternoon, when I showed up at the hospital, she'd already snuck out. "

I am speechless. I had no idea what happened to Lyra's mom. I don't know why, but I always assumed she died in childbirth or something. In a million years, I never thought that her mom just vanished, not even twenty-four hours after she was born. How was she able to just disappear like that so soon after birth? How did the hospital staff not notice? Then I realize that kind of thing happens all the time. How often have newborns been found in dumpsters or bathrooms because the mothers didn't want them? At least, the woman had the decency to have Lyra in the hospital before she just dumped her.

Then a shocked gasp escapes me as what he's said finally hits me like a sack of bricks. My eyes go wide as they snap to him. He gives me a soft smile with a kiss on my forehead. "Took you a minute, huh?" he teases.

"Jake," I gasp again.

"She's mine, Cara. Every single cell of hers belongs to me, but it's not my blood in her veins. She is my daughter, and I *am* her father. But we don't share DNA."

"You never told *anyone*?"

"No. There's no reason to."

"Jake, you – you're – I can't even put into words what I'm feeling. That's nothing short of amazing. But don't you see that's exactly why you shouldn't love me? You chose that little girl. You chose to love and protect her. Loving me will get you both hurt. I can't give you what you want or be what you need."

He pulls me closer. "I already told you, let me be what *you* need. And I can love enough for both of us. Until you accept it

172

and let yourself feel it. I can do things your way, Cara. No matter what way that is, I'll do it because all I *want* is you. And I already know you won't do anything to hurt Lyra."

I relax into him. I'm not changing his mind tonight. So I let his words wash over me, let his arms around me lull me into a peaceful sleep.

Jake

The sun blares in through the small window on my face, waking me from a fitful sleep. I was too worried about Cara to sleep well. I was afraid I'd wake up to find she'd taken off in the middle of the night.

Fortunately, she didn't even stir. I wonder when the last time was she slept so peacefully. It makes my heart warm, knowing I'm the reason.

She says she can't be what I want or need. I know she can. She just needs to believe it. She needs to realize she was a victim and she deserves love.

I prop on an elbow, just watching her breathe softly, easily. I'm not sure I've seen her looking so relaxed since she was a teenager. I'd love to give her another reason to relax.

Her lashes flutter across her cheeks. Her eyes open slowly, focusing on my face. And I wait for it.

I wait on her to realize we are in bed together. I wait for that flash of regret. I wait for the panic.

"Hi," she says softly, and I release the breath I was holding.

"How are you feeling today?" I go ahead and rip the bandage off. No sense in pretending last night didn't happen when I know it's going to be on her mind. She opens her mouth to speak. I can see the 'fine' she's about to reply in her eyes. I cut her off before she says it. "I want the truth, Cara. How are you really feeling today?"

"I'm freaked out," she says softly, her eyes leaving mine. I'm still not sure if she's afraid to be vulnerable or if she's afraid of being a burden, but I have a feeling it's the latter.

"We never did talk about what happened last night," I stroke a finger down her cheek.

"I – are you sure you want to hear?" she avoids my eyes.

"You can skip over the parts where you fucked him?" I try very hard but fail to keep the growl out of my voice.

She nods. "That is why I brought him back here. Cami and Josephine thought it would help me relax, but it never got that far."

I can't stop the internal cartwheels. I do manage, however, to just give her a short nod instead of grinning like a damn fool.

"Tell me what happened, baby," I encourage.

"We got back here. I was a nervous wreck when we got on the bus. I excused myself to the bathroom, where I took my anxiety medicine and splashed some cold water on my face. When I came

175

back out, he offered me a beer, but I didn't trust it. Guess you've noticed I've got a few trust issues," she tries to make fun of herself, but it falls flat. "Anyway, after I finally relaxed a bit, I moved to the bedroom. He came behind me and wrapped an arm around me like you did the other day. I could feel the flashback coming but held it at bay. I just kept reminding myself that was in the past. I dug my fingernails into my fist and focused on the clock on the wall, and the noises outside that weren't there that night. It took another minute or two, but it finally abated, and I thought everything was fine. Then he turned me toward the mirror and said ...." she stops talking, her bottom lip quivers and tears well in her eyes.

I pull her to my chest. I softly plant a kiss on the top of her head, giving her the moment she needs to get her thoughts together. It's a few minutes that I need too. I'm about a second away from going to find the guy myself. "What did he say, baby?"

"He said 'watch'." She says with stunted breath. "As soon as he said it, I knew." She jumps from my arms, suddenly. She whirls around to face it. "It was him, Jake. I know it was. I never saw his face. Even his voice and accent seemed different last night, but I knew it was him when he said those words in my ear. When I met his eyes in the mirror, he smirked. He knew it was me too."

My jaw clenches tightly. The man, or at least one of the men responsible for the terror she went through, was *here* with her last night. Touching her.

It takes restraint I didn't know I possessed to just sit there. I want to rage. I want to break shit. I want to find that son of a bitch and gut him. I've never felt such a proclivity for violence in my life, but right now, I could commit cold-blooded murder and not have a single regret.

I keep my features carefully schooled. This is about making her know she's safe, and raging would do the opposite right now.

I pull her back to me. "He's gone now," I reassure her. "He won't get close to you again. Not as long as I'm here."

"He's supposed to be dead," she whimpers. "I saw him lying in his own blood. How is he still alive?"

"I don't know," I press my lips to her temple, then move her, so she is laying beneath me. "I don't know. And last night might have been a coincidence, but I swear he won't get close to you again. Do you believe me?"

Her eyes war with conflict. I'm asking her to trust me without using the words. She is battling her lack of faith in herself, her ability to trust herself, even when she must know deep down she can trust me. It's a power struggle within her own mind. Finally, she gives me a slight nod. It's something. More than I had yesterday.

I lean down to kiss her forehead. I let my lips linger a moment before I draw back. Her eyes move from mine to my lips. She wants to kiss me, but she's afraid. Afraid to admit it or want it. She's afraid of the attachment. She's afraid of the emotions. She thinks she wants no strings.

She just needs that push.

I move slowly until my lips are pressed to hers. She tenses for half a second. Then she accepts my mouth. I move slowly, gently, letting her know she can trust me, not just with her secrets but with her heart. I know she didn't tell me last night because she trusts me. She wanted to scare me off. I gave her my secrets anyway. I gave her my trust so she could see that she could trust me.

Slow and gentle doesn't last long. When I hear a little moan escape her throat, all sense evades me. I bite her lip, encouraging her to open to me. I reward her for doing so by sliding my tongue into her mouth. I explore her taste just like the first time, falling completely over the edge of sanity.

I move from her mouth to her neck, nipping at the sensitive flesh. She begins to rock herself against my thigh nestled at her core. Her moans become louder when my hand finds its way under her shirt, stroking the soft skin of her hips. I press my thigh tighter into her core, allowing her to find that friction she's seeking.

I move lower down her body, catching a peaked nipple between my teeth over her shirt. I move my hand under her ass, helping her chase her release. "Let go, baby. I'll catch you," I tell her as I grab her earlobe between my teeth.

I move my hand up her shirt some more, catching her bare nipple between my fingers. "Don't ever be afraid to fall with me."

She begins to tense and shake. She opens her mouth to scream, but I catch the scream with my mouth. I continue to rock my thigh against her core as I attack her mouth. I move as the aftershocks rock her body.

When the last ripple subsides, I pull my mouth away from her. I press my forehead to hers as her sweet breath floats over my face. She looks at me with affection. I don't even think she knows how she looks at me. She's so accustomed to hiding everything, but when she's with me, that façade drops. I won't tell her. I don't want her to reinforce those walls she has built around herself, and that's what she'll do if I point it out.

"Jake," she whispers almost reverently. It's then that I realize nothing would've happened with that guy last night. She may not love me, but she's getting there. And she wouldn't have been able to go through with it, no matter who it was.

"Feel better," I grin, trying to lighten the mood for her.

She nods with a smile. "What about you?"

"What about me?" I play dumb.

"That steel pipe laying against my hip can't be comfortable," she smirks.

I kiss her nose. "Don't worry about that," I tell her. "It'll go away eventually."

"But I can he ...." she starts. I cut her off with my mouth to hers. Her fingers tangle in my hair, bringing me closer. The heat and fire burning through us are explosive. Every time we touch, it's zero to sixty in under a second. She's already burning for me, and I haven't stopped burning for her.

"Daddy, where are you?" I hear the most adorable cock blocker call out my name.

"Perfect timing," I grin down at Cara. "Another minute, and I would've had you naked."

"Another minute, and I would've let you," she tells me. I kiss her nose again.

She looks at me with worry in her eyes. "What is it?" I ask.

"I — I just don't want to lead you on, Jake. Last night — this — doesn't change anything," she tells me, her eyes moving away from mine.

I grip her chin, forcing her to look at me. "I told you last night, I don't need you to do anything. Let me be what you need."

"I'm going to break your heart," she whispers while her finger caresses my jaw.

"Let me worry about that."

"It's not fair," she argues, but there's no real fight in her tone.

"It's fair to me, Cara. I'm going to be everything you need to heal. I'm going to carry some of that weight that's holding you down. I'm going to love you until you learn to love yourself. Then, maybe then, you will be able to love me too." She sniffs as a tear falls.

"Daddy," I hear my very impatient princess yell again.

"Get up and get dressed," I tell Cara. "I'll take a shower when you're done."

She nods, and I leave the room. I see Lyra standing in the middle of it with her arms folded, looking at Angel like he's the devil. Ironically, he is looking at her like she's Satan's spawn.

"What the hell is going on here?" I laugh.

"Daddy, I can says Anel," she tells me with her bottom lip poked out.

"Look, munchkin, my name is An-gel. 'J' with a g. I'm not a butthole," Angel argues with her.

Her bottom lip begins to quiver, and Angel looks at me with panic in his eyes. "That," he points at her lip, "is why we are here. I can't handle it."

"Then why are you arguing with her?" I laugh as I pick Lyra up. She tucks her head into the crook of my neck.

"Because she keeps calling me Anal. Dude, would *you* want to be called that?"

"I'll see if Cara can help her with that," I laugh again.

"How is she? She tell you what happened?" his tone is now complete concern for her.

"She did," I affirm. "She opened up big time, but I am not telling you or anyone else what she said."

He raises his hands defensively. "I get it. You want her to trust you, but you know it's going to piss big brother off."

"Big brother can deal with it. She wouldn't have told me at all if she weren't trying to scare me off," I tell him.

"Didn't work, I see," he grins.

"Not even close. Did Henry find the guy?"

"Not that I know of. That guy was long gone in the crowd. Too many people, man. Too easy to disappear."

"Probably for the best," I tell him with gritted teeth. "If I ever see him, I will fucking kill him."

"Good to know," Angel doesn't blink an eye at my threat. "The girls have breakfast for everyone. Bring Cara over so she can eat something."

I nod and watch him leave.

"Dude, do you plan on telling me what happened with my sister?" Dane stalks after me as we head to the stage for our show.

I'm already tense as hell. The idea of leaving Cara behind while we're on stage is driving me slowly insane. I wanted to tell Liam and Henry to keep their eyes on her even if everything seemed fine, but there was no way I could without telling them why.

Dane's constant nagging, which hasn't stopped since this morning, is making the tension worse. I get it. He's worried about his sister. If I were in his position, I'd probably be just as annoying – I mean worried.

But I've told him what she told me is between her and me. I've not gotten her trust yet. I can't break it before she gives it.

"I told you, the guy triggered a flashback," I tell him again without stopping.

"And I told you I know there's more to it than that," he is practically yelling, but over the noise of the crowd, it doesn't have the same effect.

When we get to the stairs of the platform, he spins me around to face him. "That's my damn sister. I have a right to know what she told you."

I push him off with a growl. "When your *grown* sister is ready for you to know, *she* will tell you."

His fists clench at his side. He puffs his chest, glaring at me. My posture very much matches his. Two Pitbulls ready to fight. "I can't watch out for her if I don't know what's going on. Stop trying to use her trust to get into her pants."

Red fills my vision. I don't even think. I just react with my fist flying at my best friend. He stumbles back a bit, touching his mouth where blood pools at the corner. "If all I wanted was in her pants, I'd have been there days ago. *I'm* the one who slammed the brakes, you asshole."

People are gathering around us. Groupies with all access, crew members, even other bands are standing around trying to see the commotion. This isn't the time or place for this, but fucking Dane can't stop himself. My asshole best friend is on a mission and has been on that mission for ten years. But he needs to know he's gone too far with his bullshit.

"Stop trying to use my feelings for the both of you to get your damn way. You can't control everything anymore."

"You don't think I know that? I lost control years ago. I am grasping at fucking straws here." His blue eyes are glassy with tears he won't let fall. "I just want to help her."

"You have helped her, Dane. You've done everything you can to help her. Now let me help her. She gave that bit of herself to me last night. Albeit, not because she trusted me. She wanted to scare me off, but I'm not going anywhere. I have been in this for five years. Now that I have my foot in the door, I am not turning loose, and I am not going to betray that very shaky foundation. Not for you or anyone else."

His shoulders slump. He nods his reluctant acceptance. He reaches for my shoulder, giving me an apologetic look before he takes the stairs leading up the platform. I drag a hand through my hair with a heavy sigh. I feel like a shitty friend.

"He needed to hear that, mate." Ryder gives me an understanding nod. "He needed to hear that from *you.*"

"Not before a show," I point out with a groan.

"It will be fine. He'll be fine," Angel reassures me.

I nod at the both of them, then move up the stairs.

Maddox wastes no time taking the mic. He works the crowd over as only he can, getting the crowd going while the rest of us plug in.

I look over to Dane, noting the lines of stress marring his face. He meets my gaze with a tight nod. Acknowledgment that he heard me. Hopefully, acceptance that I *will* be there for her.

I am an only child. I can't relate to Dane as a sibling concerned for another sibling. But Dane has been so much more than a sibling to Cara. In some ways, to me too. And one thing I can relate to is that paternal need to protect your child. To make sure they are happy and healthy. I can understand that desire to make sure nothing ever touches them and to want to burn the world down to make everything better.

I hope I never face anything like that. The thought of Lyra going through even a fraction of what Cara has been through makes me want to take them both and hide them away from the world.

Right now, as much as I would rather make sure Cara really is okay, I have a job to do. Dane taps his stick for one, two, three, and Ryder starts the fast-paced riff of our opening song. I join in after a couple of bars with heavy bass. Angel and Dane quickly follow while Maddox steps up to the microphone. He opens his mouth, and the deep sounds of his lower register fill the space with the jaded words Ryder wrote long ago about his mother.

You're nothing without your manipulations
You tell nothing but lies to hide the bitter truth of who you are
Your world is full of hallucinations
Building deceptions to cover the pain and suffering you cause

The lyrics definitely match the angry tone of the music. Maddox's voice fills the arena like not many I've ever heard. The comparison's to the great voices of the last fifty years have been made since the band finally burst onto the scene two years ago. He has incredible range, power, and control and is definitely a sure way to know you're hearing Sons of Sin.

184

The band could've been bigger than it has already if any one of my brothers had used their influence and money. They didn't want to do things that way. They wanted to pay their dues and earn their way to the top. If anyone can't respect that, then they can fuck off. We don't need them anyway.

Even though I haven't been a part of the excitement the last few years, I've still been there. I've practiced with these guys, helped them when they were stuck on a chord progression, or couldn't find just the right lyric. Even without being on stage or in the studio with them, I know every song.

If I'd done things differently, I would've been on this journey for the entire ride. It's even possible that I would've been with Cara. But without those choices, I wouldn't have Lyra. Angel wouldn't be part of the band. He might never have reunited with Josephine.

So many things could've happened with a simple change in course. The only thing I would change is Cara. If I'd made my move, then maybe she wouldn't be suffering. Maybe she would never have ended up with the bastard that irrevocably changed her.

The rest, I wouldn't change for anything.

"I've got a song I want to share with you guys tonight," Maddox says to the audience, breaking me from my reflection. "A couple of months ago, I lost someone very important to me. I never had much of a chance to tell her that. You see, choices were made that set our paths long ago. Choices I didn't know about until I was much older. When I learned that the woman who raised me was not the woman who gave birth to me, I was angry. I was so very, very angry. If I'm honest, I still am some days. But those choices were made because my birth mother was not in a place to be a mother. What I regret most is not having the chance to tell her I love her and forgive her. That it wasn't her fault, and she did the best she could. So I'm going to tell her tonight because I know she's somewhere out there listening. This is for you, Jewel, wherever you are."

I watch as he takes a deep breath. He's struggled with this song for weeks. Wanting the lyrics and the melody to be perfect. Ryder starts slowly strumming out the haunting notes of the opening. Even though it's not our usual style, the softer notes carry a haunting power. When the lyrics come, everything stills but the song.

You were a diamond until someone stole your shine
You tried to fight your demons
But the broken pieces of your mind
Couldn't recover what was lost somewhere in time
You felt so lost and so alone
With so much weight to bear
That was was just too heavy
And you thought that no one cared
But I cared, and I'm still here without you

I'm still missing you
Though you never knew how much I needed you in my life
If we had another moment to share
It would be magnificent because I would show you I need you
I would prove you're not alone
And I would let you know just how much I love you.
But that moment just won't come
And I'm still missing you

He sings the song like it bleeds from his soul. He hasn't really expressed how much her death hurt him. Hell, except for Ryder,

186

none of us knew his birth mom. The woman we've met on occasion wasn't the same person.

This is how Maddox tells us that he's in pain. The only way he knows how. The rest of the time, he buries it in bottles and powder. But even with the influence of the drugs I know are coursing through his veins, you can hear how absolutely shattered he is.

I look to Dane on the drums and then to Angel and Ryder. They see it too. They see that Maddox is hanging on by a thread. All we can do is be there when that thread finally snaps.

The song ends. The audience has been absolutely silent. By the chorus, they'd pulled out their phones for light. Now, ear-shattering applause fills the arena. Whistles and shouts of praise tell us that everything Maddox wanted the audience to feel was felt and then some.

I look to my right where Liam, Cami, and Josephine are standing. Liam's eyes swim with emotion, making me wonder what his story is. His tough exterior of a leather-wearing, tattooed badass belies the man standing there with tears in his eyes.

Josephine and Cami are both openly sobbing. Tears run down their faces like a river.

All three faces share the same worried expressions as my brothers and me.

We get off the stage after Maddox and Ryder close out the show. The girls waste no time climbing on Mads, sobbing into his neck. He chuckles, hugging them back, then quickly brushes off their praise. In typical Maddox fashion, he plasters on a huge smile.

I notice he seems antsy. Too many feelings bombarding the guy at once. And these are all reflections of his own emotions. These feelings are for him, and he isn't handling it.

I watch as he nods over the girls' heads to us, Ryder specifically, that he is getting out of there. Fast.

I am right behind him, but I'm headed for the baby bus.

The baby bus. Like I'm not on there too. Whatever.

I walk onto the bus to find Henry sitting there looking at something on his phone. I'm still pretty irritated about last night. He should've done a better job of watching after Cara.

"Got a problem, man?" he asks when I walk past him without a word.

I reach into the fridge, grabbing a bottle of water before I give him my attention. "I've definitely got a problem, but I'm not having it out right now. Cara and Lyra are asleep, I assume?"

"Come outside," he orders gruffly, which only serves to agitate me more.

I follow him out, though. I step outside the bus but not too far away from the door. "What?" I ask without a hint of politeness.

"You said you weren't having it out in there. So have it out right here." His green eyes pierce right through me. He's trying to intimidate me, but I'm not usually intimidated by other men, even if they do have a couple inches and about thirty pounds on me. "What's your problem."

"You can't guess?" I scoff. "None of that shit would've happened last night if you'd been doing your job. I mean, that's why you're here, right? To protect her?"

He gives me a shitty grin. An arrogant one that I want to wipe off with my fist. "Your problem with me started long before last night, you jealous prick. But for argument's sake, what would you have had me do differently last night?"

I grind my teeth. I want to argue that I'm not jealous of him. That I have no reason to be. While the latter might be true, I have been jealous of him since he started. I hate that he's had all of this time with Cara that I haven't. Hopefully, that's changing, so I'm going to ignore his comments. "If you'd stayed with her, that asshole wouldn't have been able to hurt her," I accuse without hesitation. "You should never have allowed her to bring some stranger back to the bus. Much less left them alone."

"I watched her. I was close to her all night. But the girl is an adult. I couldn't stop her from bringing him back. As far as leaving them alone, what would you suggest? I stand there and watch as she fucks the guy?"

The thought of him seeing her like that boils my blood. It moves like lava through my veins as I grab him by his shirt, pushing him into the side of the bus. "Don't talk about her like that," I grind out.

"Stop letting your jealousy rule your head," he counters without attempting to get me out of his face. "If you want her, then you should tell her instead of puffing your chest out at me. I did my job. When she went in the bus with the guy, I stayed close enough to get to her. Last night, I didn't have to go to her. You did. I went after the bastard that scared her."

Fuck him. I hate that he's right. But I still don't want to admit it.

"The kid has some serious PTSD going on. She tell you that? Have you even noticed?"

189

This guy. Who the hell does he think he is? I want so badly to break his nose, I can practically feel the bone crunching beneath my fist. "I've more than notice."

"Then help her instead of standing out here marking your territory."

I release him with a shove.

I *am* being a jealous prick. I'm definitely being unreasonable, but I think I have a right to be after what she told me last night. I don't even want to think about what would've happened if none of us had been around. My stomach squeezes at the thought.

I walk back onto the bus in search of my girls. I check the bunk first, just in case, then head for the bedroom. In the middle of the big bed, Cara and my princess are wrapped around each other. The sight is so beautiful it's painful.

After a quick shower, I climb into the bed on Lyra's other side. I would love to climb in behind Cara. Wrap my arms around both of them and let the world fade away. I'm just not sure how Cara would feel about that. So I'll hold them this way and relish every second.

Cara

I wake up with a foot precariously close to my mouth. I move it slowly so I don't wake the bed hog. I look next to me to find Lyra's top half sprawled across her daddy's chest, and I realize Jake's hand is in my hair.

Looking at them, I remember the dreams of the girl I used to be. It's something Dane and I had in common. Tori, on the other hand, wanted nothing to do with relationships or kids. Ironic, she was the first of us to have a relationship, and if Zane had his way, they'd already have another baby. Or at least have one baking.

Dane has finally found his happiness. I knew he would. What woman wouldn't want a man like him? Anyone that would sacrifice so much to raise a girl they didn't have to is worth it.

Jake fits that description. I never would've guessed in a million years that he wasn't Lyra's biological father. Not that it matters. DNA does not a father make.

He'll find someone too. Someone to appreciate the wonderful man he is. Someone who will love Lyra every bit as much as he does.

The thought of him finding someone else hurts my heart. I wish I could be that girl. And that is going to get my heart broken because I will never be that girl.

One day, probably soon, he's going to realize I am broken beyond repair. My decisions get people hurt. I can't be trusted.

I feel the start of panic bubbling in my gut. I don't even know why I'm panicking. Is it because of how I feel, or is it because I know I can never have what I want?

My phone starts buzzing on the table by the bed. I quickly and quietly get out of bed and make my way to the front of the bus. The call is from my therapist. I haven't talked to him since that first day. If my brother – or the other two pseudo brothers – find out that I've been skipping our calls, they'll have me sent home. Fortunately, the good doctor or whatever he is hasn't ratted me out yet.

But there is someone I need to talk to. The only other person until Jake who knew nearly everything that happened to me. Not because I told him, but because he's the one who carried me out of that room. He's the one that pulled the trigger.

I don't even know the time difference at this point. I stopped trying to keep up about a week into this trip. I'm pretty sure he's always awake, though. He would call me for months at incredibly random hours to check on me. Until I finally stopped answering

192

the phone. He showed up at my apartment a couple of times. I pretended like I wasn't home.

I figured after a while, he'd given up. We weren't friends. The first time I ever laid eyes on him was that night. To say I was shocked that he was there to see me off when I left River City is an understatement.

This is the first time I've ever contacted him, but I need to tell him the man he shot isn't dead. He needs to know that this could all come back on him. I should've called him yesterday, but I spent most of the day in denial.

Today, I've got to stop denying what I know and tell the man who saved my life that he may be in danger.

He picks up on the first ring, worry filling his tone. "What's the matter, darlin'?"

As soon as the question is asked, I feel the tears burning in my eyes. "He's not dead," I tell him with a crack to my voice.

"Who's not dead, Cara?" His voice relays his genuine confusion.

"That man. The one who tried to hurt me. He's not dead." The panic begins to leech in my voice. I dig my fingernails into my palm, reminding myself to stay in the present.

"Cara, I killed him," he tries to rationalize. I get why. It doesn't make any sense. But then again, I don't know if he ever went back to confirm the man was actually dead.

"Christian, you're not listening to me. I saw him," I nearly scream before remembering Jake and Lyra are a few feet away, still sleeping.

"Okay, tell me what you saw," he breathes out. He's trying to understand and be patient. It's not a common occurrence among men like him.

"I saw him. Only I didn't know it was him. I just thought he was a good-looking guy interested in me. It wasn't until he spun me around to face the mirror and told me to ...." my voice cuts out. That word. So harmless and used for so many different purposes is such a trigger for me. I realized that even before therapy. It's not something I can explain to everyone, though.

"He told you to what, Cara? What did he do? Did he hurt you? Are you all right? Do you need me to come get you?"

"Christian, why do you care so much?" I ask, not for the first time.

"You remind me of someone. When I saw you hurt, I thought about it being her," he tells me. It's an answer he's never given before. I wonder what's changed. "What did he do, Cara?"

"He didn't do anything. He didn't get a chance. When he growled that word in my ear, I knew it was him."

"What did he look like?"

"What?" I ask, not understanding why that matters. Christian knows I never really saw the man.

"Just answer the question," he demands gruffly.

"Tall, like Jax tall, with dark hair and blue eyes. Had a slight accent, but I don't know what kind."

"Do you know where he is now?"

"Of course not," I hiss. "I screamed, and he ran. Liam and Maddox tried to chase after him, but he got lost in the crowd."

194

"Where were you?"

"Kyiv. Why? What are you thinking?"

"I think that it was a coincidence that you ran into him. Don't worry about him. We'll handle it from here."

"We?"

"I have to tell them, Cara," he tells me bluntly. His tone is clear. Nothing I say will change his mind.

"Can you at least tell them not to tell anyone else?" I whisper.

"They don't bring others in on business. That's what this is. Thank you for telling me, Cara."

I nod and end the call. My head spins, and heart races even faster than before at the thought of anyone else knowing what I did. What I caused.

I go to the fridge and grab a bottle of water. I set it on the counter while I grab my medication from my bag. My hands shake so violently I can't get the bottle open.

Two large, solid hands wrap around mine, removing the bottle from my grip. He opens the bottle, handing me one, then opens the water bottle as well.

I can't meet his eyes. Shame washes through me. This is why I can't be with him. Why I will never be enough. He just doesn't realize it yet. He will soon, then he will forget all about me.

And never in my life has a thought like that hurt so much.

He tips my chin up, but I still avert my eyes. "Look at me, baby." He's been calling me that a lot. I have to bite my tongue so I don't snap for him to stop. I'm not his baby. I can't be. But I move my eyes to meet his anyway. The affection shining in those beautiful eyes takes my breath away. "What do you need?"

I take a deep breath, willing myself to calm down. Can't say it's working. "I need to be left alone for a few minutes," I tell him. "I just need to pull myself together."

He shakes his head and drops his hand from my face. I take it he's letting me. Giving in already.

As I start to turn away, his arm snakes around my waist, taking me by surprise. "You're not going anywhere. I've let you avoid and ignore me. I've given you space because I thought that was what you needed."

"It is, Jake," I insist.

"No, it's not. You're not going to push me away anymore. You don't need space. You need this." He pulls me into his chest, wrapping both arms around me in a tight hug. "You need someone to remind you that you're worth it. That you're beautiful."

I give an indignant scoff as I mentally battle being in his arms. "You think I don't know what I look like?"

"I'm not talking about your face or body. I'm talking about your heart and soul. You think because of what happened to you that you're tainted. That the damage runs too deep for anyone to love you. You think you're too broken to love someone else. I know you're not."

I bury my face in his chest, tears now flowing freely. "Jake, please stop."

"Cara, you think I don't see how much you love your brother. That I haven't noticed how you are with Maddox and Ryder. Not to mention Lyra. You treat that little girl – my little girl – as if she

196

hung the moon. You're not so broken you can't be fixed, Cara. You are full of cracks and scars, but I love you for those scars and what's under them too."

I shake my head, trying to deny what I know to be true. I've seen how he looks at me. I can hear it in his voice.

"I'm going to be what you need. I going to show you love like you never thought possible. I'm not going anywhere. I'm going to be right here until you believe what I tell you. I'm going to be right here until you finally stop refusing to feel what I can see when you look at me. Just like you can see it when I look at you."

"What do you see?" I whisper.

"The other half of my soul. I saw it five years ago when I laid eyes on a sixteen-year-old girl. At that moment, I knew I was going to hell, but it will be well worth the trip. It's taken you a bit to catch up, but I knew the minute you did."

I give a wet chuckle. "Oh yeah. When was that?"

"I'll let you figure it out. When you do, you can tell me if I'm right."

"You deserve better, Jake."

"No, baby, you deserve better. I just hope one day very soon, you'll settle for me."

I am sitting on the sofa with pens and an adult coloring book. My therapist recommended I use them when I feel anxious. Something for me to focus on besides the demons in my head.

As soon as I put Lyra down for the night, they started screaming. Reminding me of the mistakes I've made. Telling me to keep my walls up because Jake won't be able to handle me.

He'll need to protect Lyra from me. Or the absolute worst, that somehow I will hurt them too. Knowing that man is still alive makes that seem like all too real a possibility.

I'm not sure if these workbooks actually help, but they don't hurt. They give me something to do besides sitting here, listening to the voices in my head.

I sit here for hours with the colorful pens, filling in the lines of the abstract design. I'm not an artist by any means. That's all Dane. But I do like to color. I like following the patterns and seeing my finished work. Kind of makes me feel like a kid. At the moment, being a kid would be better than being an adult.

A few hours later, I'm starting on my second page. Tonight, it's actually working. I've been totally distracted from the inner workings of my mind. So much so, I don't realize how late it is until the door to the bus opens and Jake walks in.

He goes straight to the fridge, pulling out a bottle of water. He grabs some paper towels, then wipes his face. His hair is wet with sweat. He reaches over his head, removing his sweat-soaked shirt, making my mouth go very dry. I realize with a shock, I've never seen him without his shirt. I knew without a doubt he'd be well-toned, but I never thought he'd look like he'd been chiseled from the marble of Michelangelo.

You can see the effects of the adrenaline from being on stage are still very much with him. More than that, he looks like sex.

My thighs clench at the thought. He always looks like sex but, right now, he could give me an orgasm just by looking at me. Especially if he keeps looking at me like he is. He hasn't taken his eyes off of me since he walked in the door.

"Wasn't expecting you to be awake," he says with a husky voice that makes my insides shake.

198

"Couldn't sleep. Too much trying to creep into my head," I tell him. I try to drop my eyes from his, but they are locked on his. I feel like a snake being hypnotized.

He walks to me. His steps, though few, are calculated and measured. Sure.

He sits next to me, taking the book and pens away, setting them on the floor. He pulls me in his lap so that I'm straddling him.

I'm unsure what to make of this Jake, who is forward with his feelings and intentions. He said he's wanted me for years. I never knew because he never showed any interest in me. I may have recognized his attraction and affection that first night of the tour, but he still never said anything. He gave me my space.

I kind of want that space back right now. My heart is doing somersaults in my chest. My stomach feels like I'm on a rollercoaster going downhill. I am feeling things I am trying not to feel. Things I desperately want to push away because they're only going to lead to pain. For both of us.

But it's the throbbing between my legs that keeps me in place. It's the feel of his hardness beneath me – that his jeans and my cotton shorts do little to conceal – that won't let me move. I somehow manage to keep my hands to myself. It takes real concentrated effort not to grind against him. Like I did the other morning, and I came like I've never done in my life.

He smirks, knowing exactly why I'm still sitting here. Knowing exactly how my body reacts to him. He doesn't mention it, though. "Why can't you sleep?"

Talking? That's what he wants to do?

I guess, considering I'm too turned on to run, his game plan is smart. "Just the memories trying to take over."

"But you slept last night," he says, brushing a stray hair from my bun away from my face. I don't even bother attempting to contain the shiver that runs up my spine.

"I did sleep last night. Tonight, I can't. I've taken my meds. I've meditated. My thoughts were taking a dangerous turn, so I decided to try these books like my therapist suggested."

"What's got you on edge, Cara?" He grasps both sides of my face firmly but gently. It's a startling contrast but so very Jake. "Why did you sneak out of bed this morning? Why were you so shaken when I found you?"

He never brought any of that up earlier today. I wish he hadn't now. I want to look away, but his grip keeps me firmly in place. My eyes close as I try to erect my walls a little taller.

"Open your eyes, baby." My eyes open, against my will, at his command. "I told you, I'm not letting you run away from me. I know for you, it's only been a short while. I've waited for just the slightest opening for years. I'm not waiting anymore. Talk to me, Cara. You know, or at least I hope you do, that nothing you have said or will say will change how I see you."

Why does he say these things? It's like he hasn't heard a word I've told him. "I had to make a phone call this morning. I had to call Christian. I should've made it yesterday, but I wasn't ready."

"Who is Christian?" His eyes stay so completely focused on mine it's a little unnerving.

"Christian is the man that saved me. I let him know he wasn't dead," a small sob lodges in my throat as I say the words all over again. "I'm not sure he believed me at first, but when I told him what he looked like, he did."

"I'm sorry it upset you. I'm sorry you're going through any of this."

"It was my own carelessness and recklessness," I shrug. "I can't blame anyone but myself for all of it. My hands are the ones that are bloody."

"No. It wasn't your damn fault. You might have made a mistake in who you trusted, but everyone has crossed that bridge a time or two. I'm a good example of that."

"It's not the same. Your decision didn't get someone killed. It didn't get your sister hurt. No one had to risk their lives to save you." My bottom lip trembles. The pain of what happened is excruciating, but it's the guilt that's crushing me.

"Let me ask you something," he tells me. "Do you think Cami deserved what happened with her ex?"

"No!" I exclaim, appalled. "Why would you even ask that?"

"Because everything your saying suggests you do. Cami was with a bad guy, but she chose to be with him. Even when he started hurting her, she chose to say. By your logic, she deserved what happened to her."

"It's not the same thing," I demand. "Cami didn't get someone hurt or killed."

"Didn't she, though? Every time she went back to the tool was like a knife through your brother's chest. Does that mean she shouldn't be with Dane? Has she not come to her senses, *she* could've been killed."

"It's still not the same," I insist, nearly shouting. "The only person really hurt by Cami's actions was Cami. My actions hurt others. If it weren't for me, they wouldn't have been there. It should've been me. Not Jasmine! Me!"

My chest heaves with each word, but my voice never gets above a harsh whisper. My fists clench tightly at my side.

His fists clench, too, right into the bones of my hip. Holding me in a punishing grip. His eyes, concerned and curious moments ago, are now flaming with fury. One hand reaches up to my jaw, this time gripping almost painfully. "Do not ever fucking say that again. Do you understand me?" he nearly yells. "Do you know that if anything had happened to you worse than it did that Dane would have lost it? His guilt is barely contained as it is. And what about Maddox and Ryder? Don't you think they've lost enough? And me? Do you have any idea what knowing you were gone forever would've done to me? I'm sorry your friend died. It was not your fault. I understand your guilt, but it was not your fault. Do not ever think it should've been you."

My heart races at the anger in his voice and the hurt in his eyes. I'm speechless. What I said was true. If I hadn't dragged her along with me, Jasmine would still be alive right now. But he's right too. About Dane, at least. He wouldn't have been able to handle it if I'd died. It's part of why I haven't told him everything that happened that night.

"What would it have done to you?" I ask him softly.

His grip loosens on my face. He pulls me until our foreheads touch. "I know this thing with us is new for you. Most days, I want to kick myself in the ass for not making a move sooner. I watched you for so long – wanted you for so long – I felt like a stalker," he chuckles when he says stalker, making me smile too. "If anything had happened to you – if I completely missed my chance, I'm not sure I would've survived. As it is, I wonder if I'd gone to you on your birthday like I planned, if any of this would've happened in the first place."

I jerk back from him in surprise. "What? Why would that even cross your mind?"

"You can't deny our connection, Cara. I know you want to, but it's been pretty clear since I showed up with Dane in River City. If I'd gone to you all those years ago, maybe you would've gone to college in New York instead of Chicago. You wanted to explore your sexuality? You could have done that with me."

"Jake," I gasp, shocked that he is taking blame for my actions on himself. He brings his lips to mine with a soft kiss. It's so sweet it almost makes me cry. "Why did you come to River City?" I whisper when he pulls away.

"I was on Dane's case to bring you home for a long time. When he told me he was going to check on you, I had to go. I needed to be there to convince him to bring you home. Kicking and screaming if need be. I needed you back home so I could take my chance."

"What happened? I didn't even know you liked me until ...." I trail off because I'm not entirely sure when I knew.

"You seemed so fragile." He brushes my hair behind my ear. "Then I started second-guessing myself. Not how I feel, but I knew there was a possibility you wouldn't feel the same way. You're so young, Cara. You still have a lot of things you probably want to do. I come with a toddler who demands most of my attention. I work at my grandfather's auto shop. The way I saw it, you'd be settling for me if you even gave me a shot. I didn't want to hold you -."

I shut him up by slamming my mouth to his. I can't shove down my feelings for this beautiful, beautiful man anymore. I still don't want this. I still don't think there is a remote possibility it could last. I'm too broken.

But right now, I can't deny how I feel.

It catches him off guard, but it only takes him a second to catch up. Our teeth clash, and tongues tangle in a flurry of want and need. My hands go to his shoulders, needing him closer. His hands move into my hair, needing the same. I'm not even sure whose air I'm breathing, but I know I need more.

I grind myself against him, needing to feel him but unable to get the relief I seek. "Jake," I moan as he begins to trail open mouth kisses down my jaw to my neck. I stretch, giving him more access to my flesh. "Jake," I cry out again with breathless pants, hoping he will give me what I want.

He leans back, stopping his ministrations. I whimper in protest. "Where's Lyra?"

I look down toward the back of the bus. "In the bunk," I tell him. "I knew I wouldn't sleep, so I wanted her close."

He stands without losing his grip on me. Those few steps to the bedroom feel like an eternity when he steps through, laying me on the bed. He settles his weight on his forearms around my head. "You sure?" he asks. Unlike last time, my answer is a resounding yes.

He nods, stepping away from me. He turns to the door, flipping the lock, then moves back to the foot of the bed. "Clothes off, Cara," he orders as he rubs himself over his jeans.

My thighs clench at the command, and my mouth waters at the outline of his erection through those skin-tight jeans. I sit up quickly, pulling my thin tank over my head, then slide my shorts over my hips until I'm completely bare before him.

"Goddamn, you're so fucking beautiful, baby," he tells me, his voice deep and husky with desire. "Now spread those legs so I can see that pretty pussy."

I groan at his words, loving the dominating tone and dirty talk. Then I remember it was my sexual proclivities that led me to Stephan, and I find myself unable to follow his demands.

"No, Cara," he snaps brusquely. "You're here with me. This is about you and me. Don't bring anyone else into it. Don't bring any guilt or shame into it. If you can't do that, we end it right now."

I bite my lip as I try to force those unwanted thoughts and feelings away. He sees my struggle. He comes to lay beside me, turning me to face him. "I don't want you to regret this tomorrow. I'm not going to give you another reason to run away from me."

"I won't regret it," I breathe. "I won't run away. Not because of this."

His eyes shadow when I say the last. "Not because of anything, Cara. I already told you. I won't say it again. Do you feel me?"

I take a deep breath and nod.

"I will make you love me, Cara," he tells me with so much resolve it knocks the breath I just took out of me. He sits up and moves back to the foot of the bed. His eyes never leave mine. "You already would if you weren't fighting it, but it's okay. I've already told you I've got enough love for both of us. I'm going to make you believe you deserve it." I watch as he removes his belt and unfastens his jeans, my tongue growing thick in my mouth as he does. "I'm going to prove to you that I can be what you need." He pushes his jeans and underwear past his hips, revealing his beautiful, thick erection that reaches for the heavens. Moisture floods between my legs at the sight of him. "I'm gonna convince you that you are already everything I want and need. You were five years ago that day in your brother's apartment. You were four months ago when you were crying in my arms in River City. You are right now, lying in front of me. Everything I never knew I wanted and have found harder and harder to live without."

He is hovering over me again. His mouth only a hair's breadth from mine. My chest heaves as I work to catch my breath. I'm suddenly very nervous. This isn't going to be a simple one-night fuck with no emotions or attachments. It can't be when he's already poured so much emotion into it. My heart thumps erratically in my chest when he grips my thighs. He spreads them wide, pushing them toward my ears. He licks his lips like he's dying of thirst and just found the oasis. He's still staring at the core of me when he says, "but right now, I'm going to ruin you. I'm going to wreck this pretty little pussy for anyone else. You're mine, Cara. Even if you don't know it yet."

I'm not sure I'm breathing anymore. Every single thing he has said has ripped the oxygen from my lungs. The center of me has been set on fire. I've never burned like this. I am an inferno of need and desire. He has demolished me, and I have no doubt I won't return from this.

I've known for a while I would never get away from Jake unscathed, no matter how hard I tried. I have been falling harder and harder by the day. Avoiding him has helped nothing. And that terrifies me. I'm not sure I will be able to handle the inevitable heartbreak.

"You've got to be quiet," he tells me as he runs a finger through my folds. "Not a sound," he demands with stern eyes when a moan escapes me. I know I'm going to fall apart fast. I have no idea how I'm going to stay quiet.

With a slightly sadistic grin, he dives between my spread thighs. My hips buck when his tongue lashes between my lips in one long swipe. He throws an arm over my waist, holding me in place. "Hold still," he growls.

He laps at my entrance teasingly, then slides it inside of me in a way I didn't know was possible. His tongue swirls and thrusts, swiping at my inner walls, and with each measure, I viciously clench around him.

My head thrashes from side to side. I throw my arm over my mouth, biting to contain the screams that are begging me to escape. When he begins to suck on my throbbing bundle of nerves, my entire body spasms.

I've never experienced such intense sensations in my life. My body is screaming with the need for release. My mind is a ball of mush, unable to form a single coherent thought.

He slides his long, nimble finger inside me slowly. He flicks his tongue over my nub, once, twice, three times while he strokes very precisely inside of me.

The pleasure is too much. It's too intense. It is bordering on pain. Delicious, erotic, pleasurable pain that has turned me into a ticking time bomb waiting for just the right moment to explode.

When his teeth clamp around that pulsating pearl, I erupt. I'm biting my arm so hard I know I'm breaking skin as the agonizing screams of ecstasy fill my lungs. My body brutally shudders. My pussy clenches so hard it hurts.

He doesn't stop until he has drained me of everything. Not until the final vicious shake of my body. Not until I can't move, speak, or think. Hell, I can't even hear or see.

I barely register when he flips me over. The sounds of foil ripping seem miles away. When he enters me in one smooth thrust, my mouth falls open, but nothing comes out.

He grips my hips, pulling nearly all the way out, then snaps his hips forward. I gasp from the pain and relish in the pleasure. The sounds of our bodies connecting echo through the silence.

My sex-drugged mind can only register the delicious sensation of being filled to the cusp. The wonderful stretching of my most intimate flesh soon has me nearing the edge of that cliff. I marvel at how close I am after that first powerful climax. I wonder if I can even survive another.

He pulls me to my knees. My over-pleasured mind takes note of him wrapping his arm around my waist, careful not to trap my arms. His other hand trails my left arm before pulling it up to his neck. He nips at the flesh where my shoulder and neck meet, then kisses the sting away.

His thrusts have slowed. He's taking his time as he reaches deep inside me. His head hits those inner nerves perfectly.

"I've wanted you like this for so fucking long. I don't want it to end." His whispers fill my ears, sounding like shouts through the quiet. "I don't want it to end, but I'm not going to last much longer. I need you to come, baby."

"I can't," I whimper, but even as I say it, I feel my inner walls clench. With every stroke, I feel him thicken inside of me. I'm teetering on the edge of that cliff, and there is no bottom in sight.

"I need it, sweetheart. I need to feel this tight pussy strangle my cock. I need it to milk me for every drop."

"Oh God," is all I can manage when his fingers begin to strum my clit. My head falls back to his shoulder. My hand flies behind us, gripping his hips as I hold on against the inferno that incinerates my body to ash. My mouth opens with a scream that he swallows with his own.

A deep, rumbling groan vibrates in his chest. His thrusts become erratic. His jaw clenches tightly, and the tendons in his neck strain. "Fuck, fuck, holy fuck," he grinds out as he pulses and twitches inside of me.

He lowers his head to my shoulder, his arm around my waist the only thing holding me up. Both of us panting. Our hearts pound, his vibrating against my back in sync with mine.

After a few more seconds, he withdraws from me, then lays me back in the bed. He walks away to dispose of the condom. I watch him do something with his phone before he returns to the bed with our clothes.

He pulls his boxer briefs back on. Then he surprises me when he puts my clothes back on me too. "Just in case Lyra wakes before we do," he tells me as he pulls my shorts up my hips.

"Maybe I should go back in there with her," I say softly, not wanting to confuse her.

"Don't even think about it," he growls. He hovers over me, brushing my sweat-soaked hair away from my face. "Are you okay?"

I smile softly, cupping his worried face. I know what he's thinking. "I don't regret it," I reassure him.

He lowers his lips to mine with a soft kiss. Seconds of sweet turn into fire quickly. The electricity between us cannot be contained. I gasp when I feel him harden against my belly.

He pulls away, leaving me breathless. "I love you, Cara. I'm not going to stop saying it or showing you until you believe it."

"Jake," I start to tell him I do believe him. I'm just not convinced it will last. Not when he sees all of me. Not when those irreparable pieces become too much. Not when he decides he needs to protect Lyra from me.

"Go to sleep." He kisses my forehead, not letting me say what I want. He slides beside me, pulling me into his chest. His arms wrap around me tightly. Almost like he's afraid I'll disappear. Guess I've given him plenty of reason to think I would.

Right now, I don't want to be anywhere else. For the first time in nearly two years, I feel safe. My mind isn't a war zone. It's actually calm for the first time in a long time. And I want to hang on to it for as long as I can.

Though one thing does stir around in my head. One thing Jake had wrong.

He doesn't have to make me love him.

I already do.

Jake

I've been awake nearly all night. Every time I close my eyes, the thought of waking up alone has them flying open.

She hasn't moved since I told her to sleep. Even when the bus started moving, she hasn't even twitched. I made sure to text the driver to use his key and flipped the latch for Lyra before I climbed back in bed.

We were scheduled to leave at four for Berlin. They told us it would take about six hours. Judging from the light peeking in the small window, we have three or four hours to go.

Cara stirs for the first time, murmuring my name. I can't stop the smile that spreads across my face when she snuggles closer into my chest.

I meant every word I told her. I'm not letting her run away from me anymore. I'm not letting her avoid me or pretend I'm not there. I'm not letting her ignore the chemistry and connection we have. I always knew we would. Why else would I become a practical stalker the second we meet?

I've given her space. I've let her do what she thought she needed, but no more. I'm done pushing my feeling aside. I'm done hiding how I feel. It's out there now. I'm not taking it back.

I'm doing things my way. The way I should've done years ago. Even months ago, when she first came home.

I told her I was going to make her love me. That wasn't entirely true. I'm going to make her *admit* that she already does. If I'm transparent, then so is she. I've seen in her eyes how she feels. I felt it in the way she clung to me the other night.

If there were any doubt about the connection and chemistry between us, tonight obliterated it. Being inside of her felt like home. It felt like where I was always meant to be. And it was hands down the best sex of my life. I've never come so hard in my life. For a second, I thought her tight pussy was going to break my goddamn dick.

I know she doesn't want to feel any of this. I know she's scared. She says it's because she will hurt Lyra and me, but the truth is she's scared we'll hurt her. She thinks she doesn't deserve happiness and love. She thinks she is too damaged.

I'm going to show her I love those broken pieces. She's not the same girl from all those years ago. Part of her is gone forever, but what's been left behind is a graceful strength she doesn't realize she has. That girl Maddox and Ryder nicknamed 'Brat' because she tended to throw fits when she didn't get her way has been replaced by a sensitive and compassionate woman that's seen too much.

What happened shattered her spirit. I would give anything to change that. But the naïveté and innocence that was stolen have been replaced by resilience and determination. Her spirit may have been shattered, but she has risen from the ashes, and those scars are evidence of her strength, making her that much more beautiful.

She doesn't see any of it. She only sees the panic and fear that cripple her. She only holds the guilt and regret of the things that happened. But she'll see soon enough. I'll make sure of it.

I must finally fall asleep because a tugging on my arm has me blinking against the light coming into the room. Two big blue eyes give me a wide grin around the fingers in her mouth. "I watch toons with you, Daddy?"

I open my arm that's not wrapped around Cara, inviting her in. She wastes no time claiming her favorite spot. I look to the two girls in each arm, and I swear to God I'd give up everything else in the world to keep this forever. To stay cocooned in this bubble where it's just us, completely separate from the rest of the world. "We can't watch toons in here. Cara is still sleeping," I whisper to her.

Lyra looks at Cara with a frown. "I not like Cara sweeping with you."

My brows dip between my eyes. I'm not going to let a toddler dictate my relationships, but that doesn't mean her words don't affect me. Especially since I thought she loved Cara. "Why don't you like it?"

"Betuz," she huffs with an overdramatic eye roll that could give a teenager a run for their money. "I wants her to sweeps with me."

I bit the inside of my cheek to keep the laugh from coming out. The tightness that was in my chest moments ago evaporates into warmth and fullness. "I thought big girls slept by themselves," I tease a little.

"Big boys does too, Daddy," she says with way too much sarcasm and sass for such a little thing.

Well damn.

Not sure how to argue with that.

"Yeah. That's true, but Cara gets scared when she's alone," I try to explain in a way she might accept.

"She can sweep with me. She not be alone with me."

Shit. I'm gonna have to fight my own kid for the girl because Cara doesn't know it yet, but she's staying in my bed. If I have to tie her ass to the bed, she's not sleeping anywhere else again. Ever.

Except, I got nothing. No argument that my too-smart toddler would understand. I feel Cara vibrate with silent laughter beside me. I look at her. Her eyes are closed. Her face is nearly expressionless. Except for the slight twitch at the corner of her mouth, I'd think she was still sleeping.

"Go to the front and find your crayons. I'll come turn on cartoons in just a minute," I tell her with a kiss on her head.

She pouts because that's not what she wants, but she actually does what I say without a tantrum. When the door shuts behind her, Cara begins to giggle.

214

I move quickly, dragging her body under mine. Exactly where she belongs. Unless it's on top of me. "You really are a brat," I tease with a nip to her chin.

"Oh my God," her giggles increase. "A two-year-old just outsmarted you."

"She'll be three in a month," I argue like that makes it better. "Why didn't you help?"

"Are you kidding? I had no argument for her. Looks like you have competition, Mr. Allen."

"I've got news for you, *Ms. Pierce*. Either way, I win. You don't get the kid without the daddy."

She bites her lip with a smile, but I see the shadows rolling in. I press my forehead to hers with a sigh. "Don't do that," I tell her, knowing where her mind goes. "You're not bad for her. You've been beyond great for her. If I thought she wouldn't be safe or cared for with you, I would never have let you be responsible for her."

She gives me a doubtful smile. She rubs herself against the erection laying between us, making me groan. "I have a feeling I know why you accepted so quickly."

I press my body further into her, grinding myself into her. This time she groans, and I smirk. "One, just because I was thinking with my jealous dick doesn't mean I didn't consider Lyra. Two, if I didn't have a little girl waiting on me in there, I'd have your ass for that little stunt."

"Jealous?" Her brows furrow. Mine mimic her not understanding what she's asking. "You said your 'jealous dick.' What were you jealous of?"

"It doesn't matter," I laugh. "Get you cute ass in the shower while I take care of the princess."

I nip her nose then climb out of bed.

She climbs out behind me wearing those tiny shorts and thin tank top. Her nipples point right at me through the material. I groan, and my dick twitches.

She giggles again. Then shocks the hell out of me with a peck to my lips as she leaves the room.

Maybe I've made more progress than I thought.

Bang, bang, bang.

"Open up, asshole," Ryder's voice calls beyond the door of the bus.

"I not an asshole," Lyra yells back as Ryder walks in with Angel.

"It is open, asshole," I yell back.

I laugh until I catch Cara's glare. "You should all watch what you say around her," she scolds.

I contain a grin at how much she sounds like a mother right now. Instead, I raise a brow at her. "Really?" I say with dripping sarcasm. Ryder smirks. Angel scowls. I want to tell her about Lyra's comment the other day, but I don't. I don't want her to think about that night at all. If it weren't for the fact that's the night she fell into my arms, I wouldn't either. I damn sure don't want to think about why the guy was there.

I know she will eventually think about it. It's inevitable, and I'm ready for when it happens. But I am not going to be the cause of it.

"Anal, Anal," Lyra jumps to him.

He grabs her with a groan. "Cara, can you please help her say my name right."

Cara smirks a bit, pretending to think about it. "I kind of think it's cute."

I love that she's joking and laughing. At the moment, the panic and tension of a few nights ago and even a few weeks ago seem to be far from her mind.

Ryder is watching her closely. He's being uncharacteristically quiet.

"Come on, Cara," Angel nearly whines which is funny as hell. "I've never asked you for anything."

"I. Says. Anal. Wight," Lyra says, gripping his face between her tiny hands.

"An-j-el," he argues with her like he always does. "Angel."

"I not want you anymore," she pouts with her arms folded across her chest.

"Aww hell, princess. I'm sorry." he kisses her cheek.

Of course, my kid isn't quick to forgive. She'll be over it later today, but right now, her pride is wounded. "I want Wywy," she throws herself from Angel's arms to Ryder. He stops staring at Cara just in time to catch her.

Angel looks absolutely dejected. He isn't overly expressive, but he loves my princess nearly as much as me. He was there every day for a while after she was born. He's changed diapers and got up for midnight feedings nearly as much as me.

Cara seems to take pity on him. "I'll see what I can do," she assures him.

"Where are you guys? We got to go," Maddox calls out as he enters the bus.

"Madsux, Anal is mean to me," she tells him when he's next to Ryder. Just as she did with Ryder, she is throwing herself into his arms.

"I just don't want to be called anal anymore. I like it, but I don't want to be called it."

"Angel," Cara hisses. "You can't say that in front of her."

"I get told I suck every time she says my name," Maddox tells him with a laugh.

"You do," he grumbles.

"Like you haven't." Maddox raises his brows with a grin at Angel. "Pretty sure you've taken it in the ass a time or two, too."

"I was stoned and drunk," Angel grumbles his defense.

"Then why do you let Josie keep doing it?" Maddox counters. All Angel can do is shake his head with a laugh.

"Oh my God. Baby in the room," Cara yells. "All of you are banned from her until you learn how to watch your mouths."

We all burst out laughing until I catch that glare again. I do not want on her bad side after taking so long to get on her good one. "She's right, guys," I agree. "We've got to start paying attention now that she's become a parrot." I take Lyra from Maddox. "Be good for Cara," I tell her with a kiss on her cheek.

"I's always good, Daddy. That why she likes sweeping with me more than you."

My mouth falls open. I look over to Cara, whose eyes have grown into huge chocolate saucers. Her face has turned the color of cherries.

"Does she now?" Angel asks with a taunting tone.

"Uh-huh," Lyra nods. "Her sweeps with me tonight, Daddy. Not you," she tells me seriously.

I can't stop the laugh this time. She has no idea that she is an absolute rat.

I hand Lyra to Cara. "I hope you didn't plan to make me your dirty little secret," I whisper in her ear with a chuckle, then kiss the corner of her gaping mouth. With my finger, I push her chin up, closing her mouth. "You're gonna catch flies."

Her eyes snap to mine, narrowed and irritated. I laugh some more as we exit the bus. I feel the heat of her glare the entire way.

"When did that happen?" Ryder asks before the door closes behind us. "Because just a few days ago, she was hiding from you and freaking out."

"Happened the same night, but it was just sleeping," I tell them.

"That is crap," Angel challenges me. "You fucked her last night, and don't bother to deny. It's written all over your face with that dopey grin."

I shake my head with a laugh. I'm not going to deny it, but I'm not going to tell them about it either.

"She looked lighter," Ryder comments. "First time she's seemed happy in years. I know you won't tell us what she said, but how is she doing? Really?"

I stop walking, looking at all of them. "She's freaked out by the other night. She thought she recognized the guy." I nearly miss it, but I catch the quick flash of acknowledgment in Maddox's eyes. "You know, don't you? Was it really him?"

He doesn't say anything. He just gives me a slight nod. Ryder and Angel both look at him with questions. "Something you want to share?" Ryder asks him with narrowed eyes.

"No. Because she doesn't want us to know. She doesn't know that I know," Maddox answers him without hesitation.

"Does Dane know?" I ask, already knowing the answer.

"No, and until she tells him, he won't find out. Same goes for everyone else," Maddox tells them all, that switch that is all authority has been flipped. "And you won't tell her I know. Are we clear?"

"I don't think she needs to know that," I agree. "It would freak her out more if she thought you knew."

"What are you jerks talking about?" Dane calls out as he walks to us from his bus.

Grins spread across Ryder and Maddox's faces, the proof of their intentions. They're about to give Dane hell.

"Talking about Jake," Ryder smirks. "He got laid."

"Can't you tell?" Angel digs in with them. "He doesn't look like he wants to punch someone in the face."

"You son of a –. As long as you're going after my sister, I told you to keep it in your pants. What the hell is wrong with you? Why would you –," he pauses midsentence when he realizes, not only am I standing here allowing him to run his mouth, Maddox, Ryder, and Angel are grinning like jackasses. "Oh God, no. I don't want to hear this. I think I'm going to be sick." He bends over, placing his hands on his thighs after he turns green.

"Don't you think your reaction is a little immature?" I taunt.

"I have two reactions. To get sick or to punch someone. Which would you rather have?"

"Let's go, guys. We have to be there in twenty," Liam calls out to us.

We nod and head to the waiting car. We have some sort of radio interview that I'm not looking forward to. Since I've rejoined the band, we've had a handful of these. When the questions stick to music, they're not bad. It's when they want the details of our personal lives that they become annoying. Not to mention the reporters and journalists that hang around the venues. I definitely have not enjoyed the paparazzi that linger around the hotels and restaurants.

One of the things I was looking forward to with this tour was taking Lyra to a few places. Creating memories with my little girl, but I've been too afraid of the chaos that might ensue. The minute it was announced I was joining/rejoining the band, they have been everywhere wanting dirt on the new/returning member of the band.

Cara has made a point to do so many things with Lyra. She has sent me picture after picture of my baby experiencing things that some never see in a lifetime. I know she probably won't remember, but those pictures will always be there.

I'm not sure how they have managed to evade the harassment because the world knows Cara is Dane's sister, but I'm glad they have. I hate to admit it, but I suppose Henry *is* pretty good at his job.

My biggest worry with coming back to the band has always been Lyra. I won't leave her behind. I also want her to have a normal childhood. I don't want her to become entitled. I don't want her to be hounded by the press her entire life. I'm still not sure how I can follow my dreams and give her that normalcy. I know it's too late to turn back now. Even if I left the band tomorrow, the world knows about me now.

The interview is going great. They focus on the music, the tour, me returning, when Maddox will start playing again, and the usual band stuff.

Then it takes a turn. The interviewer asks about the commotion the other night. Why was some random man seen running off the bus? Why did Maddox and Henry chase him? Who screamed? Why?

Maddox and Ryder play it off as nothing. They've been navigating the media and scandal their entire lives. But if everyone's faces are any indication of their feelings, then they're as pissed as I am that anyone is even aware of what went on.

Our buses were away from the festival – away from the chaos of the crowd. Maddox and Henry chasing the guy into the crowd might've been seen, but no one else would know he ran off of a bus, much less that it was mine.

When we are back in the car, I explode. "What the fuck was that?"

"I don't know," Liam answers with a scowl. "That was *not* on the list."

"How? How would anyone know what happened at *our* buses? We were sectioned off from everyone with security," Dane growls.

"It means someone on the crew or the security team is selling information," Maddox says in a tone that belies his expression. "Is it on the internet? How did we miss it?"

"It's not," Ryder says as he swipes through his phone. "Or it wasn't until fifteen minutes ago."

"Okay, all of you. Just calm down. I'll figure out who is in breach of the NDA, but for now, let's be grateful they didn't get pictures or know why he was on the bus. Cara's name hasn't been mentioned, so let's leave it at that."

Cara.

Suddenly, I realize that she's not safe. That guy was the same from her time in Chicago.

I begin to worry the guy will look for her. He knows now that she's with us. It wouldn't be hard for him to find her again. What if he recognized her as well and he wants to finish what he started?

What the hell am I thinking? Of course, he recognized her. She's not exactly forgettable. All that blond hair and those legs that go on for miles. Not to mention her big dark eyes.

I am so stupid. He didn't just stumble upon her. He knew it was her the minute he approached her.

Chills erupt over my entire body as I consider what he had planned for her. I'm getting angrier by the second and a little nauseous too.

I pull my phone out of my pocket, ready to text Maddox so I can say something without anyone else knowing.

Me: He knew who she was when he approached her.

Maddox: Probably.

Me: You think he's going to come after her now?

Maddox: Probably.

Me: You got anything to say other than probably?

Maddox: It's being handled.

Me: WTAF is that supposed to mean? I don't need your cryptic shit right now.

Maddox: I can't tell you. But I've been told that it's being handled.

Me: Who's handling it? Christian?

Maddox: How do you know Christian?

Me: Cara told me.

Maddox: He can't handle it himself without permission, but it is being handled.

Me: Permission? I don't even understand that statement.

Maddox: And you won't ever. Now drop it. She has eyes on her and people are looking for him.

Drop it. He wants me to pretend like some psycho isn't looking for her. I don't know how the hell I'm supposed to do that.

I start to slide my phone back into my pocket when it buzzes again. I figure it's Maddox with something else to say.

The name that comes across the screen is not one I was expecting. My breath catches in my throat. The anger I was already feeling turns into boiling rage. I don't want or need this shit right now.

I delete the message without even looking.

224

Cara

We are walking into a hotel for the first time in over a week. As nice as the bus may be, I am so glad to be out of it for two days. It was beginning to be a little cramped.

We didn't leave Sofia, Bulgaria, until noon because the band had another interview before they left. The guys barely have enough time to get to the venue before they have to go on. Cami has to get them ready alone because Josephine had to fly back to New York to meet with one of their clients. From what they've told me, getting grown men dressed is a lot harder than it should be.

Lyra is fussy and tired. She refused to take a nap on the bus. Her frustration is frustrating Jake, making him snappier than usual.

Something has been going on with him the past few days. He's trying to hide it, but I can see that he's tense. I wish he would tell me. Every time I ask, he tells me he's fine. That he doesn't want me to worry about him.

I know I'm adding to his stress. The nightmares are relentless. I've only had two nights without them.

Lyra has wanted me to sleep with her, but I can't. Not when I wake up in a panic every night. I can't scare her like that.

I told Jake to let her sleep in the bedroom with him, but he refused. He wants me in his bed. Every night, if I fall asleep anywhere else, he will carry me to his bed when he comes in. He worships my body, bringing me multiple orgasms before we collapse from exhaustion. I wish it were enough to stop the nightmares.

I wish he didn't insist on me sleeping with him. I hate that he sees the panic. I can only imagine what he hears. And I know he's been losing sleep.

Lyra begins to wail loudly for no reason other than she's tired. I see Jake clench his teeth, his exhaustion showing. I pick her up, rocking her in my arms as I carry her to one of the three bedrooms.

I lay with her for a while until her sobs turn to sniffles. She has the fingers of one hand in her mouth. Her other hand is wrapped in my hair. Her breathing is soft and even. I take a deep breath, letting her sweet baby smell fill me.

I stroke her hair, softly humming to her. Soothing her the best I know how.

"Cara," she says sweetly with a yawn.

"I'm right here, pretty girl." I kiss her head.

"I love you, Cara. Can you be my mommy?"

Tears sting my eyes. My words are trapped in my throat. Not that I have any. What do I say to that?

Fortunately, I don't have to. She falls asleep before I have a chance to say anything.

But I need out of here. Now. If I don't get out of here, I'm going to wake her with the sobs that are bubbling up my chest.

I slide out of bed and exit the room quickly. As soon as I shut the door behind me, I quickly cover my mouth as the sobs escape.

Those two sentences from that little girl made my heart explode in every way conceivable. It was full of warmth and joy and heartache and sorrow.

I've never felt so much love from a single person. It made me feel like I was flying to have her ask me that. I was humbled and honored.

But then the grief took over because I realized I would love to be her mommy. I can't let myself believe that could ever be a possibility. It's insane to think such things anyway. This between Jake and I won't last. And I am not in the right headspace to be anyone's mother.

My heart grieves that she doesn't have her mother. That she will never know that unconditional love that only a mother can provide. Though, knowing what I do, she doesn't deserve Lyra either.

Every time I think about that woman – if you can call her that – I get so angry. How do you walk out on your child? On your flesh and blood without looking back?

My shoulders shake under the weight of so many emotions bearing down on my soul.

"What the – ?" I hear Jake exclaim as he walks out of one of the other bedrooms. I thought he would've left by now. Within a second, his arms are around me. "What's wrong, Cara?"

I squeeze my eyes shut and shake my head. I can't tell him. I know Lyra will probably mention it, but I can't.

He scoops me up, carrying me to the sofa. He sits with me across his lap, rocking back and forth. "Come on, Cara. I can't help if I don't know what's wrong."

When I don't say anything, he continues to rock and shush me. I can feel his tension in every muscle. I know he has to go. He is probably already late.

I finally stop sobbing. It's frustrating that I'm always so emotional, but normally, it's just me that has to deal with it. I don't have to worry about affecting anyone else. I have my little breakdowns – or big ones – and then go about pretending it never happened. Since this tour has started, Jake has seen nearly all of them.

"You need to go," I tell him. "You were already running late as soon as we got here."

"Not until you tell me why you were crying." He pushes my hair off my face. He's scowling at me, but I can see the genuine worry in his eyes.

"I'm just tired, Jake," I smile weakly. "You can't keep the guys waiting."

"Don't do that," he nearly yells. "Do not shut me out. We've shared it all. Tell me why you were crying, or I'm not going

229

anywhere. I swear, Cara, I'm not in the mood, and I don't give two fucks about a damn show when you're upset."

A knock at the door keeps me from responding. I move to get off his lap, but he tightens his grip. "Leave it," he growls.

It is totally inappropriate, but his growly, demanding tone and behavior is turning me on. If we had more time, I'd convince him we should go to bed while Lyra sleeps. It would be a good way to get him to drop the subject of what's wrong with me.

But we don't have time. I'm not making him any later than he already is. Or I'm trying not to.

The knocking sounds again but louder. I cup his face in mine, trying to get the frustrated, angry man to see reason. "They're not going to stop, and then they will wake Lyra."

He releases me, but his face gets impossibly angrier. He wants to know why I'm crying, and I've been afraid to ask why he seems to be pissed lately. Seems our communication skills aren't improving.

When I got to the door, he stalks to his room. The black cloud hanging around him seems to get even darker.

I open the door to see Dane and Liam standing there. I don't get a chance to invite them in before Jake is beside me. He grips my face a little too hard, his eyes searching mine. "We're not done," he tells me. I have a feeling he's talking about more than just our conversation. I suddenly realize why he didn't want to go. His eyes soften, not much but enough for me to see fear behind the anger. He kisses me then stalks out the door.

Dane leans to kiss my cheek then asks me what's going on with him. All I can do is shrug because I have no idea.

I don't plan on taking Lyra out that night. In fact, since that night in Kyiv, I've been afraid to go anywhere. I sit on the sofa with my laptop and work on my assignments for school. I'm not sure what time I fall asleep. I just know I awake as I'm being laid on the bed.

Jake kisses me softly on the corners of my mouth before taking my lips with his. Even through the haze of sleep, I relish the way his lips feel on mine. He slowly makes his way down my jaw to my neck as he removes my shorts and T-shirt. His hands move gently over my body, kneading and stroking until he reaches my apex.

My mouth falls open on a soundless moan when his fingers stroke through my fold. He continues kissing his way down my body until his lips wrap around my nipple. My hands fly to his head, holding him in place as he continues to work my core.

I'm on the verge of climax when he removes his hand. My body moans in protest. Until I hear the sound of foil ripping.

He enters me slowly. The intensity in his eyes, in his touch, takes my breath away. He rocks into me just as slowly as he entered. The air around us is thick with emotion.

He watches me, not taking his eyes away from mine for a second. He stretches up, angling his hips to reach farther inside me, our eyes still locked. I feel tears sting my eyes from everything he is pouring into me with his body.

Completion rips through me without warning. The second my walls grip him, he falls with me, a deep groan falling from his chest.

Everything is too much. The feelings are overwhelming. I can't even describe how I feel. I am feeling too much.

The urge to run fills my chest. My heart begins to beat harder than it was seconds ago.

He lowers himself, wrapping his arm around me. "Please, don't leave me," he breaks as his forehead presses into my chest. "Please."

I open my mouth to say something. I want to say something. I need to say something but can't find the words to express myself.

"I know you can't say it, baby. Just please tell me you feel it. That you know this is real."

"I feel it, Jake," I barely rasp out.

I feel it all.

I walk out of the bedroom, dressed to take Lyra to the beach. I've let my fears hinder her. It's not fair for me to keep her cooped because I'm afraid. And I'm not missing out on the Mediterranean Sea.

Lyra has her hand in mine as we step out of the room, ready to go. All we need now is Henry.

Jake is sitting at the breakfast bar with his phone in his hand, looking at it with a mixture of worry and anger on his face. I try to keep us quiet. I don't know what's going on, but it looks serious enough not to disturb.

I set Lyra on the sofa with her book while I go to make her a few snacks. I'm digging in the fridge for a few bottles of water. When I turn around, Jake is standing right in front of me. His brows are dipped low as he takes me in. He runs his tongue over his bottom lip as his eyes travel the length of my body. I flush at his perusal.

"Going to the pool?" he asks as he runs a finger under the strap of my bikini top.

Goosebumps erupt where he touches. His gaze is so lustful, I barely stop myself from rubbing against him like a cat. "Th-the beach, actually."

He stops moving. His eyes snap to mine. I see the argument coming. "You're not going to the beach," he tells me.

"Jake, she's been confined for nearly two weeks. It's not fair to her."

He grabs me by the waist, pulling me into his chest. He brushes a stray hair away from my face with a sigh. "I don't want you out there. I don't like it."

"I'm scared too. If it were just me, I could easily hide away from the world. I've done it before, but I have to think of Lyra. You have to think of Lyra."

"I am thinking of her. I'm thinking of both of you."

"Jake, she is a little girl. She is used to daycare with friends and days at the park. Looking at four walls all day and watching cartoons isn't good for her."

"I'm not going to be able to think straight if your both out there," he whispers as he presses his forehead to mine.

A heavy sigh escapes me. Guilt threatens to consume me. "I'm sorry," I whisper back. "This is my fault. You wouldn't be worried for her if it weren't for me."

He tips my chin, so I'm looking up at him. "I'm not *just* worried about Lyra."

"I know, but − ."

"No 'buts'. Don't let your mind go where I know it wants to. Please."

"What's going on?" my brother's voice calls, making me jump.

Jake ignores him, still looking at me and waiting for me to agree to what he just said. I give him a nod. "Okay, Jake. I'll try. But you have to let us go. She needs to get out."

"Fuck," he groans. "Okay. I don't like it, but I understand what you're saying. So, how about we compromise?"

"How?" I ask curiously, wondering what he has in mind.

"We have that interview this morning. Then sound checks. We should be back around lunchtime. Wait until I can go too."

A smile spreads across my face. Lyra will love getting to spend time with her dad outside of the room. I kind of like the idea myself. "Deal."

"Are either of you going to tell me why you look so serious?" Dane asks again, sounding worried.

"No," Jake tells him with blinking.

"More secrets?" I hear the accusation in my brother's voice. I feel bad that there is so much he doesn't know, but I'm not ready for him to know. I may never be.

"They are not secrets," Jake tells him. "They're just not your business."

I tense, waiting on Dane to get angry. I peek at him over my shoulder, shocked that he simply looks resigned. I'm not sure what that means, but I don't question it.

We leave the little corner we've been in for the last few minutes and go to Lyra. I sit beside her while Jake pulls her onto his lap. Liam, who has a key to our room and let Dane in with him, sits in a wingback chair while Dane stands against a post dividing the living area from the kitchen.

"What are you guys doing here anyway?" Jake points to both of them.

"I came to tell you the interview for today was canceled and to let you know Henry has to go back to the states for a few days. I've got another guy already in place, but I know Cara was comfortable with Henry. This asshole saw me coming in here and followed." Liam tells us as he props a foot on the coffee table.

"Why was the interview canceled?" I ask while Jake says, "Who's this new bodyguard?"

Dane looks over to Liam with a raised brow. I see big brother coming to the surface. "I want to know who this new guy is too?"

"He's fine, guys. He works for the same company as Henry."

"Henry said you guys grew up together," I say. "He said you got him the job working personal security."

"I did. My sister's ex-husband owns the company," he nods. "That's why I know this guy is okay. David doesn't hire anyone that's doesn't pass his checks. Former military like Henry. His plane landed about an hour ago. He should be here in ten minutes. Didn't want him to start the job before you met him."

I hear Jake growl beside me. Liam and Dane both smirk at him. Jake's jealous streak is a little excessive but oddly flattering.

Then I realize their interview was canceled. "That means we can go to the beach now. Together," I say, grabbing Jake's arm with a huge smile. I'm genuinely excited to go now. Then an idea occurs. I look to Dane with the same grin. "Everyone can go."

"Slow down, Cara," he looks at me warily. "Cami isn't a fan of the water."

"She doesn't have to get in the water," I argue. "She can just lie on the beach."

"Cara, I'm not sure if she would want to. She really doesn't like the beach either."

"Just text everyone to come over," Jake tells him. "Let her tell everyone what she wants. Then they can decide."

Two minutes later, there's a knock at the door. Cami walks in with the rest of the guys trailing behind her. They scatter throughout the room, each saying hellos to everyone else. Like they didn't see each other last night.

Lyra climbs from Jake's lap when she spots them all. He leans back against the sofa, spreading both arms across the back when she's down. He looks absolutely exhausted. I'm sure I have plenty to do with that because of my nightmares, but something else is happening with him. Last night, when he made love to me, was intense. But the way he begged me not to leave him is still very fresh in my mind.

I have no idea where that comes from. I know part of it is the way he can read me. It's like he instantly felt my desire to run. But it's more than that. Something is weighing on him. I have a feeling I'm getting to be too much for him.

Lyra looks around the room for a minute. She looks like she's trying to make a decision. With nearly all of her favorite people in the same room, she probably is. Who she wants changes by the minute.

Finally, she goes to Angel, grabbing his pants for him to pick her up. She's held on to her grudge against him for days. Looks like she may finally be over it.

She grips his face between her tiny hand with a stern look. "I can says Angel now," she tells him seriously.

His face splits into wide smile. "Thank God," he laughs, kissing her on the cheek. He looks over to me and mouths a thank you. I smile and nod.

"Now you can help her with mine," Maddox laughs.

"Come on, guys. Let her sound like a baby a little longer," Cami tells them all. "You're going to have her in college next week with the way you're going."

"Why did you want us, Brat?" Ryder asks, changing the subject.

"I want everyone to go to the beach," I tell him hopefully.

"You want to go to a crowded beach?" Maddox asks with his brows dipping between his eyes.

"I was already going. Now that you guys have nothing to do until later this afternoon, we can all go," I nod with a smile.

"I'm down," Angel says. "Dying to get in some surf."

"Me too," Ryder nods.

"New bodyguard is here to meet before you guys go," Liam says, looking up from his phone.

"You're coming too, Liam," I tell him.

He laughs. "I think I'm going to catch up on sleep. You guys need a PR agent, and I need an assistant. I don't sleep anymore."

"I'll start making some calls," Maddox tells him.

Liam's eyes grow wide. "I didn't think you'd actually do it."

"You're overworked. If it will help you do your job better, why not?" Maddox replies with a shrug.

On the kitchen island behind Angel, a phone dings. Jake must've left it over there because it's his tone. Angel turns to grab it. He hands it to Jake, his eyes hard. Jake looks at it. His already tight face becomes more strained. He looks up to Angel, and some secret message is passed between the two of them.

My stomach clenches with worry. I can't help but wonder what Angel saw to make him angry.

We finally make it to the beach an hour later.

The new bodyguard, Matthew, showed up with his boss and Liam's brother-in-law, David, for a quick meeting that seemed to turn into an interrogation thanks to Jake and Dane. David claimed he was there to make sure Matthew could handle the job, but a few looks passed between him and Liam that said it was more. I know he's there because the guys are worried about me.

Now, I'm staring at the beautiful Mediterranean Sea. I thought the beach would be crowded, but of course, one of the guys made sure it's a private beach. It's not completely secluded. You can see people on all sides. By the way they are lingering around the perimeter, I know there is no way the guys could be out here otherwise.

I don't know when they got so huge. I feel like I've missed it somehow.

The guys take their boards to the water without a backward glance. Well, except for my brother. He can't seem to figure the surfing thing out. He stays with Cami, Lyra, and me on the beach.

238

Lyra plays with a bucket and shovel a few feet from me. Dane and Cami are shoving their tongues down each other's throats right next to me. I'm trying to be mature about it, but it's just gross to know my brother is groping his girlfriend five feet from me.

I lay back in the lounge chair and watch the guys. They look amazing on the water. It's definitely a sight.

They ride wave after wave while I keep Lyra entertained. I help her find shells. I take her into the water until it hits her knees. When the waves knock her down, I'm afraid she's going to cry, but she surprises me with loud giggles.

"Cara, I's hungry," she tells me as we walk back to the chairs.

"Hungry, huh? I made sandwiches. Want one?"

"You's gots benutbutter?" her little blue eyes look hopeful.

"Yep."

She licks her lips with a slurping sound and rubs her little belly. "I loves the benutbutter."

I laugh as I scoop her up. I carry her to the outdoor shower by the bungalow that apparently comes with the beach. I wash the sand off her little body and hands, then carry her to the tables where I have a small cooler waiting with her drinks and snacks.

A few minutes later, she is ready to go again. This kid is going to go down like a brick when it's naptime.

"Honey, if you want to go in the water, we can watch Lyra," Cami says to me.

"We will?" Dane looks at her with a frown. "I kind of had other things in mind. Besides, she's getting paid to watch her."

239

She slaps him across his chest with a hard roll of her eyes. "Dane! She can take a few minutes to herself, and you can control your libido for a few hours."

"If you can control *yours* for a few hours, then I'm not doing my job," he tells her.

"Oh, you do your job just fine," she giggles.

"I think I'm going to be sick," I mutter. "If you two can keep the innuendo to a minimum and your hands to yourself, I think I will go in the water for a bit."

"Fine," Dane huffs. "Go have fun, Brat."

Before I go, I tell Lyra that Dane and Cami will watch her and tell them if she needs to potty.

I pull off my coverup and head for the water. When I'm waist deep, I dive in the rest of the way, letting the waves take me. I swim out several more feet before I turn, swimming parallel with the beach in the opposite direction of the guys on their boards.

I'm not sure how long I'm out there. I swim until my muscles are tired, then make my way back toward shore. I come up when I can touch the bottom again, with eyes closed, wiping the water and my hair from my face.

An arm wraps around my waist, and I find myself leaning into the touch. "If I'd known this is what you had on under that little dress thing, I wouldn't have let you leave the hotel."

I giggle at the roughness of his voice. Then I realize! I just leaned in. I didn't freak out when he grabbed me.

I turn, wrapping my arms around his neck. "Why are you over here instead of surfing?"

"Couldn't resist the gorgeous thing I saw swimming around," he smirks.

"Well, according to you, you've been resisting for years," I tease him.

His hands grasp my backside in a punishing grip. "I didn't resist you. I stayed the fuck away because I knew I couldn't."

"Wonder how I would've responded if you'd said or done something all those years ago. You weren't exactly on my radar." It's a tease and the truth all at once.

"If you're trying to deflate my ego, it's not working. I would've had you then too. I wouldn't have stopped until I made you mine, just like now. I didn't resist very long at all. And make no mistake, Cara, you are mine." He dips his head down, taking my mouth in a salty kiss that takes my breath.

I am his. I just hope when he's done with me, there's something left to pick up. I won't say that, though. Instead, I look behind him at the board he's still dragging.

"Want me to teach you?" he asks with a raised brow.

"Pretty sure I'd drown," I laugh.

"Come on, you can be my Gidget, and I can be your Moondoggie."

"What?" I laugh.

He shrugs with a laugh of his own. "My mom loves old movies. I'll show you one day. Although, you're a little tall to be Gidget. Good thing I prefer long legs. Come on."

He drags me to the board, helping me on, then climbs on behind me.

"What are we doing?" I ask with a mixture of excitement and panic.

"You're going surfing."

"Jake, I'm going to die."

"Do you trust me, Cara?"

I'm not sure why, but that question doesn't feel like it's about surfing. It only takes me a second to have my answer. Another second to get over the shock of the realization. One more to come to terms with my answer. Then I tell him emphatically, "Yes."

He stops paddling us. His head drops to my back, and I feel the breath he exhales. He kisses the spot his head lays before he begins to paddle us out again. "Then you know I'm not going to let anything hurt you," he whispers. "We're not going out far. Just want to take you for a ride."

A few minutes later, a wave is coming. It looks huge to me, but Jake says it's a small one as he paddles into it. I feel when it takes us. I expect him to pop up to his feet, but he just gets to his knees, telling me to stay down. I feel him leaning and tilting as we travel on the water. The entire time I'm screaming like, well, a girl.

When it comes to an end, he's laughing so hard, we topple over into the water. When we pop up, we're both laughing.

"Oh my God," I say breathlessly, "I thought I was going to die."

He pulls me to him, still laughing. He looks lighter than I've seen him in days. Today has been good for him. "That was a tiny wave. Never knew you were such a princess."

I gape at him. "Seriously. How did you not notice before?"

"I noticed. Just thought you'd be a bit braver," he teases.

I push him lightly, but he doesn't budge, even with the waves threatening to knock us down. "I was brave," I pout. "I even kept my eyes open."

"You knew you could trust me," he says, brushing the wet hair from my face. "I know what that means, Cara. I won't take it for granted."

He leans down, kissing me soft and slow while the waves lap around us. When I start to lose my balance, he lifts me, wrapping my legs around his waist. His mouth never leaves mine until he has me on the shore. Where he proceeds to love me like no one else exists.

Jake

I make my way back up the beach to everyone, Cara tucked under one arm and my board under the other. Maddox and Ryder are back in the water. No surprise there. Cami and Lyra look like they are in the process of burying Dane alive. Angel is sitting at the table by the bungalow.

I needed today. I needed just a few minutes where the stress of the last few days didn't exist. I need to pretend like the bullshit that has blasted me the last week isn't going on.

When Cara finds out, I'm not sure I will be able to keep her. I'm not sure she will be willing to deal with the drama with everything else she has going on. And the thought of losing her when I just got her terrifies me.

It's why I needed her last night. It's why I made love to her slowly. I needed to hold on to her for as long as I could.

It's what had me begging her not to leave.

When she told me earlier that she trusted me, it was big. It's all I've wanted to hear from her besides I love you. It is probably the most precious thing she could give.

I can't break that. I can't destroy something that has taken her so long to have or give. I know I will have to tell her about the damn drama that has decided to rear its ugly head.

I just hope the love I know she feels for Lyra and me is strong enough to handle it. I hope it's strong enough to make her want to stay.

When we reach everyone, Cami looks up to us with a knowing smirk. Dane has a knowing look as well, but he's not smirking. He has a look of pain and anger.

"Daddy, I's bury Nane," Lyra looks up to me proudly. Judging by the look on Dane's face, it may be a good thing he's covered under all that sand. He grunts a bit as he stares me down. Cami gives me a wink, telling me this was her plan all along. I smirk at him. Just to add a little coal to the fire, I kiss the side of Cara's face, making her blush.

My best friend may be good with us in theory. He's even okay with us in reality. As long as he doesn't have to acknowledge anything is actually happening.

"We both know you wouldn't be so smug right now if I could get to you," he says with false sweetness and gritted teeth.

"Actually, we both know I'd still be pretty smug," I laugh. "Be nice, or I'll give you details." Cara tenses beside me. I give her a light squeeze to calm her. "You know I'm joking right," I whisper

245

into her ear. "I don't kiss and tell, but it's fun making him squirm. I see why Zane has so much fun with him."

She looks up to me. A mischievous grin stretches across her face. She runs her hand up my chest then presses her mouth against mine. "We could always just give him a show."

"What?" Dane shouts with panic. "No!"

Cara moves to my ear like she's going to nibble it or something. "It's payback for all the times I've had to watch him and Cami grope each other. Not to mention the things they say."

"Payback, huh?" I whisper while watching Dane turn green from the corner of my eye. "Only problem is you rubbing all over me has given me a situation in my shorts again, so you can't move unless you want everyone to see."

She looks down, then back up to me with a giggle.

"Oh God kill me now," Dane moans.

"No, Nane," Lyra yells as him. "That's bad."

I laugh then turn with Cara in front of me. We walk to the outside shower to rinse off. Once she has the sand off of her, she goes inside the bungalow to get Lyra's things together since we have to leave soon.

I sit at the table with Angel, who offers me a beer. I shake my head, not in the mood to mix alcohol with all the sun and water.

"You're in a better mood than you've been in days," he remarks.

"Had a lot on my mind," I tell him as I watch Lyra continue to pile sand on Dane.

Maddox and Ryder walk up with their boards, placing them against the bungalow.

"Yeah, judging by that text you got earlier, you've more than a lot on your mind. You know I saw it, so don't bother denying it."

I lay my head back with a sigh. Reality comes crashing down. "Not going to deny it. Just haven't wanted to talk about it."

"You don't have to talk about it. Get your number changed, so you don't keep getting the messages," he tells me simply.

Except it isn't simple. It never is. "I can't do that."

"You better not be thinking of saying yes," he growls. His face grows hard and dark.

"I'm not but…."

"But nothing. No. It's a very simple word. Use it."

"Angel, you know I can't just say no."

"Like fuck you can't," he yells.

I glance toward the bungalow door, watching for Cara. I don't want her hearing this. Not like this anyway.

To be honest, it shouldn't affect anything between her and me. But the drama that's could possibly be coming my way, I'm worried, will be too much.

"What's going on?" Maddox walks to us with concern etched on his face.

"Jake, so help me. She has no fucking rights to that little girl. You had them terminated." I flinch. "You had them terminated, right?" When I don't answer, Angel throws his hands in the air in frustration.

247

"Anyone want to tell me what's going on?"

"Not right now, I don't," I grit. "This is my problem. Let me handle it."

"There shouldn't be anything to fucking handle, Jake. I told you two years ago to get her rights terminated. Why didn't you?"

"Because it didn't seem right," I yell. "Peyton is Lyra's mom, whether I like it or not."

"No. She isn't her mom. Cara has been more of a mom to that little girl in six weeks than Peyton has been her entire life."

"I know. I wish I'd done what you said. I don't want her anywhere near Lyra, but I couldn't go through with it." My phone that's been sitting on the bungalow table since we arrived buzzes. I almost leave it because I know who it is.

Peyton: You can't avoid me forever. She's my baby, remember?

I grit my teeth. When Cara walks out, she immediately notices my tension. In reaction, her body tenses as well. It's like whatever I feel, she feels.

I need to talk to her about this. Peyton is a complication I didn't think I would have. She left Lyra. She left her in the hospital without a word to anyone. The last time I saw her, I was placing Lyra in her arms. The next day she was gone, and I haven't heard from her since.

When Lyra turned a year old, Angel said I should file abandonment charges and terminate her rights. It didn't feel right. I couldn't bring myself to do it. Then another year passed without a word. I didn't think it was necessary. Guess I was fooling myself.

I should've known better. I should've done what Angel said. Even in high school, Peyton was drama and trouble.

Case in point? The way she showed up at my door, claiming I got her pregnant. Maybe going along with it when I had irrefutable proof she was lying was stupid, but I was in love. Not with Peyton but with the baby inside of her. I knew from the beginning that Peyton wasn't cut out to be a mom. If she was trying to pin it on me, I knew it was because she had no idea who Lyra's real father was. She needed someone to take care of her and the baby. I decided to be that someone.

It cost me a lot of time with Cara, but I got Lyra. I made that conscious choice to let Peyton continue with her lie.

I still remember the shock on her face when I told her the paternity test validated her claim. The wheels started turning quickly. She was trying to figure out if maybe what she claimed did happen. Then she just went with it, and so did I. Because that baby was going to need someone to take care of her and love her. I knew I could do that. I loved her from that first heartbeat.

I know Peyton is only trying to stir up drama. She wants attention, and if I had to guess, money. She's probably heard I'm back with the band and thinks she can pull a fast one.

She's already threatening court and lawyers and even kidnapping charges because I left the state without informing her. Like that was even a possibility. I didn't know how to contact her. Even if I had, why would I inform someone who doesn't even know what their own child looks like that I'm going out of the country?

Peyton ensured that she can't take Lyra from me by listing me as her father on her birth certificate. I know, after nearly three years, no judge in the States would grant Peyton custody either. But that doesn't mean it won't get ugly.

Odds are it will get very ugly. She will probably have my ass picked up for kidnapping the minute the plane lands in New York if she doesn't try something sooner. She could sue me for custody, and this could be drawn out for a long time.

And all of that is why I'm worried about Cara. Will she be willing to go through that with me? Can she handle long, drawn-out custody battles and possible kidnapping charges?

She has already been through so much. Now my bullshit is just going to add to that. All because I had a freaking heart.

Sometimes it feels like the universe sends Peyton to keep me away from Cara. I know I've got to tell her, but I'm not sure I can handle it if she walks away.

"Something the matter?" Cara asks when the guys walk away. "Things seemed kind of intense out here."

"It's nothing you need to worry about, baby," I tell her pulling her to my lap.

"Are you sure?" She flushes then worries her lip. "Forget I asked that. I know it's not my business."

That's the last thing I want her to think. God, this is so damn hard. "It's not that, baby. It's exactly as I said. Nothing you need to worry about. Not because it's not your business but because I don't want it to be your problem."

Soon as the words leave my mouth, I want to take them back. It sounds like all my talk about her letting me in isn't reciprocated. That couldn't be farther from the truth. I lean against her shoulder with a heavy sigh. "That came out wrong. I don't want you to worry. I don't want you to stress out or panic. I don't want to give you a reason to run."

"What are you talking about, Jake?" she whispers, her voice breaking on the last word.

"I've told you over and over to let me in. To let me carry that weight you're carrying. I don't want to take your weight only to replace it with my garbage."

"I don't mind carrying yours." My eyes close, knowing this is her giving me more of herself. "Let me be there for you. You want me to trust you, and it's taken a bit, but I do. Now trust me."

My head snaps up. I take her face in my hands, my brows to my hair, and my eyes wide. "Fuck, Cara, I do trust you. I trust you with everything."

"You just don't trust me to stay. That's why you said that last night. You think I'm going to leave you. I know I've given you plenty of reason to think that, but why?"

"Because it's drama and bullshit I created with my choices. I'm afraid you won't want any part of it or me. I wouldn't blame you if you didn't. It's not something you signed up for. Just give me time. Let me see if I can get it sorted first. I will tell you, just give me some time."

"Okay," she whispers.

"Thank you. I swear I'll tell you. I'm just hoping when I do, there's nothing to it."

Her eyes, shining with unshed tears, dart between mine. I'm not sure what she sees, but she kisses me gently then wraps her arms around me, hugging me tightly.

God, I hope I don't lose her over this. I don't think I'll survive if I do.

"From the top," Maddox tells us all. We've been rehearsing for two hours. At the rate we're going, his voice is going to be trash by tonight.

But he's wired, his OCD is at it's peak, and paranoia at not being perfect is at an all-time high today. It happens every time he gets a call from home.

Angel is a pissy douche. He gets a little worse every day Josephine is gone. I get it, but I'll be glad when she's back. Ryder has something going on with him too. I don't know what it could be, but it has had him at everyone's throat. Throw in my bad mood, and we are four for four. Dane is the only one that seems to be having good days lately.

Angel's phone rings, cutting us all off from picking up again. "It's Josie," he tells us. "I'm taking it."

"Won't she be back tonight?" Maddox calls out as he walks off.

"In the morning," he yells back. "Still taking it. I like her more than you douchebags."

"Hopefully, his mood will improve when she gets back. It's like being around Angel from last year," Dane grumbles. "In fact, what the hell is wrong with all of you?"

"Just dealing with shit, man," I tell him as I set my bass to the side, then lay on the stage.

"Same," Maddox and Ryder say.

"I'm kind of tired of you guys keeping all your shit to yourselves," Dane snaps. The three of us look at him with identical expressions of surprise. "We are family. We unload our shit on each other, remember? Even if we know it's going to piss the others off."

"Mine's just the same bloody shit, mate," Ryder tells him. "My sister calls to tell me my grandfather is getting worse. Then I try to call him, and my mother has given orders that I am not to speak with him."

"What is her problem?" I ask gruffly.

"Me," he chuckles. "I don't play her games. If I won't speak to her, she won't let me speak to my grandfather."

"Why would you talk to her after the crap she pulled?" Maddox growls. "That was the lowest of low."

"Not talking to her is the least she deserves," Dane adds with his own harsh tone. "What about you?" he asks Maddox.

"My dad wants me to come home," he tells us.

"Why?" I ask.

"He says because he misses me," he shrugs.

"You don't believe him." It's a statement, not a question. I know Maddox and his dad haven't seen eye to eye in a long time. His dad wants him to take over the family business. He's tried to groom Maddox his entire life. Maddox has never wanted any part of it.

"I don't believe he misses me now when I've spent most of my life away from him. He had years to spend time with me. I'm not buying it now."

"All right, this little group therapy session seems to be making progress," Dane chuckles. "What about you, Jake?"

I scrub my hands over my face with a groan. "My choices are coming back to bite me in the ass," I grumble.

"Don't they always?" Maddox laughs.

"I swear to you I must be paying for something horrible from a previous life."

"What's going on, Jake?" Dane asks again.

I lay there on the stage floor with my arm thrown over my face in silence for a second. "Peyton," I tell them.

"As in Lyra's mom, Peyton," Dane grunts. "Why the hell is she a problem?"

"Because I didn't do what you and Angel told me to do," I admit.

"You're joking, right?"

"You don't have to say it. I already know. Now she's threatening to sue for custody and have me picked up for kidnapping."

"Jesus fuck, Jake," he yells. "Of all time to have a freaking heart."

"She won't win," Maddox tells me.

"I know. I won't let her, but it will get ugly. And it's going to cause hell for the band. None of that is what I'm worried about, though."

"What are you worried about?" Ryder asks.

"Cara," I sigh. "I've just gotten her to stop running or looking for a reason to run. This is a lot of drama that will get ugly. And being back in the band is going to bring a lot of attention to it. Is she going to want to stick around for that?"

254

"I'm guessing that means you haven't told her. So what? You're just hoping it will go away? You can't suck her into more drama, Jake," Dane warns me.

"I'm not sucking her into anything. Stop with that protective brother bullshit. Cara is as much my priority as Lyra," I growl.

"I am her brother. I will always watch out for her. Even from you."

"Stop. You two don't start this crap," Maddox points at both of us.

"For the record, she knows something is going on. I've told her I don't want her to worry about it but that I will tell her what's going on when I figure things out."

"How's that going for you?" Dane snaps.

"I said stop. I'm warning you, Dane. Back off," Maddox looks to him then turns to me. "You too."

"We need a break," Ryder announces. "We need a day of no interviews, rehearsals, or travel."

"You'll get your wish tomorrow," Liam tells us, coming up the stage. "You play tonight. Not again until the next night. Then we head to Italy."

I think of all the ways I can spend the day with Lyra and Cara tomorrow. I wish I could do something with just Cara and me tomorrow night. Kind of hard when the girl I want to take out is also the nanny.

Hell. She's more than a nanny. And, if things go the way I want, this will be a permanent predicament. A beautifully permanent problem. I want it to become the new normal. I want to wonder when I'll get alone time with my girl because we don't have a babysitter. Because I want Cara to be Lyra's mom in every way that counts. I know Lyra wants it too. She told me she wants it.

I just hope Cara wants it. I hope when all the drama with Peyton really starts, she doesn't take off. I've got to figure out how to keep her from running. I need to make her want us as much as we want her.

"That's a switch," Liam chuckles, drawing me from my thoughts.

"What is?" Dane ask.

We all follow the direction of Liam's nod. Angel is walking up the steps with a huge grin on his face. "Who ate the canary?" Liam asks.

"What?" Angel responds, but that smile doesn't drop. It's kind of strange. I don't think I've seen him smile that big since I met him in college.

"What are you staring at so hard?" Ryder nods to the phone in his hand.

His smile stretches wider as he hands it to Ryder. Ryder looks at the phone then back to Angel. "Seriously, mate?" he asks with his own grin.

"Okay. Share," Dane grumbles, unable to stand being left out of the loop.

Ryder passes it to Maddox. Now he's grinning like an idiot, and my curiosity gets the best of me. I snatch the phone from him to see what's so fascinating. It's hard to make out, but I know what I'm looking for since I've seen one of these before. "Well, holy crap," I laugh. "You didn't waste any time at all, did you?"

"Waited ten years. Pretty sure that's long enough," he laughs.

"What is it?" Dane whines. "Why are you all grinning like idiots?"

"Angel here has gone and knocked his wife up," I tell him.

"Seriously?"

Angel shrugs. "Looks like the band is expanding."

We all crowd around him, offering our congratulations. The guy deserves this. He and Josephine both do. It took them a long time to put years' worth of misunderstandings behind them. After all those years apart, it's good to see them together and happy.

After a few more minutes of backslaps and jokes, we get back to practice. The mood is decidedly lighter than it was earlier. Within an hour, we're all satisfied with the sound and the songs.

We go back to the rooms. I walk in to find Cara looking completely exhausted and Lyra asleep on the sofa. I look at both of them, trying to figure out what's going on.

"She's been sick all day," Cara tells me, leaning her head back.

I move around Cara to Lyra like lightning. I place my hand to her forehead. She doesn't feel warm. "Why didn't you call me?" I snap.

Her mouth falls open for a split second before snapping shut. Her eyes flash with anger and frustration. "I did try calling you," she spits, standing to her feet.

"Then you should've called any one of the guys. I know you have their numbers. It isn't that hard to get me. You're the nanny. It's your damn job."

257

Cara step right into me. When she pushes me, it catches me off guard, and I stumble back a step. For two seconds, it pisses me off – not hard at the moment – then I see the tears, and I know I've fucked up.

I move to grab her, but she jumps back.

"For your information, I tried all of you. I even tried Liam. No one answered. I called my sister because I didn't know what to do," she is yelling, and the tears are streaming down her face. I try to move toward her again, but she puts her hand up, shaking her head. "Tori said she probably has a virus. I had Matthew get her some electrolytes and some soup. Then she told me to give her a teaspoon of Benedryl, so don't try to give her any more medicine."

She turns, walking away from me. I don't even realize what she's doing until she's at the door. "NO! Cara, wait." I call out. I go after her, but I can't go farther than the doorway because Lyra will be left alone.

Dammit, I shouldn't have been so reproachful with her. No, I wasn't reproachful. I was an ass. I referred to her as the nanny when I know good, and damn well she's more than that.

All of the stress over Peyton bubbled to the surface at that moment. I took my anger with Peyton out on Cara. She didn't deserve it.

I sit on the sofa next to Lyra, rubbing her curls that are stuck to her forehead. Probably burning off a fever. I pull out my phone and text Cara.

I hear it ding on the coffee table in front of me. She doesn't have her phone. The day keeps getting better.

I lean my head back just for a second. I replay the last ten minutes and wonder if I could've been a bigger asshole.

I don't even remember falling asleep. It couldn't have been for long because Lyra is still out cold. Although, when you mix Benedryl with not feeling well, I know she can sleep for hours.

I pull my phone out of my pocket to check the time. Yep. Two hours. I wonder why Cara didn't wake me when she came back. Then again, why would she? She probably went straight to the bedroom.

I get up, trying not to wake Lyra. I head to the bedroom to check on her. I need to apologize.

She's not there. I have to leave in a few minutes, so I know she can't be far.

Right?

I try Maddox first. He and Ryder are where she went last time she took off.

"Cara, there with you?" I bark before he can even say hello.

"No," he says, sounding like he's out of breath. I can hear girls giggling in the background. "Shut it," he barks. "Why would Cara be here?"

"Don't worry about it. I'll try Dane."

"What did you do to her?"

I release a long, tired breath. "I was an ass, okay. Lyra has been sick all day. All this shit with Peyton made me overreact."

"Great. And you just let her take off," he hisses through the phone. "Call the bodyguard. Make sure he's with her."

259

My spine goes rigid at what he's saying. "You don't think she went to Dane?"

"When her boyfriend upsets her? No, she wouldn't go to her overprotective, overdramatic big brother, you idiot. If she didn't come here, then she could be anywhere. With that psychopathic stalker close by, no less."

"Goddammit," I yell. "This is all my fault."

"Damn straight, it's your fault. You shouldn't have taken your shit out on her."

"Daddy," a tiny, tired voice calls out, "my tummy hurts."

"I've got to get to Lyra."

"Call the bodyguard. I'm going to look for her."

"Daddy," Lyra starts to cry. My heart feels like it's being ripped in two by the need to find Cara and the need to make my little girl feel better.

I pick her up, cradling her in my arms. I hate when she's sick so much. But her little body tucked into mine relieves some of the tension I feel as I dial the bodyguard's number.

"Hello."

"Are you with Cara?" I ask, skipping over pleasantries. I don't feel particularly pleasant that now this guy who is probably my age, if not younger, is watching her. A guy without a kid and a baby momma to deal with.

"No, she said she wouldn't need me today since Lyra is sick," he answers with a hint of accusation.

"*Fuck.*"

"Everything okay?"

260

"No," I spit, hanging up.

I look to the table where Cara's phone sits, buzzing with texts. My irritation hits new heights when I see the messages flashing across her lock screen.

THE best friend: Have you thought anymore about what I said?

THE best friend: I meant it.

THE best friend: I've missed you. While you were away and now. Why'd you have to go with your brother?

THE best friend: I want us to try again. We were good together.

What the hell?

I haven't touched the phone. I'm just staring at it as message after message pops up. I don't know who 'THE best friend' is, but I have an idea. The thought that he's trying to get my girl pisses me off. Knowing they've been more than friendly makes it worse.

Never pictured myself as the jealous type, but I always have been with her. With all the crap I've been dealing with, I'm not exactly a picture of calm. Quite the opposite. I'm one step away from exploding.

Her ringing phone lights the fuse. His name and face flashing on her screen throw on accelerant.

I know I shouldn't answer. Even convinced myself to let it go.

It stops ringing, but the clench of my jaw doesn't loosen. My hands remained locked tight into fists. Every muscle in my body feels tight enough to snap. But I didn't answer it.

Then it starts ringing again, and all maturity and restraint fly right out the window.

I lay Lyra, who's fallen back to sleep, on the sofa. I snatch the phone off the table and walk toward the bedroom, so I don't wake her.

I tap the green icon, but I don't say anything.

"Cara, why won't you respond to my message?" he asks. And I feel like I'm boiling from the inside out. I still don't say anything. "I know you say you just want to be friends, but you know how good we are together. I want to try again. This time we're not high school kids. It will be different."

"Ever occur to you that she doesn't want you, asshole?" I growl out.

"Who is this? Where's Cara?"

"*This* is her boyfriend," I tell him. Even though she and I haven't had a discussion about relationship status, I don't hesitate. I don't need a conversation. I've told her how I feel. I know how she feels. The words don't need to be spoken. We're together. Period.

Unless I've totally ruined that with my crap attitude and big mouth.

No. She's mine. I'm not letting her run. I have some apologizing and groveling to do, but she's not getting away from me. Not because I was a dick.

I'd be looking for her right now if I had someone to watch Lyra. I only just managed not to chase after her when she ran. I should've chased after her instead of falling asleep for two hours. But I couldn't leave Lyra, and I thought she'd be back before time to leave for the show. I thought I could apologize then when she was more receptive to hearing it. I didn't think she'd runoff. Not like that.

262

"I doubt that," Daniel says with a scoff. "I'm her best friend. She'd tell me. What are you? Some roadie? I know her brother, man. One call, and you'll be out of a job. Cara's been through a lot. She doesn't need some asshole hurting her."

My teeth grind together. I work to find some modicum of composure. It's a losing battle, but I still try.

"First, maybe she didn't tell you because you're blowing up her phone, pressuring her for a relationship she's obviously told you she doesn't want. Second, you don't know crap about Dane *or* Cara. If you did, then, like I said, you'd know about me." I start to end the conversation by telling him to lose her number but think better of it. I'm already in the doghouse. I don't need to dig deeper. "She's with me. If you're her friend, respect that and respect her when she tells you no."

I hang up the call before I say anything else. Just answering the phone alone probably made my problems so much worse.

A knock on the door has me running. I sling the door open, praying it's Cara on the other side. I instantly deflate when I see Ryder's extremely irritated face.

"I'm staying here. You're going to my room," he grumbles.

"Why?" I ask, hoping Maddox has found her.

"Because apparently you messed up and she won't come here."

Relief whooshes from my chest on a breath. Then worry about what comes next sets in. I can fix this. I just hope she'll let me.

I don't even knock on the door. Maddox already had it open when I get to his room. Like he's waiting on me.

"Don't mess this up, or I'll be rearranging your face," he warns as he walks out, leaving me to clean up my mess

I walk in to see her curled on the sofa. Her eyes and nose are red from crying. I hate myself for being the cause.

She feels me before she sees me. Just like I always do with her.

She turns to look at me. The look in her eyes makes me think every wall I've knocked down has been rebuilt and fortified. "Go away." Her voice is hard and cold.

"I'm not leaving. Not until you hear me out. Until I apologize. I didn't mean what I said. I was worried, and I've been stressed, and I took it out on you." I take two steps, but so does she. I can see how badly I've hurt her. She's trying to hide it, but it's clearly written in her eyes.

"No. It's fine." She wraps her arms around her middle like she's holding herself together. Pain wraps around my heart, squeezing my lungs because I did this. "I knew it would happen sooner than later. That you'd realize I was bad for her. That I'm too much for you to deal with. It's fine. It really is, but please just go. Leave me alone. Tomorrow you won't have to worry about me anymore."

My entire body goes rigid. Glaciers form in the pit of my stomach as her words piece through my soul.

I watch her walk to the kitchen, turning her back to me. The last thing she said finally hits me. "What do you mean I won't have to worry about you tomorrow?"

"If you don't trust me with Lyra, then I shouldn't be here. I'm going home. Liam will find you a new nanny before my plane even takes off, so don't worry about that."

I'm across the room in three long strides. I turn her around to face me by her shoulders. "You're not leaving. You said you wouldn't leave, and I'm not letting you go."

The look in her eyes shakes me to my core. "I can't stay. I was here to do a job, and you're not satisfied with that job."

"Fucking hell, Cara, stop," I yell, making her flinch. "Just stop. You can't do this every time something doesn't go perfectly. You can't run every time I say something stupid or you get hurt."

"I'm not running," she yells back. "You said you didn't want me anymore."

"When the hell did you hear me say that? I never said that. You're always ready to take off. You're always ready to shut down. Aren't you tired of it yet? Aren't you tired of maintaining these walls? At keeping everyone close but not too close?"

Tears fill her eyes. I see her beginning to crumble. "I'm just the nanny, Jake," she whispers.

"You were never the nanny. You've always been more. You've always been everything." I don't give her a chance to respond. I don't allow her to deny what I've just said. To process it, analyze it, and let her demons convince her it's not true.

I pull her into my chest, slanting my mouth over hers in a hard kiss. For several seconds, I'm kissing her like I might die if I don't, and she doesn't respond. She is like a stone in my arms, but I'm not relenting. I slide my tongue across the seam of her mouth then nip at her bottom lip. When she gasps, my tongue finds her. Her hands move to my chest. I know she is going to push me away, but she doesn't. Instead, she's gripping at my shirt like a lifeline. I tug her hair to make her head fall back, giving me deeper access to that beautiful mouth. She moans as her fingers move from my chest to my hair.

She can never seem to hear my words. Not the ones I want her to hear anyway. Her brain only fixates on the voices that tell her she's too broke and too damaged. On the guilt that tells her, she doesn't deserve to be happy. On the pain that won't let go.

But I know she feels it. When I kiss her, touch her, she feels it all. The intensity of my love. The unconditional, unwavering affection that flows from me to her. The need and want and desire to consume. She feels it, and she returns it.

I move my mouth to her jaw, kissing and nipping lower. My hands glide down her body to the curve of her ass. My fingers dig into the rounded flesh as I bite the soft flesh of her neck. I lift her up. Her legs automatically wrap around mine. Her hot heat sears through the fabric of my jeans.

I walk us to the sofa, laying her down on the plush fabric. I push the hem of her dress up until it's bunched around her waist, my hands gliding between her thighs to the hot center that is slick with arousal. Her moans spur me to continue as I bite a pebbled nipple through her dress.

"Jake," she mutters, "I need you." Her pleas sound nearly as desperate as I feel. Her body reacting my mine, mine to hers, is explosive as a Molotov and inevitable as the sun holding the earth in place. Because her mind can war with her feelings and thoughts all day long, her body, however, can't deny what her heart feels. "I need you now."

I release myself from the confines of my jeans. I don't even bother to remove the little thong she is wearing. I pull it to the side and slide home. Because that's what she is. She's home.

Her heels dig into me as I press into her. Our bodies move together with need and hunger, and ferocity. Each of us chasing euphoria and wanting to prolong it all at the same time.

Her hand grips my shoulders, her nails digging into the flesh of my back. My fingers dig into her hips in a bruising hold.

I reach her chin with my other hand. "Eyes open," I command. "You can't hear my words, so watch and feel me." I kiss her hard as my movements begin to quicken. Her hips rise, meeting me with every stroke. "I fucking love you, Cara. Even when I'm being an ass. Even when you piss me off. Nothing is going to change that." She begins to clench around me as she chases her release. "I'm not letting you leave me. You belong to me. Your body, your heart, and your screams are mine and mine alone. Now, come for me, baby." Her mouth falls open with a scream of please, my name the utterance of her lips. And as she falls, so do I.

Cara

Jake and I lay there for several minutes, unable to move. Our chests rise and fall as our labored breathing begins to slow. His forehead is pressed to mine, his breath fanning out on my face. "I'm sorry," he tells me again. "I'm so fucking sorry. I've been stressed out over some shit and took it out on you."

"I should've tried harder to get you," I concede.

"You've got to stop waiting on me to be done with you, baby. Your past, my past, it doesn't determine our future. Our mistakes do not define us. They help us to learn and grow. I'll never be done with you. I have wanted you too damn long to let you go. I will chase you to the ends of the earth. But you've got to believe that. I want you – need you more than I need air to breathe."

"Why have you been stressed?" I ask him softly.

He releases a sigh that hits me right in the chest. I've seen how stressed he is. How tired he looks. But now it's like I feel the weight of it. "Peyton has decided to resurface. She's demanding to see Lyra, threatening lawyers, and kidnapping charges."

I can't stop the gasp. My eyes are wide with fear and shock. I never even realized she could possibly come back into their lives. In my naïve mind, when she left her child, she gave up any right to her.

"The irony of it all is the thing that's been stressing me out is you. I know we've never discussed what we are to each other. I've just made proclamations. But I knew you didn't sign up for ugly custody suits and possibly watching me sit in a cell for a few days. I was afraid when you found out, you'd run faster than you've ever run."

"You're facing all this over your daughter, and you were worried about my reaction?" I'm shocked, touched, and a little angry. He should be more worried about Lyra than me.

"It's a fight she can't win, Cara. She walked out of that hospital. There's documentation. I could've had her rights terminated but didn't. When it was first suggested, I couldn't go through with it. Then I just wasn't concerned. I didn't think she'd try to come back. I'm not worried because I know I won't lose. You can't vanish for nearly three years then expect to get your way."

"Jake, I –," I get cut off by the door flinging open.

"Cara Alyssa Pierce," Dane booms. Jake's and my head snap to see Dane walking into the room, his hands waving as he rants. He didn't bother to knock, and he's too busy ranting to notice the very precarious position Jake and I are in. Jake's naked from the waist up. His pants are pulled low over his hips, and he's still inside of me. Thankfully, my dress covers my chest, but the rest is bunched around my waist. "Why the hell have you been skipping therapy? We agree –," he stops talking, making a strangled sound. His eyes zero in on Jake and me. He begins to turn a very strange shade of green before turning very pale. "Oh, God, no. No, no, no." He begins to move backward. His hands up over his eyes.

"Dane, watch out," Jake calls out, but it's too late. He stumbles, falling into a sofa table with a thud, hitting his head hard on the way down.

Jake jumps up, pulling his pants up quickly while I stand up, straightening my dress. We both get to him at the same time Cami, Ryder, and Maddox come into the room.

"Dammit, Dane," Jake grumbles, checking his head. "You need stitches."

"What I need is bleach," he says with a distressed voice. "No. I need a lobotomy."

"We tried to stop him," Maddox tells us, but his smirk says he is finding the entire situation a little too funny.

"Why the hell didn't you knock?" I yell.

"Why the hell didn't you shut the door all the way? Or better yet, do that in your own room? I can never unsee that," he whines. "Part of me wants to kick your ass," he says, looking at Jake, "and the other part wants to hang myself."

"Stop being dramatic," Cami rolls her eyes. "Come on so we can get you to the hospital."

"That can wait," he waves her off and turns to me. "I want to know why the hell your therapist says he hasn't talked to you in weeks? We had a deal."

"I haven't had time," I tell him honestly. I just don't tell him the other part. I'm tired of therapy. I'm tired of talking about what happened and how I feel about it. I just want to let it go.

"Cara, that was the one thing we were serious about when you volunteered for this," Maddox says, clearly taking Dane's side. I bite my tongue to ask him if what's good for the goose is good for the gander because we all know Maddox has a world of issues.

Jake clears his throat beside me, drawing my attention to him. His face is soft and gentle, but I can already tell he agrees with them. He rubs my cheek with a finger. "Do the therapy, baby. You need it. You may not want it, but you need it."

"Why do I keep feeling like he's knows something I don't?" Dane asks accusingly.

"Because he does," I answer without hesitation. I won't ever tell Dane the details, but it's time he at least knows more happened than he thinks. "He knows lots of things you don't, Dane. He knows things I haven't even told my therapist. Before you start huffing and puffing and throwing your big brother weight around, the answer is no, I won't tell you."

His jaw clenches tightly as he turns his glare to Jake. "You already know I'm not saying anything, so don't ask."

He moves to Jake with lightning speed. I flinch, but Jake doesn't move a muscle. His chest rises and falls with rapid breath. I am expecting him to swing, so when his hand moves up, I flinch again.

My heart swells and nearly explodes when I realize that's not what he's doing. He grips the back of Jake's neck, pulling him so their foreheads touch. "Take care of her, please."

"You know I will," Jake tells him with a tight voice.

My eyes burn with emotion. Emotions I can't put into words. It's happiness that my older brother has just let go of me. He's letting another man, his best friend no less, protect me in his place. It's sadness for the exact same reason.

When he releases Jake, he turns to me. He pulls me tight into his chest, burying his face in my hair. "I have never regretted the day I brought you home for me. I will always be your big brother. I will always be here when you need me. But you need to let him love you. He's a good man, Cara. You know I wouldn't say all of this if I didn't see how much he loved you. Love him back. Don't break his heart, and he won't break yours." He says all of this in a whisper just for me. His words make the tears spill over my lashes. The emotion forces a sob from my chest.

He releases me from his tight grip. My face is still wet with tears.

"Call your therapist," he tells me as he walks away. "Or we're sending you home."

And just like that, it's like the last five minutes never happened.

"Oh my God," Josephine laughs so hard, the manicurist gives her a dirty look. "I always miss the good stuff."

"Oh, it was priceless," Cami cackles. "I wish I could've seen his face when he realized what he walked in on."

I sit in the seat next to them with a scowl while Cami replays the humiliation from the day before. I just sit between the two of them, shaking my head with a small smile on my face. It was embarrassing at the time, but I understand why everyone else

272

thinks it's so funny. Especially considering Dane's and my aversion to being subjected to the other's sex life.

On a side note, after Jake and I went back to our room, he told me about his conversation with Daniel. I wanted to be angry with him. He was out of line. But so was Daniel.

Not to mention I felt a little guilty. I hadn't told Daniel about Jake or Jake about Daniel. I hadn't told Jake because I've noticed he has a slight – astronomical – jealous streak.

I hadn't told Daniel about Jake because it never came up. We just talked like we always do. Until he started talking about us in terms of a relationship. I told him I didn't want that. Even without Jake, I wouldn't have wanted, so I didn't want to make Daniel think he stood a chance if there wasn't another guy in his way.

I should've told them both.

When that conversation was over, Jake made me call my therapist. He didn't give me much choice when he said he wouldn't go to the show if I didn't. Fifteen thousand screaming fans would've been let down. I didn't want to be responsible for that.

He started to leave to give me some privacy for the call. I stopped him. I turned on the video chat and had him sit through the entire thing. I hate admitting when I'm wrong, but I was. I needed that talk. I need therapy. Having Jake there, for some reason, made me open up more. Maybe it's because I pretended to talk to him instead.

"Okay, so I've been dying to ask," Cami looks at me with a grin. I hold back a groan at the question I know she's about to ask because the girl has no boundaries. "How is it with Jake?"

273

"Amazing," I sigh.

"Come on. We need more than that," she whines. "Is he soft and sweet, or does he like to be in control?"

"Yes," I answer because he's all of those things at once. It makes absolutely no sense to me how he can fuck me senseless and still make it feel like we're making love.

"Cara, we need details," Josephine giggles.

"What else can I say?" I shrug, biting my lip. "He knows how to play my body. Like really, *really* knows."

"Musicians are really good with their hands," Cami says. I repress the urge to gag.

"That's not all they're good with," Josephine clucks her tongue.

We laugh some more as we all agree.

Half an hour later, we are perusing the shops of Paris. It's not something I ever thought I'd be doing. I'm not sure why since I've always shopped on Fifth Avenue in New York. My big brother did a good job of spoiling me. There was more than one reason they all called me Brat.

After Chicago, my once impeccable wardrobe changed from designer labels to plain hoodies, sweats, and jeans. I tried to be invisible. I tried to detract from my looks.

I've missed my pretty clothes and pretty hair. I've missed getting up every morning, deciding what to wear. I've missed me.

We spend the afternoon browsing through several shops. Each of us buys a few outfits. Nothing too outrageous except for Josephine when she finds a pair of Valentino cage heels and a Fendi baby set.

274

"How far are you?" I ask her as she admires the beige outfit.

"Fourteen weeks," she smiles. "We didn't want to say anything until after the first trimester."

"Do you know what it is yet?"

She shakes her head with a smile. "Not yet. We haven't been able to decide if we want to know."

I nod with a smile as I admire a stunning champagne-colored dress. It's heavily beaded with fringe at the bust and feathers at the hem. The spaghetti straps and sweetheart neckline accentuate the shape of it to perfection.

"You should try that on," Cami tells me. "It would look amazing on you."

Josephine nods in agreement. "It would go amazingly with those gold sandals you were admiring."

I touch the dress, loving the feel of the beads as they fall through my fingers. "It's kind of heavy, don't you think?" I ask them both.

"I think you should try it on," Cami says again.

A woman appears at our side with a wide smile. "Your friends are right," she says in a heavy French accent. "This dress would be amazing against your skin and hair."

"You don't think it would wash me out?" I ask the three of them. "It is kind of the same shade as my hair."

"Try. It. On." Cami tells me one more time.

I look to the saleswoman, who gives me a nod.

"Okay, I will."

I buy the dress, shoes, and a few accessories, spending more on the single outfit than I spent on all my other purchases combined, but I refuse to feel guilty. I haven't splurged on myself in a long time. The allowance Dane has given me every month for years has done nothing but build over the last couple of years.

The dress makes me want to have my hair done. It's well overdue for a trim. I tell this to the girls, and they agree with wide grins.

My trim turns into a full-blown cut. My waist-length locks now fall to the middle of my back in soft layers. A few lighter pieces were added to emphasize the shade.

"Cara, you've always been beautiful, but now you look like a model," Josephine tells me, smiling.

"You look older," Cami nods, "but in a good way. You look all grown up now."

I feel myself flush at their compliments. "I needed a change," I admit. "I just have no idea when I'm going to wear this." I gesture to the dress bag.

"The guys do have the night off," Josephine states.

I can't help but laugh. "They do, but that doesn't help me. I'm the nanny, remember?"

"Angel and I can watch Lyra while you get that man of yours to take you out," she volunteers.

"We can all go. Well, except for you two, if you're keeping Lyra," Cami nods. You can practically see the wheels turning in her head. She pulls out her phone, texting, who I only assume to be Dane.

"Maddox says he's on it," Cami tells me.

276

"That's who you were texting?" I laugh.

"If you want to have a night of fun, you tell Maddox or Ryder," she shrugs. "If you want a night in, then I tell Dane. Now come on. We need to get ready."

When we get back to the hotel, Cami chases everyone out of our room. All the guys, except for Maddox, look at us like we've lost our minds. Josephine keeps Lyra entertained while Cami and I get ready.

Cami decides on a white, asymmetrical Bodycon dress that looks amazing against her olive skin and dark hair. Her smokey eyes get lined with a bit of kohl for dramatic effect. She straightens her waves then pulls her hair into a high ponytail, creating an elongating effect.

I keep my eyes neutral with a bit of wing liner. I apply a touch of shimmer to my cheekbones and keep my lips nude. I keep my hair down around my shoulder in soft waves, leaving my new style on display.

"The guys are back," Josephine says as she peeks her head in the room. When she sees us her eyes get misty. "You are both beautiful."

"Are you seriously crying?" Cami asks.

"It's just hormones. You know I've been like this for months," she waves us off.

"At least, now I know why," Cami laughs.

"What do you think, pretty girl?" I ask Lyra, who has her head on Josephine's shoulder with her fingers in her mouth.

She smiles at her around those fingers. "Pwetty."

"Think Nane and Daddy will like it?" Cami asks.

She keeps smiling with a nod.

"They're all out there waiting," Josephine tells us. "Why don't we go find out?"

Cami and I grin at each other and nod. We walk into the suite's living room, where all the guys are sitting around talking about who knows what. It could be anything from cars to tattoos to music.

"Damn!" Liam is the first to acknowledge us. "You two look sexy as hell."

The rest of the guys look up. They all voice their approval, but my eyes are only on one guy. His mouth hangs open, and his eyes are wide.

"So, we're taking the girls out," Maddox announces.

"And Angel and I are watching Lyra so Cara and Jake can go," Josephine tacks on.

"We are?" Angel asks, looking very confused.

Honestly, all the guys look confused.

"If we're going out, why haven't we been getting ready?" Ryder questions.

"Because we're rock stars. What do we need to do to get ready?" Maddox tells him. "Not like we're going to wear anything different."

"True," Ryder nods his agreement.

Dane is the first one up, pulling Cami into his side. "Am I going to be holding your hair back again tonight?" he teases her.

She slaps his chest with a laugh. "That happened once."

"Twice," he amends.

"Whatever," she rolls her eyes, but it doesn't hide how much she loves him.

"Let's go, guys," Maddox jerks his head toward the door. "We have dinner reservations first."

"We'll take Lyra to our room," Josephine tells us.

"Angel," Lyra whispers, nearly asleep already.

"Come on, Princess. You get to stay with Josie and me tonight," he takes her from Josephine with a glare. "Stop picking her up," he warns.

"I'm pregnant, not helpless," Josephine grumbles.

"And she weighs more than twenty pounds."

"Stay off of Google."

They leave, still bickering back and forth.

The rest of us follow. Maddox and Ryder stroll out behind Liam with their usual swagger. Dane and Cami go next. I watch my brother wrap Cami's ponytail around his fist, then drop his mouth to her ear, whispering some secret.

Jake grabs my wrist before I can get to the door. "You cut your hair," he notices, twirling a piece around his finger.

"It's time to make some changes," I nod.

"I hope some of those changes include me."

"All of those changes include you."

The grin that spreads across his face is blinding. His expression takes on a boyish quality I don't think I've ever seen in all the

279

years I've known him. He drops a sweet kiss to my mouth. "You look beautiful, by the way."

I nod. "I hope so. As much as I spent on this dress, if I didn't, it would be a crime."

"It's not the dress," he tells me firmly. "What you wear never has anything to do with your beauty."

I feel a blush rising from my chest all the way to my ears. I bite my lip with a smile.

Maddox made our reservations at the most expensive restaurant in Paris. If it wasn't, it should've been. It was the kind of place that would not have let them in the door had they been anyone else. Not when they were all wearing jeans and t-shirts with tattoos and piercings all on display.

The service was lovely, and the food was amazing. The conversation between all of us flowed easily. Dane and I were teased relentlessly about the day before. I was teased some more by Ryder and Maddox about their lessons when I was a kid. Dane groaned, Jake growled, and I wanted to crawl under the table.

Now we're in the VIP section of L'Arc. We were escorted straight through. People gaped and stared as we moved through the crowd to the sectioned-off space.

Maddox and Ryder waste no time ordering copious amounts of liquor. I'm not sure either one of them can even get drunk anymore, but it never seems to stop them from trying.

They pass one to all of us. Cami throws hers back as quickly as the two who lead the hedonistic debauchery. Dane watches her, grinning with a shake of his head while he tosses back his own.

When I bring my own to my mouth, Jake stops me. "You taken your medicine today?" My look of confusion has him explaining.

"You're taking benzos. I'm not letting you drink if you've taken any."

My first thought is to argue. The idea that he's telling me what to do doesn't sit well. But I know he's trying to take care of me, and he's right. My meds and alcohol don't mix. I learned that the hard way. "I haven't had any since yesterday," I tell him truthfully.

He releases my arm, allowing me to toss back the shot. "Just don't drink too many. Lyra is with Angel and Josephine, so I can make you scream as loud as I want tonight."

My eyes go wide with his words. My belly starts a simmering burn that has nothing to do with the tequila.

Before I can respond, Cami is dragging me to the dancefloor. I feel light and free. For the first time in a very, very long time, I feel like me. We laugh as we bump and grind on each other. Song after song, we dance until we're sweating and panting, and I feel wonderful.

Let Me by Zayn comes on just as I feel hands grip my hips. I don't freak out. I don't have to. I know exactly who it is.

He brings my arm up to wrap behind his head, then trails his fingers down my side. They slide slowly down the side of my breast over my ribs then my lower belly. It's a total Swayze move that has me panting.

"What are you doing to me?" I whisper.

I don't expect him to hear me, but he does. "I've asked myself that same question for five years."

We dance like that for several minutes. Even when the song picks up. It's just him and me in our own little bubble.

"Come on," he whispers, pulling me out of the club.

"Where are we going?" I ask with a giggle. I barely register the security that's surrounding us as we make our way out.

"You'll see."

He pulls me until we're out on the street. We walk quickly, Matthew following behind but not too close, making the block until we're standing at the Arc de Triomphe. Lightning flashes across the sky and thunder rumbles though the sky is clear. And it hits me, the thunder booms, and I'm not reacting. Flashbacks aren't threatening my consciousness. Memories aren't trying to push their way through. All I see and feel is Jake and my hand in his.

"What are we doing here?" I laugh as I take in the monument.

"Hopefully getting a show before the rain," he tells me as we move further into the circled path.

"What show?"

He looks at his watch then looks up to the sky. A slow smile spreads across his face. "That," he gestures to the sky.

I gasp at the hundreds of bright streaks trailing across the sky. "You knew about this?" I ask with astonishment in my voice.

"Heard about it somewhere," he tells me.

"It's beautiful," I whisper, afraid to break the spell.

"Not as beautiful as you," he tells me, tracing a finger down my cheek.

I swallow hard. Words I've felt for so long but haven't spoken out loud are on the tip of my tongue. The reason why his comments hurt so badly yesterday. The reason why I've tried too hard to guard my heart. It's been pointless. A lesson in futility. Because no matter what I've done, the feeling hasn't gone away. It's only grown stronger.

And he's done exactly what he said he would. He has loved enough for both of us. He has shown me that he wants me. He has been what I needed.

Looking up into those beautiful blue-green eyes, I wrap my arms around him. "I love you, Jake."

His eyes, soft on mine, crinkle at the corners. An amused but sweet smirk plays on his lips. "I know you do. I knew the minute you fell in love with me." He cups my face as stars continue to streak across the sky and the heavens open, and the rain begins to fall. "I never needed to hear the words. I just needed you to realize it."

His lips meet mine. Our tongues slide against each other as we stand in the middle of Paris, rain soaking us to the skin. Everything else falls away. Nothing else matters. Not the past, not the people running to escape the weather. It's just him and me.

Cliché? Maybe.

Perfect? Absolutely.

I considered taking Lyra to Parc des Buttes-Chaumont today or even Château de Versailles. Then decided to take her to the one place I knew her little toddler heart would love more than anything. It was a fight with Jake. The most crowded place in Paris was not somewhere he wanted us to go.

I realized last night, Jake has lost his anonymity. He's no longer an unknown face from the band's past. He is just as front and center as the rest of them are.

I also know that's not why he's worried. He's worried because of me. Because of who may still be out there.

Fortunately, I won the argument, and now Lyra is here with her mouse ears and a grin bigger than her face. She has hugged Cinderella, danced with Snow White, explored Alice's Curious Labyrinth, and rode the railroad. We've just finished our lunch at Casey's Corner. Matthew is helping me clean up our mess so we can get to the next adventure.

My phone rings, not for the first time today. Jake's name flashes across the screen. I roll my eyes with a laugh. He's called every half hour. I wonder how much rehearsing they're actually getting done. "Hi," I answer. "You made it thirty-five minutes this time."

"I'm just making sure you're okay," he grumbles.

"My brother isn't questioning why you're so worried?" I bite my lip. I really don't want Dane or anyone else to worry.

"He may be, but he's not saying anything. I really wish you'd just stayed at the hotel," he gripes.

"Jake, I've told you we can't make Lyra suffer. It's either I take her, or you hire a new nanny, so you don't have to worry so much."

"You've lost your goddamn mind if you think that would solve anything," he huffs. "I'm not hiring another anything, so you can go back to New York where I don't know if you're okay. I'd lose my mind, Cara."

"Then let me do this with her," I say softly. "We have Matthew here. He's doing what *he's* paid to do. We're fine."

"I have a bad feeling."

"You're just paranoid. Say hello to your daughter," I turn the phone to face Lyra. She smiles widely and rambles off what she's seen so far.

"Stop worrying so much," I tell him when I get the phone back.

"I'll try," he sighs. "I love you."

"I love you, too. See you tonight."

We end the call just as Matthew returns from removing the last of our trash. We check out a few more sights, weaving our way in and out of the crowd. Lyra has walked nearly every step. I wanted to get her a stroller, but the epic meltdown about being a big girl curtailed the idea quickly.

Now I'm carrying her. I don't know how long I will be able to carry her before my back starts screaming for relief, but her little legs are tired. I really wish I'd gotten the stroller anyway.

"I gots to go potty," she whispers in my ear as she begins to squirm.

I get Matthew's attention, letting him know we're heading for the restrooms. When we start to go in, he looks a little nervous. He has followed us every step of this trip. Never for a second has he been more than two feet away from us.

"It has to happen," I tell him, "or we're going to have another set of problems. Unless you want to join us."

That gets me a horrified reaction. "Pretty sure I'd lose more than just my job," he grimaces.

I laugh. "We'll be right back."

I pick Lyra up once her business is handled and her hands are washed to exit the bathroom. I walk straight into a wall. Except it's not a wall. It's a person, and the hairs on my neck rise.

"I'm sorry," I mutter as I attempt to get around the very large person without looking up.

"Been looking for you," he murmurs.

My brain screams at me to run, but his large body blocks my path. I squeeze Lyra closer to me. The action tells me this is not some sort of weird flashback. It's real. Very real.

I maneuver a bit, still not looking up to get around him. Relief floods me when he allows it. Relief that is short-lived when I bump into another man.

A woman steps from behind him, bring another shot of hope that she will help us. Until she reaches for Lyra. "Give me my baby."

I take the woman in with shock. Bright, familiar blue eyes stare at me. Long blond hair hangs over each of her shoulders.

I look at Lyra, then back to the woman. There is no doubt who she is, but those eyes – Lyra's eyes – are the exact same as the man I refused to look at. "I said give me my baby," she demands again, stepping forward.

Instincts I didn't know I had kick in. I squeeze Lyra even tighter to my chest with a growl I don't expect bubbling in my chest. "Keep your hands off of her."

"That's my baby," she steps forward again.

"The one you didn't want," I remind her with a hiss, backing away from her until I hit the man behind me.

His hands land on my shoulders, making my entire body go rigid. Lyra begins to cry in my arms, and all I want to do is run. But there's nowhere to go.

"Don't worry, little sister. They're coming with us."

I gasp. Sister? How is that even possible?

I don't get to ask. A hand reaches around me, covering my nose and mouth while Lyra is ripped from my arms. I struggle, fighting to hang on to Lyra and get away from the man, but it's pointless.

He wraps his arms around me, holding my arms in place as I kick and scream. The edges of the past threaten to take me under, but I will it away. I try to keep my focus on the little girl crying, reaching for me.

My vision starts to fade. Consciousness seems to be slipping. I fight with everything I have until the world around me goes blank.

Jake

Rehearsal is finally done. It's my fault it's taken so long. Between stopping to check on Cara and being distracted by the heavy feeling in my chest, I've played like crap.

I know I've had objections to Cara and Lyra going out before. Objections that were unfounded, but this time feels different. I have a really bad feeling in the pit of my gut.

Maddox catches me by the shoulder as we walk off the stage. "You going to be okay to play tonight?" he asks. To some, it might sound like he's worried about the show, but I know he's worried about me.

"Once they're back, I'll be good," I tell him. "You think I worry too much?"

"Normally, I'd say yes, but we both know who's out there. You're not worrying too much."

"I don't know if that makes me feel better or worse," I grunt.

He shrugs as we walk down the stairs. We all make it to the dressing room to find Liam on the phone. "What the hell happened?" he demands. The panic in his voice sends my heart rate through the roof. "Goddammit, this is what you were hired to prevent."

When he turns around to see all of us, his face morphs instantly. His anger with whoever is on the other end of that call fades into guilt and worry. He looks at each of us, but I stop breathing when his eyes land on Dane and me.

"Keep me updated," he barks into the phone. He lets out a sigh as he drags his hand down his face. "I'm not going to tell you not to worry because I know it won't do any good."

Dane's eyes narrow. He takes in Liam's posture and expression. His own body goes tense. "What are we going to worry about?" he barks.

"Cara and Lyra are missing," he says quietly. "You have every right to worry, but you can't panic."

"What do you mean they're missing?" Dane's voice gets louder. "How the hell are they missing?"

"They went to the bathroom. Matthew was waiting for them to come out and was attacked from behind. Tourists found him knocked out not far from the bathrooms. Cara and Lyra were nowhere to be found."

Maddox comes beside me. "Breathe, Jake," he mumbles in my ear. I realize I haven't breathed, moved, or even blinked since we walked into this room. The blood in my veins is like ice.

"We'll find them," I hear Liam say. That's what snaps me out of my stupor.

"Oh, we'll find them all right," I yell. "And when we do, whoever did this is fucking dead. When I get my hands on that fucking bodyguard, he's dead."

"The police are checking the park security footage right now. I'm sorry, Jake. You don't know how sorry I am, but we will find them."

I move past all of them, grabbing my jacket on the way out.

"Where are you going?" Angel calls out.

"I'm going to that fucking park," I call out. "I want to see that footage."

I feel someone behind me as I stalk out. "You're not going alone," Dane tells me.

I nod as I continue to stalk to the exit. We open the door, dozens of people litter the space wanting a piece of us. I don't give one shit about any person there. Security keeps them at bay as best they can, but I shoulder my way through the rest. The gasps of shock and muttering, calling me an asshole, mean nothing to me. They can think what they want. There are only two people that matter to me.

I climb into the car waiting on us. Dane climbs in beside me, Maddox in the front seat. I didn't even realize he was with us. My shock increases when Liam, Angel, and Ryder climb in as well.

I lean back in the seat as we make our way toward the amusement park. The place where dreams come true has just become the place of my worst nightmare.

Liam is tearing someone a new one over the phone. Ryder and Angel are quiet. Dane is huffing so loudly he sounds like a bear. Maddox taps away on his phone.

"Who are you texting?" Dane asks, sounding annoyed.

"Not important," Maddox tells him, his tone making it clear he won't answer the question.

Seconds feel like minutes and minutes feel like days as we finally get led to the security room. The place is huge. Monitors everywhere surrounded by equipment I couldn't work if I had to.

"Mr. Masters, good to see you again," some man says as we walk in the door.

"Thanks for helping us out, René," Maddox says as he shakes the man's hand.

None of us do a good job hiding our surprise that Maddox Masters is on a first-name basis with someone here. At a kids amusement park that is full of princesses and mouse ears.

He just shrugs us all off. He's not going to give us an answer which only makes it more curious. Though, I've recently learned there's a lot more to him than any of us really know.

"We pulled up footage of the facilities closest to where your friend was found," he tells us all. I grunt but refrain from saying anything. "We used the pictures Mr. Kelly sent over. This is where they were seen entering last."

I watch as Cara packs Lyra to the bathroom. Matthew is only a step behind them. You can see the minute someone dressed in dark clothes with a hood pulled up hits him in the back of the head. How they manage to go completely unnoticed in the crowd, I don't understand. It should've caused a riot.

"The cameras for the restroom areas can only see the corridor," he explains as he gestures to another monitor.

We watch as the guy moves into that corridor, his face still shielded by the hood. Cara comes out of the bathroom with Lyra in her arms, bumping into the man. She never looks at him, but you can see her discomfort in her body language.

"Is there audio?" Maddox asks.

"I'm sorry, sir, but no. Not here."

We continue watching as Cara moves around the guy. Another guy appears in front of her, stopping her from moving any further. When the next figure steps out, I feel ice in my veins and fire in my belly. Insidious wrath like I've never felt before settles over me.

I watch, with absolute helplessness, as Cara protects my baby like she's her own. She sure as hell is more Lyra's mother than the woman in front of her. My fists clench as I watch the man wrap his arms around her in a way that normally paralyzes her. She's not paralyzed this time. This time she fights. She kicks and struggles against the hand over her face trying to get to my little girl. She fights until she goes limp in the man's hold. The three of them maneuver around a corner through a hidden gate.

My heart feels like it has stopped beating. My knees are weak from watching my girls. Cara's body limp in the man's arms, and Lyra reaching for her, her face distorted from sobs. My world may as well have stopped spinning.

"Where did they just go through?" Dane asks.

"It's a private exit. Only accessible by employees and security."

"Rewind it," Maddox orders him. "Right before they take off with them. I want to see it again." They do as he says and then slows the footage down when he tells them to.

"Stop! Right there." He points.

My teeth grit. I don't know the man in the picture, but I commit his face to memory. I catch Maddox's attention from the corner of my eye. His lips are pressed into a thin line. His jaw clenches as he gives me a barely perceptible nod.

"Thanks, René," Maddox tells him.

"Anything else you need from me, Mr. Masters, you let me know."

Maddox nods as we leave.

"How did that help us find my sister?" Dane demands as we slide back into the car.

"It helped us to know what happened," Angel offers.

"Yeah, we saw that Jake's psychotic ex just kidnapped my sister," he blasts. "How did you ever end up with her?"

I don't answer. I sit there trying to figure out what Peyton was doing with the same man that hurt Cara. It can't be a mere coincidence. Peyton may or may not know about Cara and me, but there's no way she knew about Cara's past.

Dane continues to rant the entire way to the hotel, but I don't hear anything he says. My mind is moving a million miles a minute. I have no idea what the connection is. I don't know where they would've taken them. I feel like I'm drowning.

"Dane, so help me, God, if you don't shut the fuck up, I will lay your ass out," Maddox yells as we walk into his and Ryder's room.

I look up to see Maddox is more than a little pissed. I'm pissed. Dane's pissed. We are all pissed. But Dane's reaction to life isn't cool, calm, and collected. He's always a second away from snapping.

Maddox doesn't lose his temper often, but when he does, the result is seldom pretty.

I watch as he walks to the counter of the room's kitchen. His supply sits out in the wide open. He doesn't even bother to hide it anymore.

He does a line then another, causing Dane to explode some more. "My sister is missing, and you're getting high." His rant continues. He's losing it. Every second Cara is missing, he loses it a little bit more.

Me? I've already lost it. The second Peyton had Lyra and Cara went limp, I was done.

My rage is more focused. I'm not ranting and yelling because it won't get us any closer to finding them. Right now, I don't know that anything will get us closer to finding them. But it doesn't stop the images of what I'm going to do to the bastard when I find him.

Images of peeling off skin flash before my eyes, of carving and slicing each inch of his body. For every hair out of place on my girls will be another body part removed until he's in pieces. A darkness that's always been there just below the surface will soon be seen by this man. I may not have the resources to find him, but I know Maddox does.

I don't give a damn how high he is. As long as he can help me get my girls, he can do all the blow he wants.

294

"I am so sick of watching you put that poison in your body," Dane yells.

"Then don't fucking watch," Maddox counters.

Ryder and Angel stand off to the side, not sure whether they should get involved or not. Liam is trying to calm them both down, but he's getting nowhere.

"That's enough," I yell. "Maddox, come with me."

"You're kidding, right?" Dane yells again. "You think I'm going to let you go off and discuss this without me? You've lost your damn mind."

"I think you're going to stay here or go back to your room," I tell him, inches away from his face. "You're not helping anything. That may be your sister, but that's the woman I love and my little girl. I will get them back if it kills me, and I'm not going to do it with your ranting, raving, and bitching that solves nothing."

I leave without another word, Maddox right behind me. Angel and Ryder start to follow. "No," I tell them. "Just Maddox."

They both look stunned but stop following.

We get into my room. I lock the door behind us.

"That was him, wasn't it?" I demand.

"That was him. I wasn't sure at first, but when he looked at the camera, I knew."

"Answer me one thing. How is it you thought he was dead? Did no one think to check a pulse?"

"There wasn't time. It was all hell breaking loose. Bullets flying everywhere. Trying to get all those girls out. Matteo ordered the place burned to the ground. Even if he survived getting shot in the chest, he should've died in the fire. Only way he would've gotten out of there in that condition is –."

"If he had inside help," I finish.

"That's not our problem, though. Christian was able to send me a picture of the guy. The one from the footage at the park was too grainy. He got me his name and some information about him." The look on his face tells me I am not going to like what he has to say. I lift a brow, telling him to continue while I brace myself. "His name is Niko Novak. He was born in Slovakia. Parents brought him to the U.S. when he was twelve. He has been incriminated in quite a few crimes. Serious ones, but they never had evidence to go after him."

"How does that help us?"

"He has property all over the world. Including, right here in Paris. Odds are he's still in the city."

"This isn't a small place," I tell him wryly.

"We can narrow it down I'm sure, but there's something else you need to know." The tightness in his face tightens my chest.

"Spit it out, Maddox," I hiss.

"Novak had a sister. She was eight when they moved here. Novak had a different father than her, so they have different last names."

"Peyton," I nearly choke.

"Finding Cara was a coincidence. They've been after Lyra."

I shove my hands in my hair as my knees grow weak. "I brought this bastard back to her," I say around the lump in my throat.

"No. Peyton did. Don't know why but this isn't your fault. The only thing that you could possibly blame yourself for is taking her in in the first place."

"Not like I had a choice," I mutter.

"Didn't you?" He pops a brow knowingly.

"You know?"

"That you've been raising someone else's kid? I've known as long as you have. Did you think, when she appeared on your doorstep, I wouldn't check into it? When you said the paternity test confirmed you were the father, I knew you were lying but figured you knew what you were doing."

"Didn't have a damn clue. Still don't. But she's mine, Mads," I tell him with conviction.

"I know she is."

"Where do we start looking?"

"I've got some contacts checking into that. In the meantime, we have to deal with the press." I open my mouth to tell him I don't care about the press, but he holds his hand up to stop me. "If we don't, then we're not going to be able to focus on Cara and Lyra. Liam can handle most of it, but we have to say something. Ten minutes, Jake."

"Ten minutes." I agree.

It's been over twenty-four hours since my girls were taken. The police have no idea where to look. Maddox has been on the phone with everyone he knows. He has eyes all over watching for signs they're still in Paris, but he has people checking in other countries as well.

297

Normally, I might be curious how he seems to have all these connections. I know the guy grew up with money and power, but the people he's calling aren't entirely on the up and up.

My need to find my girls is stronger than my curiosity. I don't give a damn if he's talking to mafia kingpins or the pope. I just want my girls back.

Every second that they're gone feels like a noose getting tighter and tighter around my neck. Breathing through my anger has gone out the window. I'm a landmine waiting on the right person to step on me.

Angel has made it his business to keep Josephine and Camilla calm and distracted. Not sure it's working since they both look like they've been crying for days. Ryder and Liam are trying their best to help. They've been on the phone with European contacts all day, too.

Dane has navigated between highly agitated to worried and back. He's paced my suite so much his tracks are starting to show. He hasn't said anything else since yesterday. I don't know if he's too pissed to speak or if I got through that thick skull of his.

I've been in my room. I can't do anything but wait. I don't have contacts to call. I don't have any kind of resources to pull.

Right now, I'm sitting on the floor against the wall. I have Lyra's stuffed elephant in my hands, my head against the wall, and my heart bleeding.

I won't survive if I don't get them back. Both of them. It's not even a possibility.

The music playing through the Bluetooth changes. *I Can't Help Falling in Love* comes on. It's the song I have sung to my baby every night since the day she was born. It's the same song I've hummed to Cara when she has her nightmares.

I break. Thirty-six hours of worry and fear come pouring out. My shoulders shake as tears stream down my face. I would dare any man in my shoes not to cry. Not to feel like his world is crumbling around him.

I have no idea how long I sit there in the dark, letting it all out. I don't even realize when the song changes.

Finally, I pull myself together. I stand up, drag myself into the shower, then out of the room.

The suite is completely empty save Maddox sitting at the bar. I watch as he does a line. Under different circumstances, I'd flip over him doing that where my daughter eats, but I can't bring myself to care right now. Especially since he hasn't been off the phone for more than five minutes since everything happened.

"How are you holding up?" I hear behind me.

I turn to see Henry coming out of the extra room. "When did you get here?"

"A couple of hours ago. Hopped the first flight out when David told me the kid and the princess were missing." His eyes show genuine concern.

"Wouldn't have happened if I stopped them from going," I tell him, hanging my head. "I had a bad feeling. I should've put my foot down."

"I've watched you put your foot down with that kid. She kicks you in the shin every time," he chuckles sympathetically.

A small smile forms on my lips. "Yeah, she does."

299

"We're going to find them, man. We're going to bring them back."

I sit on the sofa with a sigh. "She was just getting some of herself back. What do you think this is going to do to her? She tell you what happened to her?"

"You already know the answer to that, but I have seen enough to recognize the signs of PTSD."

"The cause of it is the same person who has her right now," I tell him.

"We're going to find her. I've got people looking."

"Everyone has people looking," I snap.

A knock at the door has the conversation come to an end. Maddox goes to answer it.

"Madsux," I hear from the doorway, making my heart race.

I am to my feet and at the door in less than a second. I scoop up my princess. Relief floods me. It takes real effort not to break down right there.

"Oh my god, princess," my voice cracks. I look at her. She looks tired. I can tell she's been crying and on the verge of more tears, but she looks absolutely perfect. "How did you get here?"

She points at the door without taking her head from my shoulder.

"Hi, Jake," a soft voice calls out.

I hand Lyra to Maddox then move to the blond in front of me. I didn't think it was possible for me to feel angrier, but I do. I'm on her, my hand wrapped around her throat, pressing her against the wall of the hallway. "Where the fuck is she?" I growl.

Her blue eyes are wide with fear. She's pulling at my hands as tears stream down her face. "Jake," she chokes out.

"Where is she?" I yell even louder.

The doors of the other rooms open. Everyone is running at me. Dane and Henry work to pull me off her. She slumps to the floor, coughing and gasping for air.

Dane and Henry both have arms around me while Angel jumps in my line of sight. "Jake, stop," he demands.

"I'll fucking stop when she tells me where Cara is," I roar like an animal.

"She can't tell us anything if you kill her," Ryder says as he grabs her off the floor, none too gently.

"Take her to our room," Maddox tells him as he hands Lyra to Cami. "Take Lyra to your room tonight."

"No," I yell. "I need to make sure she's okay."

"And she doesn't need to see her dad like this," Maddox tells me firmly.

I watch as Cami and Josephine go into Cami's room. My little girl has tears streaming down her face. I need to be there for her. But I know Maddox is right. I am angry. Too angry. I won't be able to comfort her until I get Cara back.

"We're going to talk to Peyton and find out where Cara is. But you have to calm down first," Maddox tells me.

"I'm calm," I lie.

"You're as calm as a wolf defending the pack," Henry tells me. "You want your answers. They're behind that door, but you've got to keep your head."

I blow out a big breath, rolling my neck. I count to ten. I do everything in the span of thirty seconds to get control of myself.

Nothing works. I'm not more in control. My rage hasn't calmed. There is no logic.

"You good?" Dane asks.

"No," I tell them. "But I'll stand back, so I don't kill her."

"You know, you have always called me an irrational hothead. All of you have, and I'm not denying that. But, Jake, you have always been the most volatile. You do a good job of hiding it, but I've known you since you were a thirteen-year-old kid, pissed off at the world. You're dangerous when you're like this."

"I said I won't touch her," I grit. "Now, let's go so I can find out where Cara is."

They let go of me, but they don't let me go first. Instead, they crowd me. Dane and Henry in front. Maddox in the back. We walk through the door, my eyes instantly zeroing in on Peyton. I feel every muscle in my body coil.

Ryder is standing over her, tension rolling off him. He's pissed. They all are, but they are contained. I'm just waiting for detonation.

"Where is she?" I growl.

"I'm sorry, Jake," she sobs. "I'm so sorry. I just wanted Lyra back. I didn't know anything about Cara. I didn't know he would take her too."

"Why?" I spit. "Why, after you walked away from your daughter, did you decide you wanted her back now?"

"I realized how much I've missed," she tells me, biting her lip.

A malicious smirk crosses my lips. After she lived in my apartment for six months, I know her tells. They were never that hard to read to begin with. I stalk toward her. Dane stands in front of me to stop me from getting too close. "I'm fine," I tell him.

He moves out of the way. I get right over her, hovering my much larger frame over her smaller one. I use every inch of my body to intimidate her. "What did Cara have to do with anything?"

"I didn't know she did," she sobs. "I don't know why he wants her. When he said he'd help me get Lyra back, I didn't question it."

"Do you know what kind of sick fuck your brother is?" I ask her.

More tears fall. She shakes her head. "I had no idea."

"Where is she?"

"Goussainville," she says with a whimper. "It's just north."

"It's a ghost town," Henry tells us. "It's a ghost town. How many people are there?"

"Just Niko and his friend. Jake, you have to hurry. They're leaving tonight."

"Leaving for where?" I jolt.

"I don't know. I heard them talking. What they were going to do to her and Lyra. Even me. I tried to get them both, but Cara wouldn't come. She told me to bring Lyra to you."

"I'm calling the police," Dane says as he takes out his phone.

"Dane," I call out before he hits send. I swing, connecting my fist with his jaw, catching him completely off-guard. His eyes roll back in his head as he falls to the ground.

"What the hell was that?" Angel yells, looking at me like I've lost my mind.

"No one calls the police or anyone else. Am I clear?"

All their mouths hang open. All but Maddox. I meet his eyes, and he nods as he goes to his room. He returns carrying two nine millimeters.

"You know how to use that?" Henry asks me warily.

I take the gun, slide in the clip, and release the safety. His jaw tightens, but he nods.

"Where the hell did you learn that?" Angel asks, still in disbelief.

"Dad was a cop, remember? Learned how to use one of these when I was eight."

"He wakes up," Maddox points at Dane, "tie his ass up. I do not want him anywhere around this. He's fucking reckless when it comes to shit like this. You ready?" he asks me.

I nod.

"I'm coming too," Henry calls out as we head to the door. "You can't be sure there's only two."

"What am I supposed to do with her, mate?" Ryder nods

"Make sure she's gone before I get back."

Cara

I sit in the corner of the filthy room, struggling to keep my eyes open. I have refused to close them since I woke up here.

I'm constantly listening for Niko, as Peyton called him, to return. I know I don't have much time. As soon as he realizes his sister is gone, he'll come.

His sisters.

When my eyes first opened in this place, so many memories threatened to flood. I felt the raw edges of panic grabbing my heart. I knew I was going to be paralyzed with it.

Until I heard Lyra crying.

"Can't you make her shut up," his accented voice vibrates the thin, dilapidated walls.

305

"I'm trying, Niko," Peyton tells him as Lyra continues to wail.

"Take her back to the girl for now," a voice I don't recognize tells them.

"But she's my baby."

"One that doesn't want you," Niko says with condescension.

A second later, I hear footsteps and the sounds of Lyra's cries getting louder. The door flies open. Niko stands on the other side with Peyton behind him.

On instincts I don't understand, I race to them, needing to get to Lyra. I know I won't succeed. Not with the six-and-a-half-foot man blocking me, but I have to try.

Just as I knew he would, he grips my arm painfully, shoving me back into the corner. I watch as he takes my crying girl from Peyton's arms. He's not gentle as he carries her across the room to me, shoving her in my lap.

Lyra is quick to cling to me. She buries her face in my neck with muttering of wanting her daddy.

I want your daddy, too, pretty girl.

"Make her stop crying," he demands like it's a switch I can cut off.

"I'm not sure what you're expecting. She's tired, hungry, thirsty, and wants her father." I softly stroke her hair while she cries. Her little blond curls are nearly soaking wet with sweat.

"I'm her mother," Peyton yells.

"You're an incubator. A mother doesn't leave before the ink on the birth certificate is dry."

306

She starts for me like she's going to attack. I duck to cover Lyra's body with my own.

"Enough," Niko bellows. "You wanted her. Now go find her some food." He shoves her out the door then turns back to me. "Shut her up, or I will."

I swallow hard against the threat. She's just a little girl, but I don't see that meaning much to him.

I rock Lyra back and forth as I sing In My Arms *just above a whisper. Emotion fills me with a crack in my chest as I realize I feel every word of this song in my heart for this little girl. Tears fall down my cheeks as her sobs become soft whimpers.

I clutch her to me with a vow of getting her back to Jake. To give this little girl her daddy and the man who holds my heart in a way I never thought possible, his world. I know she's his world. His everything. Because somewhere along the way, she became mine.

Hours pass, and I don't release my hold on Lyra. No matter how much my arms burn and scream for release, I don't let her go.

Finally, Peyton walks in with a plate of sandwiches. I look at the slice of bologna between two slices of bread with a scoff. "This is what you brought for a toddler to eat. A little girl you keep screaming is your daughter."

"It's just a sandwich," she rolls her eyes. "She should be made to eat what she's offered."

"You can't be serious," I scoff. "She's three. She eats PB&J, not bologna."

"Fine," Peyton huffs like I'm being ridiculous. "I'll go find some."

"Do that," I nod towards the door. "And bring her some water before she's dehydrated."

She leaves the room, returning minutes later with sandwiches and water. Lyra doesn't eat or drink as much as I would like her to. Her normally bright eyes are full of fear and sadness that I want to take so badly.

When she finishes eating, she curls back into my lap. She doesn't fall asleep right away. She clings to me with her little fingers in her mouth, her hand tangled in my hair. She stays quiet, though, except for a shuddered breath here and there.

"I want Daddy," she sniffles. "Ands Nane ands Angel ands Madsux and Wywy."

"I know, pretty girl," I whisper to her. "I want them too. I'll get you back to your daddy soon. I promise." I try to stop the break in my voice, but it comes anyway.

Lyra looks up at me just as a tear falls from my lashes. "You is sad?"

"Yeah, baby. I'm sad," I tell her even though I should probably lie.

"I stays with you, Cara. I love you."

My cracked heart shatters with those words. Words she's told me before. Words I know she meant. But this time is different. This time I let myself feel them. I let them blanket me, wrap around me and give me strength.

I spend the night and most of the day trying to figure out how to get us away from these people. I've tried the door. It's amazing that the locks still work in this completely derelict house that is probably condemned. I consider the window, only to

308

discover we're on the second floor. It has to be a last resort because I won't let Lyra get hurt unnecessarily.

Since yesterday, the only person we've seen is Peyton which I have not questioned or complained about. Part of me hoped it meant the men weren't here. I know I can handle Peyton on my own.

But their voices carried through the house about mid-day. Every time I hear Niko's voice, my stomach drops. Nausea fills me with each word.

I wish Lyra wasn't here. I'd give anything for her to be with Jake where she's safe. But she is also the only reason I've been holding it together. She's my reason for hanging on to my control and sanity.

When the door opens, Peyton comes into the room carrying a plate of food. Behind her is her brother. She hasn't brought me food once. I haven't complained and don't plan on it. As long as Lyra is okay, that's all that matters.

But any hunger I feel is replaced by a thick, swirling knot of fear and tension when he steps into the room. I work hard to keep my expression neutral and my posture straight. I won't let him see the effect he has on me. Not as long as Lyra is here.

He doesn't say anything to me. He just rakes his eyes over my body. What little he can see, considering Lyra is in my lap.

My skin crawls with each second his gaze lingers on me. I bury my face in Lyra's hair, humming to her while she eats her sandwich. She still only nibbles.

Children may not fully comprehend what goes on around them. They don't understand what words like safe, danger, or even evil mean. But they know when something is bad. They know when they're uncomfortable.

She may not understand the danger we're in. But she can feel the tension. She is stressed and worried without knowing what it is she feels or why.

When Lyra finishes picking at her food, Niko jerks his head toward the door. When Peyton is no longer within earshot, he looks at me with maliciousness. "Tomorrow, we're leaving here. I have special plans for you. I never got what I paid for all those years ago, and you left me in quite an uncomfortable position a few weeks ago. But I enjoyed jerking my cock to images of your face."

I don't say anything at all. I don't even acknowledge he said something. He doesn't care anyway. He didn't say it for a response. He said it to scare me.

And it worked. I'm out of time. I've got to get us out of here. I don't even know where here is, but I don't think we're far out of Paris. Tomorrow, he plans to change that. I cannot let that happen.

I plot and plan several different scenarios. None are particularly appealing, especially with Lyra to consider. If I'm honest with myself, they're more likely to get us killed, but I will do whatever is needed to get Lyra safe.

Including begging Peyton. Which is exactly what I have planned when she walks into the room.

"Peyton," I whisper when she sets yet another peanut butter and jelly in front of us, "you have to help me get out of here. Get Lyra out of here."

310

Her blue eyes meet my brown ones. I think she's going to agree for a second. Instead, she just walks out of the room.

Several hours later, she slips back into the room. "Get up," she hisses.

I sit up from the disgusting mattress, bringing Lyra with me. I've had her sleeping in my arms or on my chest since we were brought here. I refuse to have whatever depravity has touched this mattress touch her.

"We have ten minutes to get out of here," she tells me. "Niko will be back by then, and it will be too late."

My heart races. He's not here. She's handed me everything in just a few words. This is my opportunity.

I quickly grab Lyra, waking her as I do. "I not wanna wakes up," she tells me as she rubs her eyes.

"I know, pretty girl," I whisper, "but we're going to go home to Daddy now."

"Daddy," she blinks, tears filling her eyes.

"Mmm-hmm, but you got to stay quiet. Okay?"

"I bees quiet," she whispers against my neck.

"Let's go," Peyton tells me, moving quickly.

We don't even make it downstairs when lights shine through the broken windows. "Shit," Peyton hisses. "They're not supposed to be back yet."

Panic filters through her voice. She's genuinely scared, and I find myself wondering why she is suddenly helping us.

She doesn't answer my question, but the look on her face has dread pooling in my gut. "I didn't know," she tells me in earnest.

311

Steps outside the front door have me shoving Lyra into her arms. "Get her to Jake," I demand.

"You have to come too," she pulls at my arm.

The door creaks as it opens. My heart hammers against my chest. "Go. Take her. Take her to Jake."

She hesitates for another second before running down the staircase. I don't wait to make sure she makes it to the backdoor. Instead, I provide a distraction. I grab a brick lying on the floor, then run back to the room I have been kept. I toss it through the window, the sound of glass shattering rings out.

It's been a couple of hours since Peyton managed to get away. She jumped into a car outside the building, taking off with gravel flying.

Her brother and his cousin didn't notice until it was too late. They were too busy making sure I didn't go anywhere.

I touch my fingers to my face with a wince. I'd gladly take another fist if it meant Lyra was safe. I'd suffer through anything to make sure she was returned to Jake. That is the only thing that has mattered.

All I can do now is wait. Wait for Niko to come for me. To finish what he started back in Chicago. To take me somewhere I'll never see my family again. See Jake or Lyra.

I'm resigned to my fate. Not because I've given up. I have no intentions of going quietly. But I'm not stupid. I will fight back, but I will lose.

I only wish I knew if Lyra was okay.

I hear voices. More than just Niko and his cousin. My stomach sinks as I wonder if they're getting ready to take me somewhere. Or worse.

I close my eyes, trying to hear what they are saying, but it's pointless. They're speaking in a language I don't understand.

A few minutes later, I hear footsteps coming up the stairs. I hold my breath. When the door opens, fear courses through me. My heart feels like Dane is playing drums in my chest.

Niko walks into the room with fire in his eyes. His stature is domineering and intimidating, causing me to back up into the corner of the mattress where I'm sitting.

He grabs me by the hair. His breath reeks of alcohol and tobacco as he breathes down my neck. I bite my cheek to stop my scream when he tugs my hair harder, licking his way up my face.

"The things I want to do to you," he growls in my ear. "Fortunately for you, my client doesn't want you used up, but that doesn't mean I can't fuck that pretty mouth."

I swallow the bile that rises in my chest. I grip the makeshift weapon in my hand, feeling it break the skin. Bastian's words replay in my head as he taught Verity and me a few basic self-defense moves. They're crude, but they stuck.

Nuts and nose.

He moves to take my mouth as my knee comes up. When he doubles over, I bring it up again, connecting with his nose. I quickly jam the shard of glass from the broken window into the first piece of flesh I can connect with, then take off for the door.

I don't make it far before a large arm wraps around my waist, bringing me back into the room. "Next time you stab someone, make sure it's somewhere it does some good."

A commotion breaks loose downstairs. He jerks his head toward the door, listening to what sounds like a brawl. I use his distracted state to dig my finger into the wound at his collarbone.

He lets out a roar, throwing me to the mattress. He comes to me, climbing over my body. His hands grab at the button of my jeans. "No. Stop. Your client," I slap at his hand and kick at his body.

"Guess I'll find a new one. Your fight makes you too hard to resist."

"No," I scream as he continues to rip and tear at my clothes.

He bends down, licking the side of my face again. "The more you fight, the more turned on I get."

He uses his body to press mine into the mattress as I continue to struggle. He leans back, tugging at my jeans. I will my body to still, afraid if I keep moving, it will only help him accomplish his goal. I close my eyes as the tears spilling blur my vision.

Then suddenly, the hands that have been pulling at me, the body that was restraining my own, is gone. I open my eyes to see he's across the room. A dark figure I can't entirely make out, stands with his back to me.

I don't need to see him, though. I know who it is. I'd recognize him in the darkest depths of hell or in the brightest light of the heavens. My soul sees him. My heart beats for him.

Every muscle in his body is coiled, ready to attack. He's waiting on Niko to make the first move. He wants him to make the first move. He's waiting like the alpha waiting for the challenge.

Niko stands with a smirk then makes his move. He charges Jake, who deftly dodges his attack, slipping behind him, wrapping his arm around Niko's neck while using the other for leverage.

Niko struggles against the hold, but the more he struggles, the tighter the hold seems to get. In an act of desperation, Niko throws himself against the wall, causing Jake to lose his grip just long enough for Niko to get free. He stumbles across the room then turns back to Jake.

Jake's eyes are dark and dangerous. He watches Niko without a word. He simply stares. It's predatory.

Niko again, unable to back down, makes his move once again. This time instead of dodging, Jake is hit. He spits out a mouth full of blood, then smiles a smile so vicious and cruel it's almost beautiful.

He swings, connecting with Niko's jaw. The larger man stumbles back a few steps, but Jake doesn't back down. He moves toward Jake with his own wild swing that Jake dodges, then counters. Blow after blow, I watch as the man who has declared his love to me for weeks fights with the man who has haunted me for years.

When Niko takes Jake to the ground, I cry out. Pleading and begging for him to let go. I start to go toward them but stop in my tracks when Jake somehow gets his arms around Niko's large neck and his legs around his waist. After more struggling, I see the fight leaving Niko until his arms are limp at his side.

I expect Jake to let go.

He doesn't.

My eyes snap up when I see Maddox and Henry run into the room. Their attention falls to me in the corner of the room, taking in my torn and dirty clothes, then falls to Jake, who is still holding on to Niko's limp body.

Maddox squats next to him, pulling his arm gently. "Let go, Jake."

Jake's eyes flash to Maddox, but it's like he's looking right through him. So much rage fills his face it breaks my heart.

I feel myself being pulled to him. I crawl across the room until I'm right beside the limp body of a man I've hated and the man I love.

I reach to him. Taking his cheek in my hand. Turning his face to meet mine. "Let go, Jake," I whisper. He still doesn't seem to see anything beyond his anger.

"I need you," my voice cracks around the words.

His distant eyes focus on me. He releases his hold, pushing the man off of him. He sits up and quickly pulls me into his chest.

"Are you okay?" he whispers, cupping my face.

"You came for me. You found me and came for me," I say with disbelief.

"I will always come for you," he tells me, pressing a kiss against my forehead. "Always."

"We need to go," Henry tells us. "Ghost town or not, gunshots aren't going to go unnoticed for long."

I stare at him in confusion. I never heard any shots. I don't say anything, though. And he doesn't answer my questioning gaze.

Jake stands, bringing me with him. He scoops me up, heading for the door.

This time the gunshots don't go unnoticed. I jump in Jake's arms but don't scream. I'm too tired to scream.

We turn to see Maddox standing over Niko's body. Smoke still swirling above the barrel of the gun. Niko's head now has multiple holes filling it.

"Not making the same mistake twice," he tells us.

Jake nods, then continues out of the house. He places me in the backseat of the SUV, climbing in beside me. Soon as the door is shut, he pulls me into his lap.

We drive through the darkness in silence. Within moments I'm leaving the same way I came to this hell, but this time when the world goes black. It's exhaustion that takes me.

Jake

We pull to a private entrance of the hotel. The trip didn't take long, but she was asleep before we pulled onto the main road. I'm not sure how I'm going to let her go after this. How I'm supposed to let her be anywhere, but in my arms after this, I don't know.

When I walked in and saw that bastard on top of her, heard her screams, I lost my mind. No one was going to stop me from killing him. I don't regret it. I regret not making him suffer. I regret that I can't bring him back and do it again. But I absolutely do not regret putting an end to him.

He tried to take everything that matters from me because Lyra and Cara are all that fucking matter to me. I've lived without money. I've even lived without the music. I don't ever want to live without them. *My girls.*

I sit in the SUV, Cara in my lap, my arms tightly around her, and think. She's been through so damn much. She really is so broken and damaged that most of the time, she can't express her own feelings. She shuts everything and everyone off emotionally, so she doesn't have to feel. Because feeling is too much.

I've tried hard to be what she needs. I've tried to let her see how much I love her with actions and words. To show her that I'm not giving up on her. That she's not too broken for me. For me, she's perfect. For me, she's everything.

She finally started to let me in. A little more every day, she would open up her spirit and soul to me. Every day I cherished everything she offered. I've been honored that she's chosen to give me this gift and swore I would never take it for granted.

Now all of this has happened. Because of Lyra's mother, no less.

There's no way she can be the same after this, but I'm faced with the unknown. Will she regress to the way she was? Keeping me at arm's length? Will she leave? I can't fucking live without her. I won't let her go without a fight, but chasing her to the ends of the earth won't be easy with a toddler.

I'll do it, though. I will follow her to hell if I have to. But what if I chase her, and she never lets me back in?

I carry her through the hotel's back entrance, Maddox and Henry following behind. Liam is in the suite sitting on the sofa when we walk in. He takes in Cara in my arms, his brows falling between his eyes.

"She okay?" he asks, but I don't say anything.

I continue walking until we're in the bathroom. I set her on the counter, her eyes red and puffy from crying. She looks toward

319

me, but she's not looking at me. She's looking through me, and my heart cracks just a little more.

I pull her clothes off. Slowly, I remove the dirty, torn garments, gauging her reaction as I do.

She has no reaction. She doesn't react when I remove her shirt or jeans. She doesn't blink as I remove her underwear.

Part of me is starting to panic at her catatonic state. I'm afraid she's had a breakdown. I'm afraid she's shutting down completely.

I turn on the shower, adjusting the temperature. Lifting her from the counter, I step into the shower and sit on the bench inside. I don't try to get her to stand. I'm not sure she could if I did. I just hold her in my lap, washing away the dirt and grime from her body.

I see bruises on her cheek. Fingerprints circle her arms. A large black mark is forming on her shoulder.

I see more fingerprints on her hips and thighs. Closing my eyes, I pray I got to her in time. I pray they didn't take *that* from her. She won't make it back to me if they did. I know she won't.

I hold her under the hot spray with my face buried in her hair. Tears I won't let her see slide down my face. All of this is my fault. She has come face to face with the person who's haunted her nightmares for a long time because of me. Because of my daughter and her mother.

She stayed with the bastard. She stayed with him so Peyton could get away with Lyra. She stayed because she knew Novak was more concerned with her than with a toddler.

She sacrificed herself for *my* daughter. Because she loves her. Because she loves me.

A shudder wracks her body, and I realize she's probably cold. I shut off the water, carry her to the bathroom to dry her, and dressed her in one of my shirts and a pair of panties. I take her into the bedroom, laying her in the bed.

I want nothing more than to crawl in beside her. To hold her close to me. Breathe her in. But I need Lyra too.

When I begin to walk away, her arm shoots out, grabbing mine. Her wide brown eyes look at me with panic in their depths. It's the first reaction I've gotten out of her since the car ride here. "Don't leave me," her voice cracks.

I walk back to her quickly, placing a kiss on her forehead while cupping her cheek. "I'll be right back. I'm just getting *our* girl," I tell her, hoping she realizes that I just called Lyra hers too.

Because, goddammit, Lyra is Cara's. Cara has shown more motherly love to a little girl that she doesn't owe anything to than the woman who grew her inside her body for nine months ever has.

Her eyes fill with tears. I don't know if it's because of what I said or because she is already starting to panic at the thought of me leaving. It makes it that much harder for me to walk away from her, even just for a second. When she nods, I go as fast as I can.

Maddox and the rest are still in the suite as I walk through. "We need to figure out how to cover that shit up," Liam says, I'm certain, referring to the bodies back at the abandoned house.

"Already handled," Maddox informs him without explanation.

"One of these days, you're going to sit down and tell me about who you really are over a beer," Liam chuckles.

"Take more than just one."

I ignore the rest as I walk down the hallway to Dane's room. Cami opens the door with a red face and eyes glazed with tears. "Jake," she gasps.

"Need Lyra," I tell her without the explanations I know she's wanting.

She nods her head quickly, rushing back into their room. She returns with Dane, who's carrying Lyra. Dane's eyes are full of questions, but he's going to wait until later. I'm not answering anything tonight. I'm also not letting him near his sister. She needs quiet and calm, and he won't be able to give that to her.

My lack of words doesn't stop him, of course. He releases Lyra to me, then follows me back to my room. I continue to ignore him, and he lets out a string of curses when Maddox stops him halfway into the suite.

I climb into the bed, Lyra clinging to my neck, right next to Cara. Cara wastes no time curling into my side, easing the knot that's in my stomach. Lyra stays on my chest but scoots just a little closer to Cara.

I can finally breathe. I have them both right here with me.

The tension in my shoulders ease. My racing heart finally begins to slow to a normal rate. The spinning in my stomach stops. And thirty-eight hours without sleep finally claims me.

I jolt upright in the bed when I realize Lyra and Cara aren't there. My heart pounds in my chest. Sweat coats my body.

Fear that I dreamed everything consumes me. That I never got them back.

I jump out of bed, racing to find them. I nearly fall, getting tangled in the sheets. I run to the door of the bedroom in a panic. I fling the door open, my lungs threatening to explode.

Then I slump against the frame. I squeeze my eyes shut as relief floods me to my core.

Both of my girls sit at the bar eating their breakfast.

I shove my hand through my hair, making sure I have myself composed before I make my way to them. I kiss my little girl on top of her head as she shoves cheerios in her mouth. She looks up at me with a huge smile.

Cara made sure she was returned to me without a scratch. Physically she was as perfect as when she was taken. Part of me worries there may be some emotional trauma, but she seems fine.

I move behind Cara, wrapping my arms around her waist. She tenses for just a second, making my stomach twist. Then she relaxes against me. I don't miss the way she pushes her own food around her plate.

I bury my face in her neck, inhaling her scent. "You okay?" I ask.

"I'm fine," she tells me softly, but I can hear that she's not.

I turn her around to face me, tipping her head up so I can see her eyes. I cup both sides of her face and press our foreheads together. "If you weren't fine, would you tell me?"

Her eyes glass over with tears. She quickly wipes them away. "I'll be fine," she changes her statement slightly.

"Don't shut me out," I plead. "Please don't shut me out. Let me be here for you."

A knock at the door draws her attention away from me. "We should get that," she tells me quietly.

"Leave it," I beg. "Just let whoever it is go away for now."

She shakes her as she moves around me. "Everyone has worried enough already."

Fuck, I can feel it. She has shut down. She is putting on that fake smile and doing the same thing she did when we started this tour. She's hiding.

She opens the door, and Dane walks in, bringing her to his chest. He glares at me over her shoulder. "You okay, Brat?"

I watch as she hugs him back. Her movements are practically robotic. "I'm fine."

"You scared the hell out of me, kid. Again."

"I'm sorry," she ducks her head like it's her fault.

I'm not letting her do that. She's not going to blame herself for something she didn't do. "You don't have anything to be sorry for, baby," I boom across the room, passing Dane my own warning glare.

He seems to realize what he just said. The reaction he just caused. He leans back, looking down at his sister. "He's right, Cara. You didn't do anything wrong. This was all Peyton's doing."

She looks over her shoulder at me in question. I shake my head minutely, letting her know I still haven't said anything to him about Novak. "I know," she tells him softly, "but if I would've listened to Jake, it wouldn't have happened."

Dammit, that's not what I want her thinking. Novak was determined. Peyton was determined. Peyton had a change of heart because she heard her brother had the same plans for her

324

that he had for Cara. It was self-preservation, but she didn't want to leave Lyra (thank God) and didn't think she'd get Lyra away from Cara. I think the only reason she brought Lyra back to me is that she had no idea how to handle her own daughter.

I pull her away from Dane without a thought. She gasps, and his jaw clenches. I grip her face on either side. I bend at the knees, so we're eye level. "You did not do anything wrong," I tell her again. "Not a goddamn thing. You will not blame yourself for this. Do you understand me?" My tone is hard. My face is probably harder, but I won't let her blame herself.

She pulls her bottom lip between her teeth with a nod. I search her eyes for verification that she hears me. I don't find it. All I find is fear and guilt.

"Speaking of," Dane coughs. "What are we doing with Peyton? She's still in Maddox and Ryder's room."

"Call the cops," I tell him. "She may not be charged with kidnapping Lyra but she sure as hell can be charged with kidnapping Cara."

"No," Cara yells. "No police. I won't talk to them."

We both look at her with mouths open. "Cara, we have to do something about her," I tell her.

"I said no. I'm not talking to anyone," she demands. Tears fill her eyes, and my heart cracks.

"This isn't just about you, Cara," Dane tells her, using his big brother voice on her. "The only way to make sure she doesn't come after Lyra again is to call the cops."

"We can't call the cops," she whispers, looking at me with desperation. "Lyra needs you."

I feel like an idiot. I know she doesn't want to talk about what happened. It just didn't occur to me why. She's afraid for me.

I pull her to my chest, pressing my lips to the crown of her head. "I won't get in trouble, baby. That's been handled."

"But Peyton. She'll say something," her voice cracks. "Or they'll want to know why you didn't call them before you came for me."

"We've already worked it out. We're going to tell them that she brought you and Lyra back."

"Then she'll get in less trouble anyway, so why say anything at all?" She wrings her hands between us. Her chest begins to lift rapidly. She's on the verge of a panic attack.

"What do *you* want to do?" I ask her.

"I want to forget all of this. Forget any of it happened."

I take a step back with a heavy sigh. An irritated sigh. I want to yell at her because this is what she does. I won't. It wouldn't do anything but push her away so I won't.

"We can't do that, baby," I tell her. "I can't do that. I fucked up by not having her rights revoked long ago. I can't let her get away with this. I have to protect Lyra."

That seems to finally reach her. Her need to protect Lyra is as instinctual as her need to breathe. If I wasn't already in love with her, I would be now. "All right," she agrees weakly. "Tell me what I have to say."

I go over everything she needs to corroborate the story. After we go through it a few more times, we call the police, then head for Maddox and Ryder's room to wait.

326

It takes the French police half an hour to show up. They question all of us for another hour. Then take Peyton with them to their precinct.

"I've got the label rescheduling the shows here and in Italy. We're heading to England in a few days. That's the best I can do," Liam tells all of us.

"That's better than nothing," Maddox nods.

It's easy for all of them to think so. They may love Cara and Lyra, but until they were in my shoes, they really have no idea how fucking awful this whole thing was.

"Where's Cara?" Dane asks.

We look around the room, realizing she's gone. My stomach plummets as I wonder how she got out of here without me noticing. Panic, just like this morning, washes over me. I wonder if this is how Cara feels all the time?

I don't waste any time getting back to our room. When I don't see her, I race for the bedroom, and I can breathe.

She's curled up next to Lyra, sound asleep. Or at least, she's pretending to be. I know the minute I climb in next to her that she's not.

I run my hand over her arm, kissing her shoulder. "Talk to me, baby."

She snuggles in closer to me, making the tightness in my chest release a fraction. When she doesn't say anything, I decide to tell her what I was feeling. "I was scared, Cara. I don't think I've ever felt fear like that in my life."

"Of course, you were," she whispers. "Your little girl was missing."

"That was part of it, but I was scared for you too. I was terrified I'd never see you again. I was scared I'd lost you forever."

I hear her sniffle and feel her shoulders shake. She's crying, but instead of soothing her, I let her cry. She needs it. "How could you be worried about me when I'm the reason your daughter was taken?"

"I already told you, none of it was your fault. I tried blaming myself too. I tried to convince myself if I'd stopped you from going that none of this would've happened, but you know what?" When she shakes her head, I continue. "I realized that this would've happened one way or the other. It would've happened because Peyton and Novak were determined. Because they knew more about us than we knew about them. None of this was your fault. It wasn't my fault."

"I was scared," she whispers. "I was scared for Lyra. I did everything I could to keep her safe. I didn't care what they did to me as long as she was okay. Every second I tried to figure out a way to get her back to you. I know she needs you, and you need her.

"She was so sad. She wouldn't eat. All she did was stay curled in my arms. She wanted you so badly, and I just wanted to give you back to her. It was what I needed to be strong."

"You did good, baby. She's just as perfect today as she was three days ago."

"When Peyton came to get us out, I knew there was no way we were both getting away. I was the one that Niko really wanted, so I shoved Lyra into her arms. All I cared about was getting her home to you. Once she was gone, I could feel the walls closing in."

I swallow hard. Questions form. One in particular. I don't want to ask. Knowing won't change anything, but, at the same time, I need to know. "Did he – did they," I struggle to get the words out. When I feel her tense against me, I fear her answer. "Did they rape you, baby?"

She's quiet for almost too long, and I feel like my head might explode. When she finally answers, I breathe again. "No. You got there before he could."

"I'm still scared, you know," I confess to her. I'm not going to keep what I feel inside. I can't expect her to tell me what she feels if I don't do the same. "I woke up, and you and Lyra weren't in bed, and I panicked. When I realized you'd left Maddox's room, I panicked. I'm still panicking here, Cara. I don't want you out of my sight. I can feel you pulling away. I know you're trying to shut everything out, including me. I'm afraid if I close my eyes when I open them again, you'll be gone. I won't survive losing you. I know you think I will, but I won't. I can't survive losing you."

She stays quiet, except for a small sigh that escapes her lips. I know at that moment, I'm right. She's quietly planning to disappear. "You would survive," she whispers. "You have to for Lyra."

"I would be going through the motions, baby. I would do what I needed to do for her, but I wouldn't be happy. I wouldn't even be content. I'd be a shell of a man without you. You're my fucking reason for existing."

"Don't say that," she whimpers. "I can't be that reason. It has to be Lyra."

"It's not the same, Cara. I love Lyra with everything in me. She will always be my priority. But the love a father feels for his child

329

isn't the same as a man feels for his woman. Don't leave me, baby. Please. I'm not above begging. You know I'm not."

"What if I can't stay?" she sobs quietly, trying her best to keep everything contained. Trying not to wake Lyra.

"Do you love me?" I ask. "Do you love Lyra?"

"More than anything," she confesses. "More than I ever thought I could love someone. It is why I want you both to have better. I was broken before. It's just going to be worse now."

I raise up on my elbows, turning her to face me. Lyra stretches next to her, but she doesn't wake. "Why? Why do you think it's going to be worse?"

"Because my head is a fucked up place to be, Jake. It's going to happen. I'm going to break."

"So you want to leave us because you *might* break from everything? I don't understand. If what happened isn't already affecting you, then why are you so upset?'

"Because I know the only way to protect both of you is to leave. When it finally happens, you don't deserve to pick up the pieces."

It all clicks. That distant look. The way she seems like she's there, but she's not. All a far cry from the girl I found last night, fighting against her attacker. I don't know why I didn't see it before. She hasn't been affected more by this attack. If anything, last night, she seemed stronger. She's just afraid that it hasn't come yet.

I climb out of bed, pulling her with me. She's reluctant, but she allows it. I walk us into the bathroom, facing us both to the mirror. "Look at yourself," I tell her. "What do you see?"

"I see me," she answers.

"Do you look fragile? More so than normal? Do you look weak?" She shakes her head. "Did you feel weak and fragile when you were being kept there?"

She bites her lip as she stares into my eyes. "I started to panic a few times but pulled myself together for Lyra. I knew I needed to be strong for her."

"Lyra wasn't there when I walked into that room and saw you fighting against a man twice your size.

"It wasn't a battle I was going to win," she tells me dryly.

"That's not the point. You weren't the same defeated woman we brought home from River City. You were strong and resilient and refused to back down. Do you feel weak now?"

"No," she admits.

"The only person in this room right now that is weak, baby, is me. You've brought me to my knees. Figuratively and literally. You? You've begun to pick up the pieces and put them back together."

"Because of you and Lyra," she confesses.

"Then why the fuck would you think leaving is the best option?" I spin her around to face me, no longer being gentle. She's not fragile, not anymore. I should've never treated her that way.

I lower my mouth to hers, kissing her like I haven't seen her in years. Kissing her like this is the last kiss I will ever get. It only takes a second for her to respond, her tongue tangling with mine. I slide my hands down her body, gripping the back of her thighs. I lift her, setting her on the bathroom counter. Our hands are tangled in each other's hair and clothes in a feverish demand.

High pitch crying has us both pulling away with a pant.

"We should check on her," Cara tells me.

"We should," I nod. I pull her with me back into the bedroom.

My little munchkin sits in the middle of the bed, her face wet with tears. We each climb in on either side of her. She quickly climbs into Cara's lap. I pull them both into mine. "What's wrong, princess?" I ask her.

"I's not know where you was," she tells us both.

Cara and I lock eyes. Looks like my little girl is the one who's been the most affected. In my stupidity, I just assumed she'd bounce right back like nothing happened.

"I – uh – I think maybe we all need to talk to that therapist of yours," I tell Cara.

Her eyes are wet again as well. "I'll call him this afternoon."

"Cara, not yeave me," she mumbles into Cara's chest.

Shock registers on her face before absolute adoration. Her tears spill over her lashes. "I'm not going anywhere, pretty girl. I'm here forever."

My spirit flies with the words from her lips. Words she says to my little girl but tells me with her eyes.

Forever.

That's good because that's exactly how long I plan on keeping her.

Epilogue

Cara

I watch as the guys all make their way to the stage. Excitement and pride flood down to my marrow as they accept their awards. Awards they have earned and deserve.

Best Rock Album? Check. Best Rock Performance? Check. Album of the freaking Year? Big fat check.

All the guys stand on the stage with wide grins. Except for Angel, who's back in New York with Josephine and their brand new baby boy for the next few weeks before he hits the road with the band again. Good thing they always seem to have a backup member these days.

Their two-month world tour has been extended to include Canada, Australia, and the U.S. They've been on the road for seven months with seemingly no end in sight. They don't seem like they're ready to slow down either.

I've been in nearly every state and every country these last few months. It's been an amazing experience. But more amazing is how much more I love Lyra and Jake every day. It hasn't been easy by a long shot.

After everything happened, my nightmares stopped. Once the initial shock wore off, I knew what happened wasn't my fault. I also found myself thinking that the whole thing was my redemption for Chicago. I did everything in my power to keep Lyra safe. I would've died to keep her safe.

But Lyra's nightmares started. Every night for weeks, she'd wake up screaming. Every night Jake or I would sing her back to sleep. She's been sleeping with us for weeks.

We tried over-the-phone and video chat therapy with my therapist, but she needed more. After a recommendation from my therapist, Jake hired someone to come on tour with us for Lyra. She's been traveling with us for five months and really seems to help Lyra. She's insistent that Lyra sleep in her own bed, but neither Jake nor myself are quite there yet.

I rub my growing belly, knowing the time will come soon enough.

Yep. I'm pregnant. Not on purpose, mind you. But that day on Maddox and Ryder's couch, we kind of forgot the gift wrapping. Jake and the other guys have taken every opportunity to torment Dane with the knowledge that he walked in on his niece or nephew's conception.

I remember telling Jake. I remember being scared to tell him.

334

I stare at the pregnancy test on the counter. This is the fourth one. I'm pretty sure after the first, there wasn't much point of another, but I can't believe what I'm seeing. We've always been careful. I don't know how this happened.

I also don't know how I'm going to tell Jake. Or how he's going to react once I do tell him.

I've been feeling like crap for a few weeks now. It wasn't until Cami asked if I had any tampons that I even realized I was late. And oh boy, am I late. I've missed two periods without realizing it.

I hear the door to the bus open. I quickly grab the test, throwing it under the counter. He never looks under there for anything.

I know I've got to tell him, but I need more time to work up the courage.

"Hey, baby, where are you?" he calls out when he doesn't see me right away.

I jump out of the bathroom with a finger to my lips. "It took me forever to get her to sleep," I warn him.

"I'm not trying to wake the princess. I just wanted to know where my hot girlfriend was," he chuckles. "You done in there? I need a shower."

I nod, letting him by. When he's in the bathroom, I run off the bus in search of Cami or Josephine. I need a girl to talk to about this.

I pound on their door. Cami opens it with a confused look on her face. "What's going on?"

"My brother in there?"

"No. He went to go over something with Ryder and Maddox."

335

"What about Angel?" I don't need him hearing this either since he'll run right to Jake. Or Dane.

She shakes her head. "He just took Josephine out for lunch."

I push my way past Cami once I know she's alone. When the door closes behind her, I blurt out my news. Her eyes grow wide along with her smile. "Oh my God! What did Jake say?"

"I haven't told him yet. I'm freaking out, Cami. He's going to be upset," I babble.

"Why would you think that?" she frowns. "Have you two talked about it before?"

I shake my head. "Come on, Cami. How could he possibly be happy about it? He just got his music career back."

She narrows her eyes at me as she grabs my shoulders, turning me to sit on the sofa, then crosses her arms over her chest. "What does the band have to do with anything? He doesn't have to leave the band just because he has a baby. He kind of already has a kid on tour."

I huff. She's not listening. "Exactly, he already has a three-year-old. He won't want another."

"Do you hear yourself?" she asks with a cocked brow. "You are inventing reasons he'll be upset. You get that, right?"

"I'm not," I pout. "After everything that's happened the last few months, this isn't ideal timing. I'm in therapy because my head is a mess. Lyra's in therapy because of her mother. Hell, Jake is in therapy because of the three of us. He doesn't need something else to stress out over."

"Cami, is Cara in there?" I hear his voice call outside the bus.

I look at the door then back to Cami, panic washing over me. "Stop that," she scolds. "That man loves you. That man has loved you long before you even thought to love him. Ideal timing it may not be, but he's going to be over the moon. The only reason he'll worry is if he thinks you're not happy about it. Are you happy about it? Isn't that what this is really about? Not Jake freaking out, but you're freaking out?"

"What if I'm not ready to be a mom? What if I suck at it?" I confess.

She shakes her head with a laugh. "That's something you need to work out – with Jake – but you're already a mom, Cara. You've acted every bit the part since you stepped onto that plane five months ago." Jake's voice calls out again. "Stop creating problems that aren't there. Talk to him."

Jake walks onto the bus, looking right at me. His eyes flash with something, but I'm not sure what. I swallow at the unfamiliar feeling. I always know what he's thinking.

"I'm going to find Dane," Cami tells us. "You two should talk."

Jake steps aside so Cami can walk past him, but his eyes don't leave mine. "We got something to talk about, baby?" he asks, but his tone is more telling than asking.

I swallow around the worry in my throat and do what I do best. Or at least I did until him. "Where's Lyra?"

"Still sleeping. Quinn is watching her," he tells me.

"She's here to be her therapist, not her nanny," I tell him, pretending to be upset.

"Yeah, well, her nanny *vanished, and I needed to have a talk with my* girlfriend. *Cami seems to think we need to talk too," he pauses, waiting for my response, but I'm pretty sure I've*

swallowed my tongue. *I need to tell him. I know I do, but I don't know if I'm ready.* "No? You just gonna disappear from the bus the second I step into the shower without a word?"

"I – uh," I stammer, not knowing what to say. *I've just realized I have a pattern. When I freak out, I disappear from him. Probably not the best thing.*

"It wouldn't have anything to do with this, would it?" he reaches into his jacket pocket, pulling out the empty pregnancy test box.

Crap! Apparently, I can have the forethought to hide the results but not dispose of the rest of the evidence.

I feel my face grow warm as I gnaw on my cheek. I struggle to meet his eyes as my heart pounds in my chest. I'm not sure what to say. *Five minutes ago, I wasn't ready to say anything, but I can't lie to him.*

He sits next to me on the sofa, pulling me into his lap. "Are you?" he asks, his brows furrow into a deep V as he forces me to meet his gaze.

I still can't seem to find words, so I just nod, tears stinging my eyes.

"You're not happy about it?" he seems to be choosing his words carefully. *He's not giving anything away about how he feels.*

Finally, my brain decides to communicate with my mouth. "Are you? Happy, I mean? I know this isn't the best timing. We haven't even been together that long. You already have Lyra. You've got your music back. I'm a mess. Why would you be happy? I'm probably the last person on earth who should have a baby. I still have panic attacks and nightmares. You still have to hold on to me just so I can breathe. I –."

338

"Cara, shut up," he orders because apparently, when my mouth starts working, it really starts working. Then he starts laughing at me. "You're freaking out on me. I knew when I found the box in the trash, you were freaking out. You're overthinking like you always do."

"It's not overthinking," I yell. "It's a big deal."

He laughs again. "No shit. I think I've got a pretty good idea how big a deal a kid is."

This makes me laugh, and I realize he's right. I'm definitely overthinking. I'm panicking over something that could be – should be good. "You're not mad?"

"Hell, no," he exclaims. "Timing may not be ideal, but is there really a such thing? I love you. I've loved you for so damn long I wouldn't know how not to. You're it for me. The thought of having babies with you has always been there."

"I just don't know how it happened," I confess. "I know I'm not taking any birth control or anything, but we've always been careful."

"Except that one time on Maddox and Ryder's sofa," he chuckles.

"Well, damn," I join him. "How did I forget about that?"

"Marry me," he whispers.

My mouth falls open for a second before anger takes over. I remove myself from his grip with a glare. "Are you joking? You're asking me to marry you now? What the hell is wrong with you? I'm not marrying you just because I'm pregnant."

"Overthinking, again," he points at me with a smirk that only pisses me off more. Until he's on his knee, pulling a small box out *of his pocket. I suck in a breath, knowing he didn't get* that *because I'm pregnant. He found out ten minutes ago. There's no way he would've had time.*

He opens the box, revealing a simple diamond on a platinum band. My hands fly to my mouth. My heart begins to gallop. "Jake, what is that?"

"I've had it for a bit," he tells me with a smile. It's shy and humble. "I didn't want you to think I was asking you because of everything that happened with Peyton. I've been trying to plan the perfect time to ask, but it's kind of hard to do in between shows. Cara, I love you so fucking much. First time I laid eyes on you, I knew I had to have you. I also knew that would get me sent to jail quick," he shakes his head with a laugh. "I felt like such a goddamn creep. I did good and kept my distance but damn if it wasn't hard. Then it seemed like everything that could get in the way did. And despite all of that, my feelings for you kept growing. You're the one. You were the one when you were sixteen, and I was twenty-one, and five years later, you're still the one. That night you told me you loved me, that was the best day of my life. I feel like I've waited a lifetime for your feelings to catch up with mine. I don't want to wait another lifetime to make you mine in every way possible. So, Cara Alyssa Pierce, will you marry me?"

Holy shit. How do you say no to that?

Easy. You don't. But my brain has lost communication with my mouth again, so all I can do is nod.

With a wide grin, he slides the ring onto my finger then pulls me into his arms. "I can't wait to tell your brother he was there the moment the little bean was made," he laughs.

I swat his arm. "Don't you dare," I warn sternly.

"Oh baby, I'm gonna do more than dare. I'm gonna enjoy the fuck out of it."

I snap out of the memory with a grin, only to realize Lyra has escaped me. She is running down the aisle toward the stage. The audience laughs as she climbs the steps, making a beeline for the guys.

"I think she just stole the show," Cami laughs next to me.

"I think you're right," I grin.

The guys accept the award, each thanking all the appropriate people. But it's Jake, I listen to as he holds Lyra. "I want to thank my wife for making it possible for me to get back to my band and my dream. I love you, baby."

Yeah, that's right. We're married.

Three weeks after he proposed, they played a show in Vegas. We didn't want to wait. We've done everything in this relationship in fast forward, so why not this too. We both know there is no one else for us, so why wait.

"That man is gone for you," Cami tells me.

"I kind of like him too," I grin as he returns to our seats.

He grabs my hand, pulling me out of the row. "Let's get out of here," he tells me.

"What about the rest of the show?"

"I could care less about the show. I just want to be with my girls."

"I like the sound of that," I tell him as we leave behind the crowd of people, the glamor, and the glitz to our own little corner of the world.

341

Jake

"Come on, baby," I encourage as I wipe the sweat from Cara's exhausted face. "One more, and you'll be done."

Tears run down her face as she cries out in pain. It is absolutely killing me to see her like this. And I am helpless to do anything but hold her hand.

"I can't, Jake. I'm so tired," she tells me breathlessly.

She has been in labor for nearly twenty-four hours. The last four have been the most grueling, and I'm not sure how much more she can take.

They tried giving her an epidural. For whatever reason, it hasn't affected her. She has felt every second of this, and if it isn't over soon, I might go crazy. But I'm trying to maintain my composure for her.

"Come on, Cara. One more big push, and you'll be there," the doctor tells her. "On the next contraction, give me everything."

"Ready?" I ask her, brushing her hair from her face.

Determination fills her eyes. She gives me a nod. I hold her hand on one side while the nurse is on the other. She gives it everything she has left, then collapses back into the bed.

Cries fill the room, and the biggest fucking smile spreads across my face. "Want to cut the cord, Dad?" the doctor asks.

No hesitation on my part. I follow the instructions the doctor gives me with pride. Then they hand me my son.

Brown hair covers his little head while eyes dark as coal looks up at me.

"Is he okay, Jake?" Cara asks me, worrying lining her face.

"He's perfect, baby," I reassure her.

"Let us have him for just a second, then we'll give him right back," the pediatric nurse tells me.

I hand my beautiful boy to the nurse then return to my wife. My exhausted and so fucking beautiful wife. "You did so damn good, baby." I kiss the top of her head affectionately

"He's really okay?" she asks again, still nervous.

I nod. "Got all ten fingers and toes. And you heard those lungs."

She smiles with relief. "Get Lyra," she tells me.

"I'm not sure they'll let her back here."

"I don't care. I want my daughter to meet her brother," she demands. There will be no arguing with her, and I don't want to. Every time she calls Lyra her daughter, my heart swells to the point of explosion.

"What Momma wants, Momma gets," I gladly concede.

I walk out of the delivery room to the lobby, where everyone is waiting. They all stand, waiting on me to tell them something. I laugh at their expectant expressions.

"You didn't come out with a baby," Dane accuses. "She's not still in labor, is she?"

I can't help the smile that splits my face. "Nope, but she wants her little girl."

343

"Aww, come on, man," Dane whines. "We've been waiting for hours."

Cami slaps his chest with a shake of her head. "Lyra, are you ready to go see Mommy?" Cami asks her.

She bobs her head quickly. "I got a brother now, Daddy?" she asks me with wide, curious eyes.

"Yep. Want to go see?"

She runs to me, grabbing my hand just as precocious as ever. "Come on, Daddy."

I lift her into my arms, and we make our way back to the delivery.

"Sir, she can't be back here," I hear a nurse call out to me. I just keep walking back to Cara's room. I shake my head with a laugh as I hear her begin to follow me. "Sir!"

I walk into Cara's room to find my boy at her chest. The nurses see me walk in with Lyra on my hip. They grin, probably imagining their co-workers who've followed me into the room frustration. Dr. Anders looks over at us with a smile.

"I was wondering how long it would take before Mom and Dad brought you back here, Lyra?" Dr. Anders tells her with a smile. She learned months ago, where we go, Lyra goes.

Lyra isn't paying any attention to her. Her eyes are solely focused on Cara and the baby in her arms. She jerks her body in the direction of Cara. My cue to move.

I sit on the side of the bed, looking at my beautiful wife. She's always been so damn gorgeous, but right now, there is nothing in the world that could make her more beautiful. Nothing she could do that could make me love her more. Though I suspect I will anyway. Every day I love her more than the day before.

"Meet your baby brother, pretty girl," Cara whispers.

"I'm a big sister," Lyra returns her whisper. The awe and reverence on her face is endearing.

Cara opens her arm, the one not holding the baby, inviting Lyra in. She looks up at me with those baby blues asking permission. "Just be easy," I tell her as I nod for her to go.

Gently and more slowly than I thought my princess was capable of, she crawls into Cara's side. I watch as she ooh's and ahh's over her brother.

Love, raw and powerful. All-encompassing love. I am filled to overflowing with so much of it.

There was a time I didn't think I'd get any of this. I thought the choices I made would keep me from having it all. I was okay with that because, without those choices, I wouldn't have my princess. She is every bit my child as the dark-eyed boy in Cara's arms.

But fate has a funny way of bringing things full circle. I got the girl, scars and all. This girl loves my princess as much as I do. She loves me in a way I'm not sure she would have, had things gone differently.

I got the career I've always wanted. But even without that, I would be the happiest man in the world because I got the girl and the family. I have it all. And it couldn't possibly get any better than this.

Break Me Down

Sneak Peek into book 4 of Sons of Sin

Available for preorder on Amazon

Exhaustion settles deep in my bones. Another double shift is over, and I am dead on my feet.

I walk into my tiny two-bedroom apartment with our dinner. "I got Chinese," I yell. "I'm taking a bath first. My back is killing me."

I walk into the small bathroom to start the water. I adjust the temperature to as hot as I can stand. I add some lavender bubble bath and light a few candles. I inhale the scent as I strip out of my uniform. I can't stop the groan when I submerge myself into the hot water.

I lay there for a while, allowing the day to fall away. I relax until all my fingers and toes are pruny and the water turns cold.

Finally, I drag myself from the bath, putting on my warmest fleece pajama pants and an old hoodie. I love this hoodie. It holds so many memories. Memories I'll never regret.

I walk into the kitchen, finding the take-out boxes left open. "You could've closed the boxes back up," I yell.

"Sorry. I forgot." Tyler says.

"Don't talk with your mouth full," I laugh, getting a grin in return.

I sit on the sofa with my plate of food. I turn on the television, not even caring what's on. The first thing on the screen is a music award show, and the band on the stage makes my heart drop. People I left behind long ago are accepting awards they deserve. They've always deserved them. Talent like theirs doesn't come along every day.

I think back on memories which those boys – men. Remember the laughs we had. They were the closest thing I ever had to a family. They accepted me and all my flaws. They didn't judge my purple hair or the piercings. They never thought anything about the tattoos. I laugh at the thought. How could they when they all had their own?

"Who are they?" Hunter asks, sitting beside me.

"Sons of Sin," I answer.

"They seem really popular. How come I've never heard them?"

"Because you don't listen to music," I tease, then instantly regret it.

"That's because you won't let me, Mom. Why do they look like the guys in your photo album?"

I swallow hard. "Because they are," I tell my son.

His head snaps back to the screen, then back to me. His eyes swim with questions. Questions I've ignored and avoided for too long. Questions I knew would bite me in the ass one day.

"But that means –," he trails off.

"Yeah, baby. That's your daddy."

347

Books in this Series

Goodbye Is a Second Chance

Bed of Nails

Shooting Star in the Rain

Break Me Down (Winter 2022)

Shed My Skin (Winter 2022)

Other books by the author

Fighting for His Life

Protecting His Night

Preserving His Truth

Taking His Victory

Acknowledgments

This has been by far the hardest book I've ever written. It probably wouldn't have been finished without so many people encouraging me and pushing me forward. I can't begin to name all the people who help me through each book, and I am so thankful that the lists keep growing.

My beautiful friend Sionna, you keep me laughing every day and continuously help me break down the walls of writer's block. You listen to my rants and distress and keep me moving forward. You, also, so very graciously read through each line over and over, helping me through my disaster of proofing and editing. I don't think this would get done without your help. The mutual admiration society is alive and strong.

C. M. Danks has been my biggest cheerleader from the first book. I often joke that I could write about dog shit, and you'd think it was a bestseller. But it's your love of my work and devotion that makes me want to continue on this crazy journey. Your unyielding loyalty to those who deserve it is something I aspire to, and I am grateful to call you a friend.

Anita, you have slid into my DMs and never left. I am so very grateful for you. Your messages of encouragement have gotten me through rough days. Our talks about our love for books have sent me to some great ones, and the wonderful music you send daily to inspire us is the highlight of my days.

Devin Sloane, you are beautiful. Our talks are probably some of the most real conversations I've ever had with someone I've never met in person. You have a kind and beautiful spirit that invites people to open up. We've laughed and shed a few tears in the time since we've been introduced, and I couldn't be more grateful.

Tempest, my little squirrel, you're heart is so soft and tender. You deserve to be loved and appreciated for the beauty of your mind and your spirit. Thank you for the beautiful book you have written, for the support, you have given, and most importantly, for you.

Nedra, our conversations are kinky and quirky at times. You've made me laugh and given me great support with Jake. You are brave, bold, and beautiful. Thank you for being my friend, and thank you for loving my guys.

Susie, you are amazing. You've swooped in and made it your mission to push me to be my best. You've taken it upon yourself to learn things just so you can help me. For that, I cannot thank you enough.

Charm, my beautiful friend, you've read and encouraged every single book. You love all my guys without fail and support me through it all. I couldn't do this without you.

Sandy, L.C., Hana, Kel, Daria, Michelle B., and so many others I know I am forgetting. Thank each of you for loving my little universe. Without you, I wouldn't be here.

About the Author

Nola Marie has been writing her entire life but has authored nine books in the last year, four of which are published as her steamy mafia romance series, The Men of River City. Currently, she is working on her Sons of Sin series, which promises to be just as bold and exciting.

She also holds a bachelor's degree in IT Management and an MBA in Leadership and Strategy.

She has spent her entire life in Louisiana and absolutely loves everything about it, from the crawfish to the swamps. She has a hard-working, completely devoted husband that encourages her to do what makes her happy, three smart, kind, intelligent children that are her best friends, and an assortment of pets.

When not spending time with her family, she reads, writes, listens to music, does amateur graphic design, and plays video games.

Printed in Great Britain
by Amazon